When I Let You Go

LILY FOSTER

SHOREFRONT BOOKS

Also by Lily Foster

THE LET ME SERIES

Let Me Be the One

Let Me Love You

Let Me Go

Let Me Heal Your Heart

Let Me Fall

When I Let You Go

THE BLACKBIRD SERIES

When the Night is Over

Your Hand in Mine

Ghost on the Shore

All Your Life

This is a work of fiction. Names, characters, places and incidents are either the product of the author's imagination or used fictitiously. Any resemblance to actual persons, living or dead, events, or locales is entirely coincidental.

When I Let You Go
Copyright © 2018 by Lily Foster

All rights reserved. No part of this book may be reproduced in any form or by any electronic or mechanical means, including information storage and retrieval systems, without written permission from the author, except for the use of brief quotations in a book review.

First paperback edition February 2018

Cover by Cover Me Darling

IBSN 9780998916705 (paperback)

* * *

Shorefront Books

When I Let You Go

Prologue

MARGOT COLE

Calm, confident—victorious even. To our esteemed guests, and to the fawning simpletons who stopped mid-stride to admire the scene, that's how I appeared.

After more than half a lifetime in this world, I'd perfected the art of masking my emotions. No one did it better than me. But today I was struggling. I was in danger of showing some cracks in my normally bulletproof veneer.

The flashbulbs snapped as we exited the Rolls Royce Phantom sedan. Me in a champagne-colored Carolina Herrera original that I'm sure the Times reporter would portray as timeless and understated, and Vince in a classic, custom-made Brioni tuxedo. At fifty-four, Vince could easily pull off the slimmer cut that was now in style. His light brown hair still looked boyish, with only a smattering of gray hairs visible at the temples. And damn him, the gray hairs and the subtle laugh lines around his eyes only added to his looks. He was the personification of power and sex.

Vince took my left hand in his and rested his right hand on my lower back. His hold was comforting and possessive as he guided me up the steps outside of St. Ignatius Loyola, my childhood parish. Latecomers congratulated us as they made their way up the side steps, hurrying in as the organ began cranking out the opening chords of Pachelbel's Canon.

Standing tall on the corner of Eighty-fourth and Park, the outside was austere, modest, nothing to look at really, but the inside was magical. As a child I remember sitting between my grandparents on Sunday mornings, transfixed as I stared up at the ornate ceiling, the gilded altar, and the beauty of the stained-glass windows. The homily delivered by the Jesuit priest no more than background noise, while the angelic voices rising up from the choir paired with the booming, sometimes eerie melody of the organ captivated me. As we entered the vestibule today, though, my heart sank. The feeling intensified when my oldest and dearest friends kissed me on the cheek and happily went on about how this day was long in coming, joking about the joining of two dynasties.

I should be happy.

They are perfect for one another.

I tell myself this repeatedly.

Mother of the groom is the hassle-free, luxurious role, and we'd already done our part, hosting an elegant rehearsal dinner. Our family powerful enough to close a Michelin star-rated restaurant on a Friday night in New York City for a private party.

Rehearsal dinner. It was a small wedding really, with just over one hundred guests. It was a fabulous evening because nothing else would do. My name and my image, carefully cultivated over the last three decades, had cemented my place among the effortlessly stylish ladies of society long ago. Everyone raved about the food, the flowers, the beauty of the bride-to-be and how perfect she looked on his arm. No one noticed that my son drank just a little too much that night—heaven forbid. When the volume of his voice rose slightly higher than that of his friends, I made sure to have Vince place a commanding hand on his shoulder as he offered him a club soda in a way that left no room for argument.

Standing on our balcony looking out over Central Park this morning, I simultaneously laughed and shook my head, taking in how utterly perfect this day was. I admired the beauty of the leaves dotting the lush green trees, the ones that were just starting to turn that gorgeous shade of cranberry as autumn took hold. Looking up to the sky, I saw only azure blue. We Christians joked that they *were* the chosen people—it seemed there was rarely a Rosh Hashanah or a Yom Kippur when the sun wasn't shining. With not so much as one white, fluffy cloud in sight, today was no exception.

The hollow sense of victory took me back to my own wedding day. Unwilling to let myself dwell on everything I was losing, while smug in the knowledge that I, Margot Clarke, had played the game by my own set of rules and won.

* * *

Vincent Cole was a fixture of my childhood. Our mothers, lifelong friends, had conspired to marry us off the day I was born, nearly three years after the day Vince arrived on the scene. We attended each other's birthdays, Communions and graduations, and we vacationed in the same spots every summer and during winter ski breaks. But he was three years older than me and ran with the boys, only stopping to tickle me into fits when I was a young child, and when I was a little older, to scare me during nighttime games of Ghost in the Graveyard that played out on the estate grounds of family friends.

We were the next generation. A group of around fifteen to twenty that ran into each other throughout the year, whose parents conducted business with one another or chaired committees together. We spent long, lazy weekends together at summer homes on the Vineyard or in Southampton, and spent winter breaks lounging poolside in Palm Beach or skiing in Aspen. Since most of us came from small families—to be an only child was commonplace—our group was like an extended family.

Vince was just one of the group, a boy I paid only a passing interest in, until he wasn't. That summer he turned sixteen, when I first noticed the faint stubble on his chin and the bronze skin stretched over muscles that made him suddenly seem a man, that's when I took notice. But at thirteen I was a child, not yet developed, still wearing a modest one piece at the pool, and not entirely sure that I wanted to trade in playing Marco Polo and catching fireflies for sneaking off into the woods to do Lord knows what.

It was that summer, though, that I started to watch and I started to change. I experimented with make-up, started wearing a training bra even though it was wholly unnecessary, and shaved my legs for the first time, leaving bloody nicks around my ankles and knees after Juliet Hastings made fun of me in front of everyone at her pool one day.

"Margot, wax much? I can almost braid this." She squealed for dramatic effect, pulling on one hair until she yanked it out by the root.

My face was crimson as I looked around and took in all the boys laughing. The girls looked up to Juliet because she was older and because she acted like she knew everything. And while I was embarrassed, I had a sharp tongue at that age and managed to land what I thought was a decent comeback. "Thanks for the advice. Hopefully you'll make a great beautician someday since things aren't working out so well at Choate."

I'd hit the target but also made an enemy. And I'll admit it was a low blow. After all, there were few among us who weren't excellent students. Most of us were not only bright, but excelled at sports and spoke a foreign language at least well enough to enjoy our European vacations. Juliet was beautiful and worldly, but the only reason she was able to hang on at her exclusive boarding school was because her parents had money and a whole lot of influence.

I noticed Vince crack a smile at my comment, though, and for his approval I'd take whatever retribution Juliet was sure to dish out.

Soon I'd be heading off to one of those faraway places. I was afraid of leaving home and also hated the idea of leaving Todd to fend for himself. My little brother needed me. But staying local for high school was unheard of. No, I'd be shipped off to Miss Porter's come next August, just as my mother had been when she was fourteen.

That night, as groups of us wandered around the property, the youngest playing games, the older ones far out on the dock smoking their smelly cigarettes, Millie Dalton and I wound up in the loft of the boathouse, asking the Magic 8 Ball questions about our future.

I loved Millie. She was unlike any of my other friends. She was proper when out in public, but raunchy and crass when it was just us and she was looking to make me laugh. *She* wasn't asking the ball if she'd marry a handsome millionaire one day. No, Mille was asking if her first lesbian experience would be in high school. When the ball answered: *Signs Point to Yes,* she followed up with, "Will I enjoy carpet munching?"

Half the time I didn't even know what she was talking about, I just knew she was being outrageous and I liked it.

I was just about to ask a question when Millie clapped her hand over my mouth and looked at me wide-eyed, urging me to keep quiet. We'd been perched up there in darkness, enjoying the séance like atmosphere for our game, so when the soft glow from a lantern illuminated a corner of the downstairs space, we knew we had company even before we heard their hushed words and laughter.

Juliet was giggling as she shimmied out of her shorts and tank top. Vince commanded, "Keep quiet!" as he tugged his polo shirt over his back and off.

Millie and I sat spellbound, peering over the side to look down at them. Vince's body was muscular and tan, with a light smattering of hair growing on his chest and below his navel. He hardly looked like the same boy from last summer. Now I figured he was over six feet tall, and his voice, once light and playful, was a low growl as he undid his shorts and ordered Juliet to lay back.

She did as she was told, reclining back on the lounger. Juliet let her legs fall open as she beckoned him, crooking her finger when she whispered, "I've thought about you every night since New Year's Eve. Have you been thinking about me?"

New Year's Eve? Ohmigod! Vince was fifteen then. And the party was at my family's home in Palm Beach. Did they do *this* in my house? The thought horrified me and lit me up with jealousy at the same time.

Juliet giggled again, as if Vince was tickling her as he slid her underwear down over her hips. Right before Vince lowered his head between her legs, he said, "Seriously, Juliet, you act like an idiot when you smoke. Maybe you should stick to vodka."

My head jerked back up when Millie tugged hard on my wrist. Stunned, I'd forgotten she was there with me or what we were doing before this moment. She mouthed the words, "Oh my God," wide-eyed as she stifled a laugh. I mouthed back, "What should we do?" Millie gestured to her criss-crossed legs to indicate that she wasn't going anywhere. She was enjoying this show and seeing it through to the end. I had to stifle my own laugh when Millie mouthed, "Carpet munching," pointing down at Vince.

I wanted to leave but I really didn't want to at the same time. I didn't have access to this type of education in my life. While Millie freely shared that her dad had a stash of Penthouse magazines tucked away in his study, my home was devoid of anything like that. And my days were full between school, tennis, riding lessons and volunteering to keep my Nana company two afternoons a week. It's not like I had time to read the Danielle Steele novels my mother kept hidden away in her nightstand drawer.

So my attention was drawn back downstairs, where Juliet was moaning and rubbing her own breasts as Vince braced his hands against her thighs and pressed his face into her. *That* would feel good? I had my legs pinned together watching them, unable to imagine that letting someone put their mouth there could be enjoyable. But she sure seemed to be enjoying it. She unclasped the front of her bra as he wiped his mouth on his forearm and moved back up over her.

"Hmm, these are nice," he hummed as he sucked and licked her nipples.

I felt like I didn't even know Vince at all. Who was this person? And I was envious of Juliet, envious of the differences between us that were now so very obvious. Once as rail thin and boyish as I was, Juliet had now sprouted boobs, her hips were curvy, and her legs were long as they wrapped around Vince's waist—long and hairless. And she was shameless; she seemed to actually like it when Vince looked at her naked body.

"Are you gonna give it to me?"

"At your service, baby," Vince said as he stood and grabbed his shorts from the ground, fishing something out of the pocket. Then, as Juliet watched, he slowly slid his underwear over his hips and down. I'm sure my mouth was hanging wide open in shock when I caught sight of him. I'd seen Todd's, but the kid was practically a baby, still only eight. Vince, oh my—the size of him stunned me.

He slid what I quickly determined to be a condom over himself and then started to lower his body back down. He stopped abruptly and gestured to Juliet when he said, "Turn over."

When she whined, "Why?" he snapped, "Turn over...Head down, ass up."

Millie poked my shoulder, snapping my attention back to her as she mouthed, "Ho-lee shit."

My heart was pounding and my eyes immediately broke away from Millie's to look back down.

"Tell me something dirty," he commanded, and when Juliet responded with some generic line like, *Do me baby,* her voice muffled because her face was now mashed into the chair cushions, Vince smirked, looked up to the loft, locked eyes with me and winked.

I shrank back, eyes wide, looking to Millie with urgency to let her know we'd been caught, only to see her leaning back now, lost in her own world, her hand pressed between her legs. Really? Was I the only sane person left on the island? I kicked her leg, startling her as I mouthed, "He saw me!"

If you didn't know Vince well, or even if you did, he could be intimidating. So Millie and I sat completely still for the next five or ten minutes, dead silent as we heard grunts, moans and the sounds of skin slapping against skin. We sat immobile until the two of them were dressed again and gone.

I couldn't get that exchange out of my head, Vince practically barking at Juliet, demanding that she say dirty things to him. Her obedience rewarded with a condescending smirk. I wasn't a fan of Juliet's. She used me for target practice today and it wasn't the first time she'd publicly ridiculed someone. But the whole scene left me confused. Why would he want her to look foolish? Was it payback for what she'd done to me?

Who was this new Vince?

He was either a monster or he was my hero.

I couldn't sleep until I rested my hand between my own legs that night, rubbing as I thought about Vince and Juliet. The next morning I was bone tired as I stood on the grass, peeling an orange as I watched Todd splash in the pool.

There was a gentle tug on my braid. "Enjoy the show last night?"

My cheeks were hot but I fought to square my shoulders and face off with Vince. "Nothing special. She might be Juliet but you're no Romeo."

He liked that one, a smile stretching clear across his face as he looked me over from head to toe, so slowly that I fidgeted under his inspection.

"I can't wait, Margot."

"For what?"

He shook his head, biting his lower lip and eyeing me with what...wonder, laughter, longing?

"I just can't wait," he repeated as he shoved his hands in his pockets, turned and walked away.

* * *

Off to boarding school I went after the following summer. At fourteen, I was tall and gangly, flat-chested, angry about the state of my body and resentful of my mother's attempts to make me into a bona fide debutante.

She was proud of my grades, I guess, but I got the sense that the number of invitations I received to social events was far more important than my intellectual development. And while my mother tolerated my love of horses, she didn't understand how I could enjoy spending afternoons at the stables, turning down offers to go shopping or to get pampered at her favorite hangout, the spa. While I was anxious about living away from home, I was relieved to escape Mother's scrutiny.

Being away gave me some reprieve, but as I got older, her interest in my social status and my "prospects" intensified. Millie's mother certainly didn't seem concerned with whether or not she was dating at sixteen, whereas my mother seemed to be plotting my exercise regime, my outfits and my outings.

There was more to it than the quintessential overbearing mother wanting a good match for her only daughter. There was a *lot* more to it than that.

Because my parents did nothing to censor the screaming matches that had now become a daily ritual in our home, I heard my mother threaten divorce whenever big sums of money disappeared from their accounts, which seemed to happen at fairly regular intervals. And I overheard my grandparents admonishing my mother over my father's reckless spending, about his gambling problem being an embarrassment to the family.

I eavesdropped on that especially bad day, the day when they handed down the verdict: No more. They wouldn't hand over another penny. Grandmother tsk-tsked, Grandfather raised his chin in the air and shook his head, both looking down on their only child as a disappointment. Clearly, Mother had made a bad choice in marrying my father.

I would not be permitted to make a bad choice.

Vincent Cole, my mother reminded me ad nauseam, would one day be at the helm of a very successful company. He was so handsome, wasn't he? An accomplished sailor, a top student—as we speak he's preparing for a semester abroad in France, he's fluent after all.

She forgot to list womanizing gigolo on his dossier.

It's not like I followed his every move, but I did listen with interest whenever his name came up. I hadn't seen a whole lot of Vince in the past three years. He was older. Family vacations and parties were traded for summer backpacking trips through Europe and college semesters spent in Virginia as well as abroad. But I was a part of the same set, so I'd hear bits and pieces. And from what I'd heard, Juliet was one in what became a very long list of conquests. At twenty, it was common knowledge that he was linked with girls he could go to jail for "knowing," as well as women who had graduated from college years before. There was even a rumor circulating that he'd had a steamy affair with one of his married professors. I believed it. But when I finally saw him again, it was hard to reconcile the person before me with the legend.

I'd just finished my junior year of high school. I was seventeen and excited to leave on a two-week trip to Spain with Millie and my best friend from school, Madeline Paulson. The trip was touted as a gift from my parents and would be my first time leaving home unchaperoned. Why my parents trusted three teenage girls traipsing around Europe without any adult supervision, I'll never know, but this type of trip was not unusual. To keep up appearances, my grand-parents had shelled out for the best hotels, deluxe transportation between cities, and tickets to a range of cultural events. They also gave me plenty of spending cash, knowing we would need some money to get up to no good in proper fashion.

A few days before we were scheduled to leave, the Daltons had a get together at their place in Southampton. My father would bitch and moan every time we had a function out this way. Fearful of flying unless the plane was heading to Reno or Vegas, my father would not take a helicopter or small plane out east like everyone else did. No, we were stuck in traffic the entire ride out on the Long Island Express-way. For over four hours I listened to my parents bicker as Todd stared out the window absently.

I was worried about him. My bubbly, sometimes hyperactive little brother had become quiet and introverted since I'd left for boarding school. When I was home, which was now rarely, I noticed he spent hours on end alone, playing video games. Occasionally I'd join him, trying to take some interest in Super Mario Brothers, but it was so inane and pointless. I'd tell my mother they shouldn't let him space out alone all day playing that nonsense, but I think she was happy to have him occupied, no matter that he was turning into a zombie right before their eyes.

Two more years and he'd be shipped off to Exeter. While I liked the idea of Todd being pulled from this self-imposed exile he was currently in, I worried about him in that environment too. The boys at those prep schools were like Vince for the most part: accomplished, confident, popular and athletic. Todd was none of those things, and I feared he'd be eaten alive by those future masters of the universe. But I didn't really dwell on it too often, though, or give him the attention he deserved. I was seventeen and selfish to a certain extent, consumed with the minutia of my own life.

Millie let out a whoop when we finally arrived, dragging me to her room to show me the skimpy dresses she'd bought for the trip, going on about all the clubs and parties we were going to hit in Ibiza and Valencia. We made our way back downstairs eventually, chatting with the other kids who came along with their parents. It was a small gathering. I was happy to see Todd off playing with Juliet's brother, and even more thankful that she was nowhere to be seen. Vince's parents were here, but no sign of him.

Vince's mom, Catherine, was simply beautiful. My mother was attractive and very well preserved, don't get me wrong, but Catherine Cole was otherworldly. She had sunshine-kissed blonde hair, blue eyes, and dewy skin that looked as if it belonged on a woman a full decade younger. She was slender, but not in the way the other women were. My mother and the others were bony and pale, side effects of the strict diets they adhered to. I think my mother subsisted on nothing more than grapefruit, iceberg lettuce salads and vodka, and it showed. She was also a fan of the newest craze: monthly colonics. So gross.

Catherine was different. Her trim waist and defined arms were evidence of her daily yoga practice and afternoons spent mucking out the stalls in her stable.

"Margot, sometimes I have to remind myself that you're not a little girl anymore. Look at this figure! And so tall! You're just stunning."

I truly loved Catherine Cole. Unlike my mother, who lived to point out my flaws, Catherine seemed to notice only my good qualities.

She squeezed my hand. "I saw you ride at Fieldstone in June. How's that going? Are you planning to ride in college?"

"I'm not sure, but I really have to make a decision soon. Part of me wants a city campus experience, and riding won't fit in with that."

Total bullshit.

The only reason I was looking at schools without an equestrian program was that finances had become tight as of late in the Clarke household. Boarding horses was outrageously expensive. Add to that the riding wardrobe, trainers, competition entry fees, veterinary bills —the list of expenses was endless.

Our money came from my mother's side, and last year my grandparents had essentially cut my mother off. My grandparents weren't cruel, though, so we never presented to the outside world as penniless. Todd and I still attended schools that cost quite a lot of money, and people were falsely led to believe that my parents were more than comfortable when, for example, they were able to treat me and two friends to an extravagant holiday for my seventeenth birthday. But I was well aware of the financial strain. And my mother was in quite a pickle. She couldn't rein my father in. His gambling habit was out of control, if you believed what my grandparents were saying, and his penchant for upscale Vegas call girls was another expensive and embarrassing problem. But divorce him? It just wasn't done. And when he was around, even though I was growing to loathe the man, I'll admit he was a charming companion who doted on my mother in front of their friends. Apparently, that was all that mattered.

I'm thinking Catherine Cole, as my mother's one and only true friend, was privy to all this.

"I can understand that, Margot. And look at Vincent...I was certain he would pick a school where he could sail, but he seems quite content landlocked in that part of Virginia."

"How is Vince? I feel like I haven't seen him in ages."

"He's busy, that's for sure. His father has him by his side during every school break, getting him ready to take on Cole Industries." She smiled wistfully. "Sometimes I wish I could go back in time. I'm not ready for him to be all grown up, to not need me anymore. And I worry that it's all so much pressure."

"Vince seems like he can handle anything."

I blushed after I said that, but I meant it. In my eyes, Vince was intelligent and sure of himself. I imagined his transition from college boy to corporate leader would be seamless.

"He does," she said, "but mothers just can't help but worry. You'll see for yourself one day."

Mrs. Hastings sidled up to us, giving me a passing glance while saving her beaming, enthusiastic suck-up smile for Catherine. "So I hear Vince enjoyed his semester in Paris. Juliet was so happy to meet up with him."

Catherine's look turned glacial. "I didn't know Juliet was in Europe last semester."

"Oh yes, I'm sure I mentioned it. My brother and his wife are in London so that's been her base, but she's been all over the continent this year having a fabulous time."

"Just...living it up? You mean she's not in school?"

Juliet's mom stiffened. "She's taking a gap year. Bryn Mawr didn't really live up to her expectations."

I wanted to snicker. Anything that required mental effort wouldn't be Juliet's cup of tea. Juliet was a social animal who preferred to devote her time and efforts to shopping, perfecting her tan and partying like she was in training for the Olympics. And Catherine's reaction filled me with a certain kind of evil glee. Girls like Juliet weren't up to snuff as far as the Coles were concerned. She was wealthy beyond measure but she was vapid. I don't know about Vince, but his parents certainly wanted better for him.

I piped up. "Where is Juliet now?"

"Oh! You might just run into her. I hear you'll be heading to Spain with Mildred."

If Millie overheard, I think she would have accidentally on purpose spilled a drink on Mrs. Hastings. Mildred—who on Earth would name a child Mildred? Millie had taken to telling people her name was short for Milan. She said she'd rather be taken for a pole dancer than a crusty gal who wore granny panties.

"Yes, Mildred and I are leaving on Wednesday," I answered loud enough so that Millie could hear. I saw her face scrunch up from the corner of my eye and I smiled, knowing there would be payback for that later on.

"Well, you'll have to meet up with Juliet," she said, dismissing me as she turned back to Catherine. "And where is Vince? I haven't seen that darling boy in months."

Catherine looked to me when she answered, "I'm hoping he'll pop in tonight. He's out east visiting with a friend in Montauk."

"Montauk? Might as well be Timbuktu. To me, the Vineyard is *so* much more enjoyable. All this traffic...It will take Vince an hour to make his way from Montauk. And I'm sorry, but I'm just not crazy about the crowd out here."

Millie's mom, Martha, was now standing with us, her face tight as she took in the insult. "My family has been coming here for three generations now. It's home to me."

Mrs. Hastings tilted her head, smiling. "Of course it's simply fabulous here, Martha. I just mean that to *me* it's not as quiet and peaceful as the Vineyard."

"I love it here," Catherine said. "And I love that I can actually swim in the ocean before Labor Day. The water is always so dreadfully cold in New England."

Mrs. Hastings looked positively perplexed. "I haven't been in the ocean since I was twelve."

It was nearly eleven by the time Vince sauntered into the backyard with a friend. Tan, muscles well formed from days spent surfing and sailing, casually dressed in khaki shorts and polo shirts—they both looked as if they'd just walked off the pages of a Ralph Lauren advertisement.

I watched as he surprised his mother, lifting her off the floor into a bear hug, the smiles that passed between the two of them proof of the close bond they shared. The other mothers fawned over Vince like they always did. He was the golden boy of our crowd. I watched as he chatted up the ladies, charming them. He was like a politician, turning from one to the next, flashing each a smile and laughing on cue. He popped from the ladies over to his father and the other men, accepting the congratulatory pats on the back, conversing with ease and confidence. Was he aware that everyone seemed to bask in the glow of his presence?

And I couldn't help it, when he finally made his way over to me I felt grateful to be acknowledged.

I'd purposely moved off to the side when I first saw him. I wasn't going to stand there as if I was on some damn receiving line like the rest of those girls, waiting like puppies for Vince to pat them on the head. My back was turned to him as I pretended to look on with interest while Todd and his friend climbed a tree.

"Margot?"

I turned and gave him my carefully thought-out and practiced greeting. The one that told him I was happy to see him but not too concerned about him one way or the other.

"Hey Vince, how are you?"

He didn't say anything back for a full minute. Count it out, sixty seconds—it's actually an agonizingly long stretch of time. He spent that time taking me in from head to toe.

"Wow," he said to no one in particular. Then he gifted me with the softest smile. "You're beautiful, Margot."

I looked down at my feet, not knowing what to do with that, and then crossed my arms over my chest when I could feel my body responding to him. *You're beautiful, Margot.* All my false bravado washed away by those three words.

"And that sweet blush makes you even more beautiful," he said as he gently coaxed my chin with his finger, forcing me to look at him.

"C'mon, Cole, we've put in our time. Let's go."

Vince's friend was rude—good looking but rude. He didn't even introduce himself, just stared at my chest as he spoke to Vince. It was clear from his tone that he found his current surroundings tiresome and boring.

"Gimme a minute, Carter."

Carter threw his head back, exasperated. "It's another half-hour to the Drift. If we don't get there soon, we're gonna be waiting on a fucking line with those townie losers."

Vince rolled his eyes. "We won't be stuck on line. Wait for me outside."

"Hurry up," Carter said as he started walking. "I don't want to leave those dirty Quogue girls waiting."

Vince laughed and then called after him, "And don't light up, asshole...You're driving." He reassured me when he took in my wide eyes. "Don't worry, we're not driving back out to Montauk tonight. We'll find a place to crash."

He didn't understand—I was still stuck on the dirty girl comment.

"So, Mother mentioned you're heading over to Ibiza?"

Calm, cool Margot was replaced by a teenager excited to go on her first unchaperoned adventure. "I'm so excited! Have you been there, Vince?"

"Yeah, a few times," he answered offhandedly. "Listen," he said as he took my hands in his, "just be careful."

My pulse was hammering as I nodded absently. "I will."

His look was suddenly stern, threatening even. "I mean it, Margot. It can get out of control. And some of the guys..." he trailed off, shaking his head. "I heard Reginald Pierce is going to be there with a few of his buddies?"

I was confused by his tone. "Yes, he called me last week. We're planning to meet up."

"He's a sick fuck, Margot. You're *not* meeting up with him."

With anyone else I would have argued or laughed in their face. I did not like being told what to do. But for some reason when Vince spoke, I listened, nodding my head like an obedient child.

"Promise me," he demanded.

"I promise."

"Good." He moved in closer, so close that his chest grazed mine.

Vince leaned down, just barely touching his lips to a spot on my neck right underneath my ear when he whispered, "I don't want him or anyone else touching you."

Oh.

My body was frozen in place but burning up on the inside.

"No one touches you," he said before he backed up a step.

"Vince!" Carter called from the road.

His smile was soft again. "I gotta go."

I stayed there off to the side, partially hidden, needing some time to regain my marbles.

Was I under his spell? Yes and no.

Vince was always somewhere, lingering in the periphery of my consciousness. The memory of his lips on my neck, and those possessive lines whispered in my ear were replayed many nights as I lie in bed alone. But he wasn't around. More than another year passed before I even saw him again.

* * *

At nineteen, as a college freshman, I was now fully on the young socialite circuit. But even though I was entering adulthood, I was still firmly under the heel of my mother. The Junior League Winter Ball, the Young Frick Fellows Ball—didn't matter if I had a massive paper due or I was in the middle of finals. I was to come home, don whatever couture get-up my mother had hand picked for me, and then I was expected to be fabulous. To see and be seen.

At school, though, I had my own life. I had a boyfriend.

Mother didn't know about him.

He didn't understand these mandatory social obligations, and thankfully, had no interest in joining me. That was for the best. He'd mock everyone decked out in their tuxes and couture dresses, snorting lines in the bathroom—all in the name of raising money for homeless people, starving artists or some other worthy cause. I felt like a hypocrite when the pictures were printed in the Times for all to see, with me mugging it up for the cameras along with the rest of them. Wearing twice as much make-up as I normally would, my high heels and shimmery dresses in stark contrast to the unassuming jeans and tees I wore on campus.

Jesse.

Even his name was cool. He was a singer, a songwriter and a musician—double helping on the cool. And he loved me. He played guitar and fronted a local alternative rock band, but the first time I heard him sing was in Church.

The Sunday night Mass held on campus was informal, led by Father Tim, who could not have been a day over thirty. We were encouraged to call out our intentions during the Prayer of the Faithful, and hugs were given to every other person in the basement chapel when the Sign of Peace was offered. The first time I heard Jesse sing, it was a soulful rendition of *O Love That Wilt Not Let Me Go*. If he asked me to go skydiving without a parachute as he played the closing chords of that song, I would have dropped everything and followed him. He was gorgeous, passionate, so intelligent that it floored me, and he was comfortable in his own skin.

Less than one month after that night in Church, I was head over heels in love with him. I spent entire weekends naked in his bed. I happily swayed front row in small, smoky clubs as he played songs written just for me. I held on for dear life, laughing as we sped along on his vintage Triumph with the wind whipping my hair.

I dreamed of our future. But we imploded just ten months after our love affair began.

I asked him to come to my parents' annual Fourth of July bash on Martha's Vineyard, sure in the knowledge that he was booked for a gig in Hyannis. So when he strolled out onto the pool deck that evening wearing a threadbare Kiss t-shirt and cargo shorts slung low on his hips, I nearly fainted.

Back on campus, my heart would have been beating double time with lust at the sight of him, but here? I quickly surveyed the scene, taking in my mother's scrunched up nose, Millie's waggling eyebrows and Bunny's smirk. I swear, it was as if the music had stopped, people froze in place and every conversation halted mid-sentence. He could not have looked more out of place if he tried. As he scanned the group for me, I saw the corner of his mouth tick up in an amused smile as he took in the crisp khaki shorts, seersucker pants and the bright hued polo shirts, each and every one with the collar turned up.

We were done the moment Jesse's eyes landed on me. I tried my best to smile and put on a surprised yet delighted expression, but back then I was a terrible liar. My unease and embarrassment were easy to read.

He didn't seem to care that my parents made no effort to hide their distaste when I introduced him, and he was unreadable when my so-called friends practically laughed in amusement when he told them he was from Dorchester. He could just have as easily said Boston, but no, Jesse made sure to clarify to everyone that he was born and raised in the most economically depressed part of the city. The only person who was civil and friendly towards him was Vincent Cole. He approached, shaking hands, introducing himself as Vince as he handed Jesse a beer, simultaneously taking a sip from his own longneck bottle. And while Jesse was cordial in return, his hard eyes never once left mine. When Vince left us, Jesse downed the rest of his beer, tossed it into the trash so that it made a loud clanking sound, and then turned to leave without another word.

"Jesse, where are you going?" I asked, knowing full well what was happening. Fully aware that I couldn't fix this or undo the damage.

He was walking down the long driveway as I nervously trailed behind, trying to catch up to him but wary of actually doing so.

His head shook from side to side. "Never in my life, Margot...I've never felt like that before. I can't fucking believe it, you're actually ashamed of me."

"I am not!" He let out a cheerless laugh. "Come back, Jesse."

"I'd rather chew glass than be around you right now."

"Where are you going?" I asked desperately as he kept making his way down the driveway with long, purposeful strides.

"It took me nearly two hours to get here between the ferry and the long ass walk. What a fucking waste." When I caught up to him and grabbed his elbow, he shook me off and then rounded on me, pointing in the direction of my grandparents' sprawling home. "Go back, Margot. Go back to your life."

"I'm sorry, Jesse. Please, just wait a minute," I pleaded as he turned and continued walking.

"Nothing to wait for...We're done."

I felt as if I'd been kicked, as if the breath had been knocked right out of me. I staggered back and sat on the front steps for I don't know how long before Bunny sat down and handed me a glass filled to the brim with Chardonnay.

Bunny was my roommate. We were soul-sister close since that first day of freshman orientation. From a Main Line Philly family herself, her upbringing was similar to mine so she understood me. But while she seemed to genuinely like Jesse, I always got the feeling she was humoring me. Like she thought our relationship was nothing more than me taking a walk on the wild side, living out some bad boy fantasy. She'd tag along when I watched him play, sometimes hooking up with a bouncer or one of his bandmates. But drunk and calling out to me over the bass and drums, Bunny had once laughed as she informed me that Jesse and I had less than a snowball's chance in hell of making it.

"I'm sorry I giggled when he showed up, that wasn't cool. But that outfit, Margot! I just, I thought you would have prepared him."

I was too busy gulping my wine to be annoyed with her.

"Where is he?"

"He broke up with me. He's gone."

"Aw honey, I'm sorry. You know how I feel about the whole

thing, but I like Jesse. He's a good guy. And he loves you. I'm sure you can work this out, but—"

"What?" I interrupted. "But make sure I get the approval of the tribe first?"

When Bunny didn't answer, I looked up to see her staring reverently at Vince. No words passed between them as she instinctively got up and abandoned me, leaving room for Vince to take the now vacant spot next to me.

"Trouble in paradise?"

"I'm a terrible person," I said to no one in particular.

He lowered his head and reached over, slowly dragging his thumb over my jaw to catch a wayward tear. "No, you're the best kind of person, Margot. You follow your heart. Not one of those girls back there would even look outside of our set. Sometimes," he shook his head, "sometimes I feel like I have a target on my back when I'm around this crew."

"You *are* kind of the crown prince. I think my mother would actually mud wrestle Juliet Hastings' mom for the honor of being your mother-in-law."

I had a quick laugh as I visualized that scene, but then just as quickly I began sobbing—and I mean ugly, wet, chest-heaving sobs.

"Hey," he soothed, drawing me in close as he wrapped his arm around my shoulder. "Do you love this guy?"

"Yes."

I would come to realize months later that my quietly murmured yes, that one simple word, set the course of the rest of my life into motion.

Before Vince got up and made his way towards his new toy, a pristine black BMW convertible, he squeezed my shoulder, kissed me chastely on the temple and said, "Then I have my work cut out for me."

Three years later, at just twenty-two, I was a June bride. I was the envy of nearly every female along the Eastern seaboard between the ages of eighteen and thirty, about to embark on a month-long European honeymoon before taking my place alongside my husband as the prototypical supportive corporate wife.

I was Mrs. Margot Cole.

* * *

Twenty-nine years later, Vince and I take our place of honor in the front pew. I look to my only child, my son Dylan. He is my life's work. As he turns to watch his bride make her way up the aisle, his expression mimics mine: smiling, confident, winning. There's something barely perceptible around the eyes, though. And I'm sure if I had a mirror, I'd see the same look reflected in mine: resignation.

As the priest recites those solemn words, "I now pronounce you man and wife," I think to myself: *I've done it. I've ruined his life, just like my mother ruined mine.*

Chapter One

DYLAN

I've only cried four times in my life, not counting skinned knees or the time I got kicked in the nuts for telling a girl she was fat in the fourth grade.

The first time was after I'd caught my father cheating on my mother, balls deep in his secretary. I also cried as I left Church on that cold March morning, trailing behind the coffin that had my cousin Will trapped inside. Then there was that shitty night. Alone in the back seat of a cab, a few tears escaped on that weary ride back to the airport, just having lost her. Now this, the fourth time, I am drunk, staring ahead at nothing in the pre-dawn hours of my wedding day.

I'm going to go through with it. There's no reason not to.

Cecilia has been patient, waiting five long years for me to commit. She didn't pester me when the wedding invitations from friends dwindled, only to be replaced by baby shower invitations and birth announcements. No, she didn't say anything at all. It made me angry. She was telling me right from the start that she would acquiesce to me at every turn, that my needs surpassed hers, that she would do anything just to be with me.

I kind of hate her for that.

Several hours later, I plaster on a mega-watt smile as my bride enters the Church flanked by her mother and father, who just happen to be my parents' closest friends. She looks beautiful in her cream colored dress, and I approve of the choice—Lord knows she would have been risking a lightning strike if she'd tempted fate and worn white. Her dress is classic but fitted just right, letting the world know that while the future Mrs. Cole is elegant, she's packing some indecent curves underneath that fabric. Her silky chestnut hair is piled above her head, revealing her long, sensuous neck, and her make-up is understated because she knows that's what I prefer.

As she gets closer, my jaw strains with the effort it's taking to hold my smile in place. I let out a relieved sigh, happy for the opportunity to regroup for a moment when Mr. Tate pulls me into a tight hug, whispering, "Take care of my baby girl," before joining her hand with mine.

I will take care of Cecilia.

I said I would, so now it's my duty to do so.

She has to nudge me when the priest raises his head, looking to me, waiting for me to repeat those tired, time-honored vows. A week prior, Cecilia had sheepishly asked if I'd like to write vows of our own, ones that were more personal. I balked, said that went against tradition. But truth was, I knew I could spit out the standard lines with ease, in sickness and in health and all that. Express feelings of love and devotion for Cecilia in my own words? I was a good liar, but even I couldn't fake my way through that.

So we exchange the rings that served as symbols of our love and—ahem—fidelity, dance to our first song as man and wife, and accept the toasts to our lifetime of happiness.

The only way I can get through it is to down another shot of

Macallan, close my eyes and picture *her* face as I fuck my wife on our wedding night.

Chapter Two

SEVEN YEARS LATER...

DYLAN

"You know I'd love it if you could come with me, but I don't want to pull you away from what you've got going on here. Seems important...What is it again?"

She looks at me with a doting, loving expression. "I'm co-chairing the Juvenile Diabetes Research fundraiser with Samantha Paulson. It's in two weeks. I put it on your calendar, but please make sure that dimwitted secretary of yours doesn't book anything for the weekend after next." I look back at her with what I imagine is a blank expression. "Don't worry, *I'll* make sure she's up to speed," Cecilia amends. I don't take care of trivial bullshit like that and she knows it. "There's just *so* much to do, but I hate the thought of you traveling all alone."

I almost laugh out loud at the predictability of it all. I ask you to join me, you decline. I ask again while subtly reminding you of your other obligations. You hem and haw—decisions, decisions. And then it's settled. I go on my merry way, solo and unburdened, while you stay in New York, tending to your charity ball nonsense or whatever other inane pastime you and your fellow Stepford wives are currently into.

I hate the thought of you traveling alone.

What Cecilia really wants to say is something along the lines of: *If I don't come with you, I know you'll be nailing that twenty-five-year-old account executive from the Zurich office, and I hate the thought of that.* And she's right, I will be. In fact, I've already called lovely Lara and told her to clear her schedule for the next four days, giving her the play by play of all the dirty things I plan to do to her in my suite at the Baur au Lac.

Just pretending to want Cecilia's company is enough to reassure her. "It's up to you, CeCe."

"Ugh…I'd really love to go but do you mind if I stay here? I really do have *so* much to do."

"It's fine, I'll be busy anyway. Probably wouldn't be much of a vacation."

The buttons on her blouse come undone slowly, one by one, and then she lowers the zipper on the side of her fitted pencil skirt. Underneath she wears a corset-style bra and a tiny scrap of a thong. Cecilia still has a tight, well-toned body, long legs and firm tits.

She sinks to her knees in front of me. "If I won't be seeing you for nearly a week," she purrs, "then I have to give you something to remember me by." She undoes my belt, lowers my zipper slowly and pulls my cock out, stroking me until I'm hard.

Cecilia does everything I like. She touches herself as she sucks me off, and takes me deep into her throat when I push her head down as I thrust up into her mouth. She'd basically do anything to please me. Let me take her any way I want, wherever and whenever I want. Cecilia is my wife but acts like she's my sex slave, always looking to keep me interested by suggesting things that are edgier, riskier. For our one year anniversary, she organized a threesome. On my thirtieth birthday she planned a trip to Paris, arranging a night at an upscale sex club. It was the kind of place where couples paid ungodly sums to protect their privacy while either swinging or being voyeurs as members of parliament, models, business titans and socialites mingled and got it on wearing masks and little else.

It wasn't always like this. I'd known Cecilia my entire life and I genuinely liked her. There was a time when she had interests and opinions. And even though deep down I always knew she'd come running if I snapped my fingers, I found her to be intelligent, ambitious and kind. I used to admire her. But I set a chain of events into motion that night so many years ago, the night I tapped out a text as I sat in first class on the last flight back to Chicago. I needed comfort after I'd just gone and fucked up my life—lost *everything*. I never should have reached out to her, but I did. And that's when things began to change. Without meaning to do it, that's the night I set about ruining Cecilia.

I upended her world. Her pursuit of a master's degree was halted mid-way through her program. Finish school? We traveled too much. Start her own career? How could she when I needed her by my side, handling my calendar and our social obligations? Her days became just like those of every other insipid society princess in our social set: work out at a trendy gym that offered the newest pilates-spin-cardio fusion bullshit routine that cost more per session than feeding a homeless family for a week, pop into the dermatologist's office for whatever fountain of youth procedure that was currently the rage, shop, lunch with friends on wine and lettuce leaves, and then service your husband in the evenings *if* he bothered to come home and see you.

Wash. Rinse. Repeat.

My poor, dull wife—she just didn't get it. There was nothing she could do to keep me interested in a monogamous relationship with her. The only woman who had the slightest chance of reining me in was long gone.

Back then, back when I had Kasia in my life, I fought hard against my baser instincts. I hired plump, middle-aged office managers and personal secretaries. I always traveled alone, conducting business during my business trips. I lived to please her. And if I'd just had some more time to grow up, I know I could have been the man she deserved.

But I fucked up royally back then, and I've been paying the price ever since.

"What time is it?" I groan into the phone, registering Cecilia's name on the caller ID.

"Oh honey, I'm sorry! It's just after eleven here. I just got back from dinner with Melanie and Samantha." Cecilia sounds giddy. I'm estimating she's good for at least three glasses of Cabernet right now. "I just wanted to tell you that I love the flowers."

"CeCe, it's five in the morning here. I have a meeting in two hours. I'm glad you like the flowers, but can we talk later?" I manage to sound annoyed even though I'm blissed out and smiling. Lara is nudging me with her bare ass, grinding against my morning wood.

"Ok baby, I just really loved your note. You know that I feel the same way, right? You are my one true love, Dylan."

What the fuck was she babbling about? "Did you girls have a lot to drink tonight?"

"No, I only had two glasses of wine! Maybe I'm just feeling sentimental tonight...Missing you. And that note, well, it just made me feel loved. I love you, Dylan."

Lara was now sucking hard on my thumb and rocking her hips with more force. "I love you, too." For that, Lara scrapes her teeth against me so hard that I nearly let out a yelp. I barely manage to choke out, "I'll be home tomorrow," before hanging up on my wife.

Chapter Three

DYLAN

"Do *you* want children?"

Melanie sits across from me, sprawled over one of the two deep leather chairs opposite my desk. People literally sank into those chairs, which was intentional on my part. Made my adversaries feel even weaker in my presence as I sat tall behind my desk. Even if we stood eye to eye, which was a rarity, I typically had a good half foot on them once they took a seat.

"Hmm...do I *want* them? No, but I'm going to do it. I mean, I don't know how much longer I can put him off. Jon is being a major pain in the ass about it lately, not to mention his mother. I hate that bitch." Her mood brightens when she adds, "Anyway, I'll have nannies. It's not like I won't be able to live my life, right?"

At least she doesn't sugar coat her opinions to make them more palatable to others.

Melanie Pierce, now Mrs. Melanie Sheffield, is a close friend. Maybe my closest friend, even though I don't like what that says about me. Not that I wanted to hang out with her often, it's not that kind of friendship, but there is a level of comfort in our relationship that I have with no one else. Melanie knows almost everything there is to know about me, just as I know all the depraved and lurid details of her life.

We grew up together, a generation of overindulged rich kids, just as our parents had grown up together decades before. We attended the same parties, vacationed together and even spent four years together at the same university. She's a close friend of Cecilia's, and Melanie used to date my fraternity brother and friend, Christian. For years, I liked to think of me, Christian and Melanie as members of our own little secret society. We were like-minded free spirits, and didn't see how the rules of relationships applied to us. The nights I wound up in Christian's bed with Melanie sandwiched between the two of us were too numerous to count.

I guess everyone has their come to Jesus moment, though, and mine was the day I realized I was in love with Kasia. Christian's was the day he walked in on his stepfather tapping Melanie. And Melanie? I don't think she's had that moment yet.

"Is CeCe nagging you again?"

"No."

"Good." Melanie arches her back, pushing her chest out in the process. She's still issuing the invite even though I haven't partaken in quite a while. "I told her that shit is annoying. And what's the rush anyway? We're thirty-five. No one has kids until their forties nowadays."

I smile and laugh. "That's a lie."

She winks. "I know. I'm actually surprised Bunny and Margot haven't worn you down yet."

"Mother doesn't push at all. Bunny and Paul have made some subtle remarks, but they stay out of our business for the most part."

"Ah, must be nice...I'd love to be able to put the fear of God into everyone like you do."

"I don't scare *you*."

"No," she says, licking her lips, "you don't."

"I guess it wouldn't be so terrible. I know Cecilia really wants a baby. It's just—"

"It's just that you just want your baby growing inside of someone else's fat, stretch mark-riddled stomach. What does she have, like, eight kids now?" When I fix her with a look, she tries to placate me in her own sweet way. "I know you, Cole. I know that behind that hard-ass veneer you're still nursing a broken heart. Kind of makes me sick, if I'm being truthful."

"You don't know what you're talking about."

First off, she has four children, not eight. And the last picture I saw indicated that she's bounced back from every pregnancy just fine. In fact, she's never looked more beautiful.

"Right," she shoots back, making no effort to conceal the eye roll. "Bet if I knew your password, I'd find some encrypted file on your laptop with a photo collage of that girl. She wasn't all that, Dylan."

"Just for the record, none of that pining away crap is true, but admit it, Melanie, even you wanted to fuck her."

She throws her head back and laughs. "I'll own up to that...Kasia had some body."

At the sound of her name, a familiar memory pops up. I'd been stalking my prey for days, obsessed with the practically naked girl in that picture since I first saw it. She was lush, sinful and innocent all at once, and I had to know her. I smiled remembering her smart mouth when I finally caught up to her, butchering the pronunciation of her name. *It's not Kah-see-ah.* She tried to act bored but I caught the gleam in her eye. I wanted to suck her face like an animal when her soft lips finally spoke her name, so much sexier, pronounced like Sasha with a K.

Everything about that girl brought me to my knees. And I realized I was now rubbing a spot on my chest, easing an old, familiar ache when Melanie cut into my stroll down memory lane.

"But you and I both know it wouldn't have worked out. Kasia

barely had any time for you, and you're a pampered little bitch who expects to be waited on. I repeat, never would have worked."

Yes, I would have made certain it did.

I stand up to signal that our little chat is over. "You and Jon are coming over for dinner Friday night?"

"Guess I'm being dismissed," she says as she struggles to extricate herself from the chair. "Yes, we'll be there. Please invite that sweet little junior VP of acquisitions or marketing or whatever."

"Who?"

"I don't know...Allen or Andrews or Anderson or something?"

I sigh. "He's getting married next month, Mel."

"Are you telling me *not* to let him bend me over the table in your wine cellar like he did last time? I can just picture his cute little fiancé trying to get in good with all the executive wives while I was deep throating her man."

I can't help but laugh. This girl is like my brother-in-arms. We're more alike than I'd ever care to admit.

"Love you, Mel. I'll see you Friday."

* * *

"You're florist is really exceptional, CeCe. Do use Violet's on Columbus?"

"Yes, they did the table arrangements, but this one is from Dylan."

A few women are standing in the entryway, admiring the towering vase of bright orange long-stemmed roses interspersed with willow tree branches. I'm not one to even look twice at that sort of thing, but I've recently taken a keen interest in flowers. She looks over in my direction, smiling wistfully when she adds, "He sends me flowers every Thursday, like clockwork. I don't know where he orders from...I'm never here when the delivery comes in."

"It's so different," Delia Parker remarks.

The dreamy look on Delia's face is courtesy of the card that came with the flowers. The card Cecilia has left prominently displayed in the arrangement. The card that reads: *I'm so lucky you chose me*. The card I did not write.

Four weeks.

I don't have time to deal with this. I *run* Cole Industries. I make decisions that impact workers, consumers—global economies for fuck's sake. So given the relative insignificance of this issue in comparison to what I deal with on a daily basis, I hadn't given the notes that came with Cecilia's weekly flower delivery much thought. She never used to display the cards, the ones with the generic, impersonal note I dictated to my secretary in haste long ago—something along the lines of: *To my darling wife*. Same note for the past seven years. Come to think of it, those were the same words my father attached to the bouquets he sent Mother. Why mess with tradition?

Better question: Why is someone looking to mess with me?

You are the best thing that's ever happened to me.

Everything is better when I'm with you.

Last week's delivery came with the best one yet: *I'm the man I am today because of you.*

That shit is not even remotely true.

* * *

"Kimberly, come in here."

My newest secretary is about to be fired. How dare she take it upon herself to write that romantic bullshit to my wife?

Friday night after everyone left, Cecilia asked me—dead serious —to *make love* to her. I blame the notes. Before the damn notes she referred to our physical relationship as what it was: fucking. I was never a fan of the phrase to begin with. *Make love* is what sappy soap opera actors crooned to one another back in the eighties. It was phony, fake and downright elderly in my opinion. Hell, I loved Kasia with everything I had, and never once did I use those absurd words on her.

"Mr. Cole?"

I reconsider when she enters my office looking a little shy, a little nervous, and very fu—nope, not going there. Maybe she can just rectify the situation and we can move on.

"You've been with Cole Industries nearly a month, Kimberly."

"Yes, Mr. Cole," she answers, smiling with confidence.

"I know this job is a lot to take on, and you've been meeting my expectations so far."

"I'm glad to hear that."

"But you have to know, I'm particular about how things are done. I have to trust that you can anticipate what I need and that you don't take it upon yourself to make changes I haven't authorized."

She's young, straight out of a top undergraduate program with a major in English Literature. Both of us know she was lucky to land a job like this with that useless major. The job is demanding—*I* am demanding—but she's very well compensated. And aside from this issue, I did think she was adjusting well and doing a good job. And the sex reference was in poor taste; I no longer dipped my pen in the company ink. But if she was looking to make her mark by screwing with my personal life, I'd be firing her sweet, round ass without a moment's hesitation.

She furrows her brow. "Did I do something wrong?"

Damn, I like her pouty, scared look just a little too much for my own good.

"Depends...Did you make any changes to my weekly flower delivery?"

"No! White lilies on the reception desks throughout the office Monday mornings and a varied seasonal arrangement delivered to your personal address every Thursday afternoon." She shakes her head, eyes wide. "No changes."

"Good. I need you to check in with the florist. Tell them I want the standard message. And let them know that if they can't get the order right then we'll find another vendor starting next week."

"I'll do that right away, Mr. Cole."

"Thank you."

"Anything else?"

"Make a reservation for five at Delmonico's...Thursday night, eight o'clock. Confirm it with Tom Farrell's secretary."

Chapter Four

DYLAN

I'm grateful Tom's younger brother is going be tagging along tonight. Brendan, someone I've always referred to as "kid," is twenty-seven now and currently killing it at a private equity firm. Just upgraded to a sweet loft apartment in Tribeca and he's living the life.

It's not that Tom, Caleb and Ben bore the crap out of me nowadays—actually they do, but I love them like brothers—it's just that with Brendan around, there's less likelihood that the conversation will veer into Dad mode. Every once in a while I have to suffer through a few minutes of preschool acceptance drama, junior lacrosse league politics or some other bullshit, but for the most part I think it goes unsaid that kids and marriage are not acceptable topics of conversation at our monthly steak dinner.

"To the groom!"

So much for that.

We all clink glasses, toasting Brendan, who just pulled out a ring box to show off a big-ass square cut diamond. He's set on proposing to his girlfriend next week. I paste a smile on my face but I'm not feeling it. Hearing Brendan talk about his girl and looking around the table at the other three, all of whom are absurdly happy, leaves me feeling hollow.

I feel bad for myself but worse still for Cecilia. I'm a shitty husband. I know it, she knows it. But we pretend. She pretends I don't fuck around behind her back, I pretend to be grateful to have her as my partner in life, she pretends that she's not aching for a child, and I pretend that I'm on board with starting a family someday soon—just not this very minute.

Every day I pretend.

I pretend that I'm not miserable and really fucking lonely.

* * *

Turns out the night wasn't a total wash.

I convinced my fellow thirty-somethings that it was beyond lame to go straight home after dinner. We had to go out and celebrate Brendan's impending nuptials. It wasn't difficult to lure them to Le Bain.

Shuffling into my apartment much, much later, I decide that I should take the spare room. I reek of booze and weed, even though I don't partake in the latter anymore. Pot isn't legalized in New York but you'd never know it. You could get a contact high in some of the confessional booths in this city—people light up everywhere. Cecilia would be irked if she thought I was toking without her, and she's not a fan of whiskey breath, or worse, whiskey dick.

I laugh to myself as I slide off my already loosened tie and toss it onto the entryway table. If I was capable of feeling shame, I'd say I embarrassed myself flirting with that insanely hot coat check girl tonight, but I'm thinking she was down with it. Usually I wouldn't dream of putting myself out there like that—I've been on Page Six enough times to know better—but there was something about her.

Making my way into the bathroom, I set about brushing my

teeth, making three attempts before successfully landing the toothpaste onto my brush. Yep, she was hot, but so what? So is every other girl who works the trendy bars and clubs of lower Manhattan.

In my drunken state I'm gonna call her Gia, because she looked like a Gia. Gia had dark brown hair that draped halfway down her back. It was shiny, and I remember that I wanted to nuzzle into it just like I used to bury my face into the pelts of my mother's soft sable coat when I was a kid. But while Gia's hair looked soft, her eyes didn't. No, those bourbon brown eyes rimmed in gold looked like they belonged to a street cat. And when I first approached her without a coat to check, she'd pretty much bared her claws at me. I think she actually told me to "beat it," like I was some annoying loser wasting her time. A manager who was nearby overheard and came over, practically tripping over his words to make sure I wasn't offended. He shot Gia a stern look and was about to lay into her before I stopped him cold, assuring him that Gia was doing an excellent job. He walked away but turned back to glare at her twice.

"Guess you're a VIP, as in: very irritating patron. My boss looked like he was about to drop down to his knees for a second there." When I went to speak, she raised her palm, cutting me off. "And don't expect me to say thank you for saving my ass. It's been one day and so far I hate this job."

"The tips must be good."

She rolled her eyes. "Right, when guys like you come up to ogle and flirt without a coat on."

I didn't even know where my suit jacket was at that point, or else I would have checked it. I loosened my necktie, pulled it over my head and handed it to Gia. "Here, I'm trusting you with one of my most valuable possessions."

She shrugged as she took it from my hand and then turned it over to check the label. "It's ugly, but you're right, it probably cost more than my entire outfit."

"My personal shopper would be insulted."

"Oh Gawd, please tell me you don't have a stylist. I was starting to think you were cute."

Cute? Nope, don't think that word has even been used to describe me.

"What's the matter with hiring someone to shop for me? Real men don't waste time shopping for clothes."

"Agreed," she said, nodding, assessing me. "But it makes you seem like you're way too into your appearance. If you have a personal shopper then you probably have a manicurist and some chick who waxes your eyebrows."

"Hah, you don't know diddley when it comes to me. I bite my nails, thank you very much, and I have no need to wax my eyebrows." She had her lips wrapped around a straw as she sipped her drink, trying her best to rein in a smile. I was focused on her lips, which is the only way I can explain the line that followed. "I do wax my balls, but that's just common courtesy."

I think she actually snorted some of her club soda when she laughed, and she couldn't stop giggling as she dabbed at her top with a napkin. I wanted to dry her off, trap those few stray droplets that landed on her collarbone. I wanted to wrap that long hair around my fist and coax her head backward. I wanted to trace my lips over her neck and inhale her scent.

I was drunk, but not drunk enough to overlook the fact that this girl was not for me.

The tough girl act was pretense, nothing more. When she laughed, you saw all that was vulnerable underneath. Yes, Gia was sexy, but moreover, she was young and innocent.

Not for me.

I drop my belt onto the bathroom floor, the buckle making a loud clatter, and then make my way back out to the foyer to see if I left my phone where I dropped my tie. The tie she left an imprint of her lipstick on before sticking her tongue out at me and tossing it back in my face. Hot little brat. My phone, my phone—I want to see if I got Gia's number. I think I might have. No, I remember now, she made some comment about being young enough to be my kid's babysitter before snapping a selfie and telling me she was giving me something for my spank bank as an act of charity. Good sense of humor, too.

I have to blink and focus hard to open the photo app on my phone. There she is, wearing one of those tight black dresses they make all the girls wear. Supposed to make the help blend into the background, but that backfired with Gia. She's a true beauty. Taking in the smile she's flashing, I suddenly feel guilty because there was something else about her—she was nice. She admitted to being out of her element when she confessed this was her first night working the club. And she pulled at the hem of her skirt every few minutes, trying in vain to stretch the scant few inches of fabric lower to cover more of her legs. The simple gesture telling me that while she was no doubt aware of the fact that she was sexy, she wasn't all too comfortable being noticed in that way.

I dropped a hundred in her cup when she turned away from me to get someone else's coat, and then left her without saying goodbye.

I toss my phone back onto the table, feeling dejected, and it lands with a thud, hitting the vase that sits in the middle. "Fuck," I mutter as it teeters. As I reach out to steady it, I bang into the table and the vase goes toppling. There are purple flowers everywhere, the floor is soaked and the vase is done for. Nothing worse than glass in your foot, so I scoot back on my ass, away from the mess I've made. I'm so tired. I contemplate just curling up right here on the floor, but press the heels of my hands into my forehead to try and shake myself out of this. When I open my eyes, they fix on a small card sitting amid the broken glass. The writing is smudged but I can still make it out.

My heart beats for you.

Oh, *hell* no.

* * *

I might have been shitfaced when I got home last night, but that card is the first thing I think of when I pop out of bed running on three hours sleep. I regret my standing seven o'clock appointment with my sparring partner for a split second before jumping in the shower to start my day. I feel like hitting someone this morning and I need to sweat the booze out of my system. After my workout I plan to head into my office and lay into Kimberly. What the fuck? That was a pretty simple task. The access to eye candy isn't worth it. I need a plump, middle-aged, competent den mother-type to run my office. I'll get on that right after I send Kimberly on her merry way.

Chapter Five

DYLAN

Apparently I'm getting soft in my old age.

Two sniffles from Kimberly and I'm reassuring her that she'll be happy working in the marketing department and that her year-end bonus will stay the same, even though she doesn't deserve a penny of it. And me, *I'm* the one marching down Madison Avenue on the warpath looking for H&A Florists.

I nearly pass the understated storefront. It's housed on the ground floor of a residential building that looks old and stately, kind of like the Dakota. There's a small gold plaque with H&A Florist and Landscape Design inscribed on it. From the location alone I imagine they have a lot of upscale clients, but it comforts me to know they'll definitely take a hit losing my business. And I want to personally inform them that they will never be considered for a vending contract for any business connected with Cole Industries.

Take that, motherfuckers.

I pause and take a deep breath before entering because I like to project an air of relaxed control at all times—can't do that when you're red in the face and foaming at the mouth. But I *am* livid. I can't believe I'm taking time out of my day to deal with this trivial shit, and I'm fuming mad because someone obviously thinks this is funny—that fucking with Dylan Cole is funny.

I'm taking deep cleansing breaths when five minutes have passed and no one has ventured near the counter to help me out. I was actually starting to feel slightly blissed out when I first walked in. There's soft jazz music playing, it feels like I've wandered into some secret garden with clusters of greenery and colorful blooms filling the space, and the smell is incredible. But now I'm back on the warpath at Defcon level one.

The sound of someone singing gets louder as I make my way towards the back. And to call it singing is being kind. She's facing away from me, her hands busy arranging a towering bouquet of black roses. I'm transfixed for a moment, taking in the odd beauty of the coal-black flowers, appreciating how artistic the girl is, and simultaneously wondering what moved someone to order such a macabre arrangement. I'm also transfixed by her ass. She's moving her hips back and forth slowly, head cocked to the side, wearing short shorts, a snug belly- baring shirt and she's barefoot. It's November.

When she goes to hit a high note, butchering the Etta James hit, I'm snapped back to the present. And when she ignores my umpteenth *Excuse me*, I slam my hand down on a work table to get her attention.

"Eeep!" she shrieks, spinning around and knocking the vase off balance with the motion.

She looks startled and I'm rendered speechless.

"What the eff?" she barks, narrowing those freaky cat eyes on me. "Gia?"

Chapter Six

VERONICA

"Who the hell is Gia? And are you stalking me, psycho?"

"No, no...I'm not stalking you. I'm uh—"

The shears are behind me. Reaching back, I slide one hand along the surface of the countertop until I've got them. I'm on Madison and Seventy-first, not exactly dangerous territory, but I'm a woman and I'm alone, and this guy is much bigger than I am.

"I'm calling the cops!" I warn him as I swing my weapon in front of me, the pointy blades facing towards Mr. GQ. Holy hell, why do all the good-looking ones have to be creeps?

He takes a step back and puts his hands up to convey that he means no harm. At the same time his expression hardens. "I've been waiting up front for five minutes. Does anyone in this store understand the concept of customer service?"

I don't know why it feels so difficult to look him in the eye, but it does. It feels like he's boring holes into me. The other night it was with this intense kind of interest, but right now he's looking at me with something that borders on animosity, hatred even. In avoiding his glare, I'm now taking in what lies at my feet: the broken Simon Pearce hand-blown glass container and two dozen rare Turkish Halfeti roses, a few of them too mangled to salvage. Henry is going to lose his shit.

"I'm gonna lose my job."

He shoves his hands into his front pockets, impatient. "What was that? You're mumbling."

I bend down to pick up the roses, thinking about which vase will do, now that I have fewer flowers to make the arrangement look full. I already know that this customer, prissy fuck that he is, will be calling Henry to complain. He's a well-known restauranteur and knows his stuff, flower-wise. He has a standing weekly order and likes what's unique, expensive and hard to find. Henry used to insist on making his order personally, but recently began trusting me to design arrangements for his more demanding clients. And today Henry and Alex trusted me with the entire store while they check out a property in Rye. I don't want to give them a reason to regret their decision.

"Still can't hear a word you're saying."

Speaking of prissy fucks.

Through clenched teeth I ask, "Can I help you with something or are you just here to screw with my head?"

His jaw tenses as he looks around. "I'd rather speak to a manager."

"Well, I'm all you've got."

"This is your shop?"

"No. I'm in charge today, though."

Taking my own statement to heart, I take a deep breath, muster up a quasi-smile and gesture for him to follow me to the front. I wince in pain as I take another step towards the register, knowing that a sliver of glass is firmly wedged in my left heel. Why the hell did I take off my shoes?

Catching a glimpse of myself in one of the many mirrors that line the store's walls, I shake my head, taking in the getup I'm sporting. I look like I should be pumping gas instead of tending to customers in one of the most exclusive zip codes in Manhattan. Usually I change before opening up for business, but I was excited early this morning when I saw Henry's notes on the black rose arrangement. I dove right in, feeling creative.

Mr. GQ looks uncomfortable now, taking me in as I hobble along, careful not to let my left heel hit the floor. "Are you all right?"

I wave him off. "I'm fine. Just not the way I like to start out the morning. You startled me and I, well," I look down at my clothes, shaking my head, "I didn't even realize it was past ten."

"Look, maybe I should come back tomorrow when your boss is here."

"No! Look, I'm sorry if I was rude before but really, I can handle your order or any concern or issue or whatever it is." Great, now I'm rambling. "I just...This is a weird coincidence. It is a coincidence, isn't it?"

He turns his face to the ceiling as if he's asking God for patience. "Of course it is. I certainly didn't track you down and follow you to your job...I mean your second job."

Without meaning to speak out loud, I mutter, "My third."

His eyes are kinder now. "You're industrious."

"Why did you call me Gia?"

He shrugs his shoulders. "I have no idea. I was pretty drunk the other night. I thought that's what you told me."

"I never told you my name."

"I never asked," he shoots back, smiling now.

"It's Veronica."

"That fits." He pats the countertop. "Hop up. I'm pretty skilled at removing glass."

When I hesitate, he takes me by the waist and deposits me onto the counter. He takes my foot in his hands and I feel the sensation zip from my heel to the very top of my inner thigh. He doesn't notice my reaction. He's intense as he inspects my foot, then reaches into his suit jacket to pull out a pair of reading glasses. I try to stifle a giggle but fail. He looks like an insanely hot version of Clark Kent.

"No making fun of the old guy allowed," he says without taking his eyes off my foot. "Just wait until you turn thirty-five. One day you can read the newspaper, next day you can't."

"You wear them well."

Before I can even register what he's doing, some sound like *ahh* comes out of me on a breathy exhale. He's crouched down and licking a path across my heel. Oh. My.

"What's that for?" I rasp.

"It must be small." He licks again and then swirls his tongue around one small spot. "Got it," he says, raising my foot up again and peering at it as he pushes both thumbs against the spot. "Hold still."

Hold still? Not a problem. I can't even breathe.

He looks at me triumphantly as he holds out his index finger, the tiny shard perched on the tip. "It's amazing that something this small can cause so much pain."

"Thanks. Let me guess...You're a surgeon, right?"

"Not even close, but maybe I missed my calling."

The air shifts between us again, the tension from before returning. He takes a step back and I hop off the counter, thankful when I locate my shearling lined slip-on boots.

"So, um, how can I help you?"

"I'm having a problem with my weekly delivery. I've had the account for years so I'm not really sure what's going on."

"Your name?" I ask nervously as I boot up the computer. I've been taking on more of the day-to-day operations lately, making the arrangements and scheduling the deliveries, so if there was a screw-up it was probably my screw-up.

"Last name's Cole. The delivery is to the San Remo. Seventy-fourth and—"

"Central Park West. I know it."

I made those arrangements, and with care, goddammit. The last one I made was my favorite to date: deep purple peonies packed together with boxwood stems adding some deep green contrast. It was simple but luxe. His order had a big budget: three-fifty a week for a basic home delivery, so I always had lots of room to let my imagination and creative streak run wild.

"You didn't like the last arrangement?"

"It's not the flowers...Tell you the truth, I don't even look at them."

Ok, asshole.

He stares down at me then, jaw set. "I need to know who's writing the notes."

I'm sure I've taken on a deer in the headlights look. "What's wrong with the notes?"

"Someone's taking the liberty to write whatever the hell they want." His face is growing red with suppressed rage. "I have an order. There's a standard note with that order."

Holy shitcakes. "It was me. I just...Henry said it was, um, a guy who sends flowers to his, uh, wife every week. You have a wife?"

Mr. GQ looks away, digging his hands deeper into his front pockets.

Guilty much?

"I'm cancelling the order, effective today."

I stare at the computer screen, taking in the size of the order. In total, between the corporate and residential deliveries, this guy is shelling out roughly eight grand a month. He's basically covering the store's monthly operating expenses. If I fuck this order up, even my cousin Alex won't be able to save my ass if Henry wants to fire me. Hell, if I owned the shop *I'd* fire me.

"Please don't do that. I make your arrangements. I wrote the notes. I just thought—"

His eyes are cold when he snaps, "You didn't think."

"The original note just sounded so lame. I figured I'd spice it up."

"How old are you, twelve? Do you have any idea what you've done? You don't stick your nose into someone else's relationship."

His words sting for just a moment before I have the urge to laugh in his face. My anger is a slow burn, steady and growing as I picture some clueless wife at home, while her husband, this jerk standing in front of me, spends his nights trolling the clubs for barely legal cooch. I want to tell him that his note—*To my darling wife*—is bull-shit, something only a guy with a giant stick up his ass would write. I want to tell him that only a phony, only a *cheat* would write that. But I hold my tongue. Alex and Henry put their trust in me and I'm not about to let them down.

I swallow all that down and say, "I never meant any harm."

He looks embarrassed, and dammit, he should look embarrassed. Is he taking a stroll down memory lane right now, recalling his borderline lewd behavior from the other night? Trying not to stare at my tits, but failing miserably as he sucked on the lime from his tequila shot for way longer than was necessary? At the time, I'll admit I thought he was funny, beyond hot and even a little sweet. But now? Now he's just another creepy married guy stepping out on his wife.

"Probably better if I take my business elsewhere."

"I'm asking you not to do that. This was *my* mistake." I have to pause for a deep, steadying breath because I *hate* sucking up to people. "I made the mistake and I'll make sure the orders are correct moving forward." I can tell he's not going for it so I throw myself a Hail Mary. "Please, I need this job."

He studies me for a moment and then lowers his head. "Look, I know you think I'm a jerk. I just..." He shakes his head and takes a second before continuing. "I don't think you understand...You couldn't possibly understand my life."

Is he joking? Doesn't this guy realize he is anything *but* compli-cated? He's a dime a dozen. Another cheating husband—nothing more, nothing less. But the customer's always right, isn't he?

"Absolutely. Just like you couldn't possibly fathom the crap I have to deal with on a daily basis." Like I said, groveling is not my strong suit. "So, can we let bygones be bygones, Mr. Cole? You don't cancel your order or go to my boss, and I won't wax poetic ever again."

I'm doing my best to give off the cool and unaffected vibe, but my nerves are shot.

He keeps me waiting for a long moment before nodding. "Okay." His expression is sheepish when he says, "Maybe the note should say something like...*Thinking of you*."

"Done."

He flashes me a smile that's more shy than cocky as he turns to go. "This is the weirdest morning I've had in a long time."

"Ditto."

"Take care of yourself, Gia," he says before walking out the door.

$$\mathscr{Chapter\ Seven}$$

DYLAN

Thinking of you.

Every time I see the cards, I think of her. Now they peek out from very simple, drab arrangements. The fiery colors, the stark contrast of bare branches, the lush greenery spilling out over the lip of the packed vase—all of that is gone. The compositions are now sterile. Lost that loving feeling, if you will. This week it's yellow roses and that cheap crap they stuff in between. Baby's breath, I think they call it. And the card, once hand written, is now plain white card stock with a preprinted message in Times New Roman font.

Gia.

Veronica.

I don't think she has a hand in making the flower arrangements anymore.

I left the office early after that debacle at the flower shop because as far as productivity goes, I was useless. I had my driver take Madison that afternoon, even though it took us out of the way. Had him pull over across the street from the shop, making some lame excuse about needing a minute to type out a few emails. It took just ten minutes before I was rewarded with a glimpse of her. She was fussing with something in the front window display and then walked outside to see it from the sidewalk. Gone were the cutoffs and tank. She was now in a sleeveless bright red sheath dress that ended mid-thigh. The girl obviously didn't feel the need to dress for the weather. She still had on the short fuzzy boots, but all I could see was leg, long ass legs. Her hair was pulled up now, showcasing her neck. Made her look older but it didn't change the fact that she was young—too young.

I wanted to see her again but I wasn't a fool and I wasn't weak. After that day I banned myself from driving down Madison Avenue and I banned myself from late night drinks at the club that was once my favorite.

* * *

My mother hates it when I put my phone on speaker, but I'm so done with this day and it's late. I stand and put my jacket on, say yes to whatever it is she's asking me to do. "I'll be there."

"Your father and I can't make it, Dylan, so I appreciate it."

"What's up with you two lately? Lots of trips, getaways…Is it like second honeymoon time?"

She lets out a cheerless laugh. "Nothing like that."

"Everything all right?"

"Of course, sweetie…Just so busy. You know your father, so many obligations."

No, I didn't know. I'd basically taken on all of my father's business-related obligations. Nowadays my father came into the office three times a week, max. I really didn't know what he was doing with all his free time.

Christmas at their house was weird this year, now that I think about it, with my father ducking out to take calls every hour or so and my mother pouring the chipper on extra heavy. I didn't give the distance between them so much as a passing thought at the time, but now her tone was making me uneasy. "You sure nothing's up?"

"You would know better than me, dear. You see your father every day. I'm lucky if I get one dinner a week and a few hours on Sunday after he saunters in from playing golf."

I clam up. I know that my parents' relationship isn't perfect, no relationship is, but this sounds different. Margot sounds angry in her own passive, controlled way.

"Are we still on for dinner tomorrow?"

We have a standing Tuesday dinner date at some little hole in the wall Italian place on the East Side. Sometimes having to carve that time out of my schedule was a drag, but now I was feeling like a serious sit down was in order.

"Would you mind terribly if we skip this week? I'm thinking of heading up to the Vineyard. There's a yoga retreat I've been hearing about and they have a spot that just opened up last minute."

"You and Bunny getting all Namaste?"

"I'm going on my own. It's more of an individual thing."

"I get it," I say, even though I do *not* get it. Margot never does anything alone. She raises the troops and she's always the one-woman planning committee for girls' getaways, family vacations and dinner plans. I want more of an explanation but keep myself in check. "Sounds good. How long will you be gone?"

"Just five days. I'll be back on Monday so keep next Tuesday night open."

"You, me and Dad?"

"Just the two of us, Dylan. Tuesday night is our thing. It's the only time I get you all to myself."

Something is most definitely not right in Colesville.

"And remember to keep this Thursday afternoon free. I'll call your secretary and give her all the details."

"Yep, I'll be there." I feel the need to add, "I love you, Mom."

* * *

By Thursday afternoon I'm seriously on edge. My father spent two hours in the office on Tuesday, didn't show at all on Wednesday and left before noon this morning. I caught up with him as he was leaving to ask how my mother's yoga retreat was going. He tried to cover, but I could tell he had no idea what I was talking about.

My father has a sense of integrity in all things except his marriage. That fact was established long ago. And while I used to feel superior to him because of that, I no longer feel I have any right to judge him —for obvious reasons. My mother is no one's fool; she knows about his extracurricular activities. We don't speak of it, but she knows. I preferred not to give it much thought, but always figured they had an understanding. Whatever is going down between them now, though? This is different.

So I'm irritated and distracted as I walk into New York Hospital, wondering what the fuck he's done this time. But I carry on, shake hands with the doctors and hospital administrators, and pose for pictures with the nursing and recreational staff that work the new Catherine Cole Pediatric Wellness wing. My mood softens as I listen attentively while the hospital's CEO sings my mother's praises, and I even take to the podium myself, saying a few words about my mother and her devotion to carrying on a cause that was close to my paternal grandmother's heart. Catherine Cole, registered nurse—for years my mother has worked tirelessly to raise funds to help children across this city in my grandmother's name. For her, I can suck it up and put on a happy face. My mother deserves that and so much more. I even hang out and play ping pong with a few of the kids, literally taking it on the chin when a little cutie named Ava nails me in the face not once, but twice.

The Chief of Staff, Dr. Norris, walks me to the elevator, making a case for even more pledge dollars from Cole Industries to fund some research project. I'm only half listening, but nodding my head in agreement anyway, still high from the positive energy those kids gave off. It's like everyone says, children are resilient. That little Ava was rail thin, pale, and had a giant patch of hair missing from a recent surgery, but still her smile stretched from ear to ear when she aced me on a serve.

My smile matches Ava's as the elevator doors open, but then drops when I catch sight of a young woman leaning against a wall in the lobby with her face in her hands. Her body shakes with the force of her sobs. A young doctor makes his way over to her before I can get there. She shakes her head and takes a deep breath, refusing whatever help he's offering. I'm about to continue on my way when she moves her hands to wipe at her face.

"Out of the way." I gesture to the young doctor who's now cemented by her side. "Veronica?" At the sound of her name she looks up at me. Her eyes go wide before she breaks into a new round of sobs. "Here." I offer her my silk pocket square and place an arm around her shoulder. Crazy, but the thought of comforting her makes me feel like a man, makes me possessive and territorial. I shoot a look to the young doc that says: *Run along, son*, and he does as told.

"Veronica, tell me what's wrong."

She blows her nose and takes a shuddering breath. When she attempts to speak, she collapses into herself again, weeping as she says, "I'm sorry," over and over again.

I pull her into me and hold her tight, suddenly sad myself. Not just because she's in pain, but because holding her feels so good that it hurts. That's how fucked up I am. Holding a girl who is practically a stranger makes me feel the all-powerful pull of goodness and love, while I have a wife at home, and holding her makes me feel...nothing.

"Shh, I've got you."

She sinks into me, still crying. I may or may not have kissed the top of her head. Probably did because then I feel her stiffen. She draws in another deep breath before she nudges me back gently and whispers, "I'm ok, really."

I take a step back and clear my throat, trying to rid myself of the ridiculous thoughts I'm entertaining. Veronica isn't mine to hold and I'm probably the last person on the planet she'd seek out for comfort.

She goes to hand me back the used pocket square but thinks better of it, stuffing it into her purse. "What are you doing here?"

"I was here to, uh, dedicate a...Nothing, just corporate stuff."

I'm not about to tell her that over the years my family has donated enough money to have several wings of this hospital named after us. That would be a tad too douchey.

"Do you have a friend admitted here? Or family?"

"Family," she states flatly.

"That's rough."

"My cousin...She's been sick off and on for the past year or so. But she was getting better, you know? She was in some clinical trial and she was doing great. The past two weeks, though...I could tell. I knew she was getting weaker. But Kasia always puts on a brave face. She's always smiling, never complains, never—"

Now I'm the one leaning against the wall for support. "Kasia?"

She nods. "Yes, my cousin. She's the strongest person I know."

I look at Veronica, dumbstruck as she pulls her shirt sleeve down to wipe at her eyes again. My God in heaven—Veronica and Olivia, Kasia's little cousins. This very girl sat in my lap one Christmas Eve long ago, chewing my ear off about wanting her own horse, the injustice of not being able to wear nail polish at age seven, and arguing that genies were, in fact, real. And my Kasia. The thought of her suffering in any way feels like a punch to my gut.

I'm sure I look pale and lifeless when I ask, "What's wrong with her?"

Veronica doesn't notice the odd catch in my voice or the cold sweat that's breaking out across my forehead. In a muffled voice, she answers, "Brain cancer." To no one in particular, she adds, "I don't know how they'll manage without her. Her babies are too little to lose their mother."

"She has children?"

I'm still hoping this is some other Kasia. Some other girl, not mine.

"Four."

"Fuck!"

My foul mouth snaps Veronica out of her funk. "Listen, thanks for, um, everything. I appreciate it, although I feel kind of foolish now."

"Please don't thank me, and you have no reason to feel embarrassed."

I have to make a conscious effort to stop raking my hands through my hair repeatedly like a deranged lunatic. "Are you going up to see her now?"

"Just leaving," she answers, her expression matching the gray sky and cold January rain that waits just outside the lobby's revolving glass door.

"I'm stuck here for a while longer but my driver is outside. He can take you home."

"Definitely not going there," she mutters. In response to my concerned look, she adds, "Long story."

Veronica shakes her head when she looks down at the thin sweater she's wearing. Again, not dressed for the weather. Without a coat, she'll be soaked to the skin within a minute.

"He can take you wherever you're heading."

"Are you sure? I've been crashing in the apartment at the back of the store. That's all the way across town."

I already have my phone out, texting instructions to my driver. "I insist."

I watch her walk out the door, now underneath the protection of the umbrella my driver has opened and waiting for her. My eyes are fixed on her until she's ushered into the car, safe and dry. Once they pull away, I stand there for I don't know how long, as if my feet are bound by cement. My world has been rocked off its axis.

Sick on and off for the past year.

A year.

My first instinct is to call Tom Farrell, my oldest friend and the closest thing I have to a brother. But fuck Tom. He *knew*. I'm sure he's known this entire time—sat across from me at dinner, sat by my side at every Giants home game this season, spent an entire weekend skiing with me and a few of the guys just this past month—and that piece of shit didn't see fit to tell me that Kasia was dying? Fuck Tom, fuck Darcy, fuck Caleb. Fuck every single one of them that claims to be my friend.

Dr. Norris is exiting the elevator, leaving for the day when he spots me.

"I need to get some information on a friend. She has cancer, brain cancer."

"That's an odd request, Mr. Cole. Are you all right?"

I feel out of it, so I'm sure I look the same. "I'm fine," I answer, collecting myself. "I just ran into someone who relayed the news to me." I take a deep breath and fix him with a hard stare that's meant to convey there won't be a dime for his damn pet project if he doesn't help me out. "I need you to tell me her prognosis, and I have to make sure, absolute certain that everything possible is being done for this woman."

Well, HIPPA laws be damned. He nods his head in the direction of the elevator, and within five minutes we're in an office on the tenth floor, the oncology ward.

"Her name?"

"K-A-S-I-A. Last name M-A-Z-U-R."

"Must be a mistake...We have no patients registered under that name."

I close my eyes, realizing my error. She hasn't been Kasia Mazur in a long time. I know exactly how long too, because I remember getting good and drunk, sitting alone in my apartment with all the lights out and the shades drawn on her wedding day.

"Last name is Wozniak."

He's quiet for a few minutes, clicking from one screen to the next, looking at images, reading test results. He takes his glasses off and looks up at me. "Glioblastoma, late stage. Surgery with recurrence less than one year later. She took part in the AMG-103 clinical trial."

"Speak English."

"Your friend has an aggressive type of cancerous brain tumor."

"What about the clinical trial?"

"She was a marginal candidate at best. Immunotherapy. Frankly, I'm surprised she was included. But unfortunately, it doesn't seem like it worked for her."

"You said she had a recurrence one year later?"

"Yes. She was initially diagnosed, hmm, let's see...February. So she's just coming up on two years. Seems like her initial symptom was blurred vision."

"Is she terminal?"

His eyes are kind when he says, "I'm not her doctor but her condition, yes, it is terminal."

I swallow, unable to speak until I clear my throat of the sadness and pain. "Is she here now because she's dying?"

"No. She's in the middle of a round of chemotherapy and was dehydrated. From the doctor's notes it looks like she'll probably be discharged home tomorrow or the day after."

"So the chemotherapy will help her?"

"It can prolong her time." He shakes his head when he adds, "There's no cure, Mr. Cole."

"That can't be right."

"I assure you, Mrs. Wozniak has been given every cutting edge treatment option there is. Her treating physician is Dr. Poole. He's the head of neuro-oncology. I can tell you, it was quite a coup when we lured him away from Duke. She couldn't be in better hands."

"Her room number?"

"I can't tell you that, Mr. Cole. What I've already done...It's pretty much illegal."

I don't need him to tell me. As I'm making my way back towards the elevators, I see a hunched over figure standing at the end of the hallway. I'd know him anywhere. And whereas I've only ever felt a long simmering hatred for the guy, in this moment I actually wanted to hug Jake Wozniak, to let him know I understand the heartbreaking pain he must be in right now.

Chapter Eight

VERONICA

"This is fine, right here."

Before I can hop out and make a run for it, he comes around with the damn umbrella again. This is going to be awkward. I knew before I got in the car that I didn't have my keys to the store on me. Alex and Henry are away so I was planning on prying my way past the flimsy grate that covered the window near the rear service entrance. Can't really do that with Jeeves here on my heels, now can I?

"Thank you again for the ride. Good day."

Did I really just say *Good day* to the man? Like I'm an extra on the set of Downton Abbey or something?

"It's raining, Miss Veronica. Mr. Cole would be displeased if I didn't see you inside safely."

Safe. I was just beginning to grasp the concept again. Kicked out of my home a few months after my seventeenth birthday, I've basically been couch surfing my way through the past three years. Don't go feeling bad for me, though. I've been lucky. I had Larson at first, and then I had friends to lean on. And this past year, when things got really rough, I swallowed my pride and knocked on a once familiar door. I thank God when I think back to that moment, when the extended family I was estranged from for so long took me back in with open arms, no questions asked.

This entire day—what a mind fuck. Jake asked me to babysit for the kids until my aunt and uncle came to take over. I decided on a whim to pop into the hospital to bring Kasia some magazines. Showed up only to overhear the doctor talking to Kasia and Jake about palliative care—treatment to ease her pain and make her last few weeks or months as good as possible. Weeks! I actually staggered on my feet when I heard the doctor, calm and reassuring as he spoke to them, and took in Kasia and Jake, sitting side by side on her hospital bed, holding hands and nodding, absorbing the blow together. Then Kasia, comforting me like I was one of her babies instead of it being the other way around. I couldn't wrap my head around it. And to top it off I run into that guy again while I'm blubbering like a child? That jerk, that fraud—the very married Mr. Cole. I want to hate him, but sinking into his embrace today, he made me feel cared for and protected.

But care and comfort feel like a chokehold right now, with this man hovering over me with his circus tent-sized umbrella.

I collect myself and turn to him. "Tell Mr. Cole I've arrived, safe and sound."

I enter the side entrance gate and close it behind me in a way that's meant to say a final adios to the driver. He gets the message, nodding his head once before retreating back to the car. I spend the next forty-five minutes standing in the driving rain, cursing my stupidity and wincing as I break two fingernails before I'm finally able to break into the store.

I make a mental note to speak to Alex and Henry about the lax security.

* * *

"Yes, Liv, you heard me right. And yes, mother knows and she *still* hasn't called her sister or gone to visit her niece in the hospital." I cut her off when she starts in on defending my mother. "I can't, Liv. I can't listen to you make excuses for her."

"Do you even care about how hard this is for me? To be in the middle all the time?"

"You're not in the middle because I'm not asking you to take sides. I *never* asked you to, even when Mom stood by mute as my *father* kicked me out onto the street for no reason."

"You can never just let things be...Everything's always a fight."

I have to choke back my tears, knowing that my little sister, my Olivia, is most definitely not in my corner. She never was. She was the obedient child and I was the bad one. By now she probably believes all the crap my father's been spewing about me over the years: the ungrateful child, the immoral girl, the whore.

"I have no desire to fight with you, Olivia. I'm just letting you know that if you want to see Kasia, you have to make the decision to do that soon. She would welcome you with open arms. Everyone would."

"Mama and Papa said they don't acknowledge us as family."

Mama and Papa—*really*? Olivia, you're not five years old and we're not in the old country. That's what I *want* to scream. Instead, through gritted teeth I say, "Dad is the one who doesn't acknowledge them. I know you were young, but you have to remember it was Dad who cut ties with them, not the other way around."

"I feel like I don't even know her anymore."

Now the tears fall unchecked. Olivia was eight when the battle lines were drawn. She really doesn't know Kasia anymore. She doesn't remember how Kasia told us fantastic stories, made up on the spot, the two of us snuggled up with her in bed all those nights spent at their home in Greenpoint. She doesn't remember days spent in the Central Park Zoo, the tea parties Kasia happily suffered through, or the afternoons spent styling our hair and dressing us up for her mock fashion shows. She doesn't remember how much Kasia loved us and doted on us. She doesn't remember our cousins Alex, Tomasz and Michal anymore. She doesn't know our aunts and uncles. She doesn't know Kasia and Jake's beautiful children. And three years have passed since I was told to never step foot in our home again. She no longer knows me.

"I love you, Olivia, I always will, but you're making a big mistake."

She sees my father through the same lens as my mother. They make excuses for him. Yes, he's flawed but he's a good man, a hard-working man. One who makes sure his wife doesn't have to work. One who makes sure his daughter has the very best.

They love him but they also fear him. The truth is that my mother doesn't work because he won't allow it. He wants her at home, the dutiful wife. If my mother makes her own money, she'll have a voice. If she has friends, she might come to rely on someone else. Can't have that. And Olivia, she is perfect because she has to be. If Olivia steps out of line there will be hell to pay. Anyone who challenges him is the enemy. I'm the enemy.

The memory of that day is etched into my soul, every last detail. I remember the car slowing down as my entire body went rigid. My tennis coach's confused look as he watched my father run in and out of our home, coming out each time with his arms laden, tossing shoes, books, clothing, my jewelry box, my bras and underwear—my every last possession strewn across our front lawn. I remember digging my fingernails into his forearm as he went to exit the car, my silent plea not to get involved. My father's eyes honing in on me from across the street, one finger shaking as he pointed at me, accusing me, while the other hand held tight onto a notebook. My breath hitched when I recognized it as my journal. It held my dreams, my plans for my big, grand life. On its pages I'd detailed the minutia of my daily existence. I wrote about how difficult my AP Chem class was, how much money I made in tips at my new job teaching rich preschoolers how to play tennis, and how I dreamed of attending college out west so that I could be as far away as humanly possible from my *controlling asshole of a father*. And—kill me now—I wrote in detail about how awesome it was when I finally let my boyfriend feel me up for the first time.

That explained why my father was shrieking, red faced and spit flying as he cursed me as an ungrateful, filthy whore.

It also explained why my boyfriend had a busted lip and looked in the opposite direction, obviously shaken up but dismissing me coldly when I went to approach him before class that next morning.

"If you ever want to meet up to talk, Liv, just grab coffee sometime or whatever, call me."

I hang up, sure in the knowledge that she won't be reaching out anytime soon.

My family is fractured beyond repair.

Chapter Nine

DYLAN

"You look great, Mom."

And she does. No makeup, hair down, dressed in some comfortable but chic cotton stretchy getup. The kind probably advertised as dye and chemical free, made in an ethical, sustainable and sweatshop children-free way. And yes, there's a spiritual crystal or some shit dangling from a silver chain around her neck. Gesturing to it, I smirk. "Source of your chi or chakra or whatever?"

Clutching it and smiling, she answers, "It *was* a lot of new age nonsense. And I'll admit I was rolling my eyes that first day. But then...I don't know, it made perfect sense to me." She focuses on her napkin, unfolding it slowly and placing it in her lap before looking me in the eye, calm and direct when she says, "I needed this...I've been struggling lately, Dylan."

"Struggling how?" I ask, even though I have a pretty good idea of what Margot Cole's struggles entail.

She takes one of my hands in both of hers as she leans across the table and whispers, "It's my cross to bear, not yours." Leaning back, she smiles, adding, "And as silly as it sounds, a week of doing nothing but meditating and reflecting did make me feel all peace, love and harmony."

We share a quiet laugh, toasting as we sit across from one another at our regular corner table. But this whole thing isn't sitting right with me. Maybe it's not my place, and maybe everything with Kasia has me fucked in the head and acting all weird and emotional, but I can't just sit here and pretend anymore.

"Dad had no idea you were gone."

"That's because I moved out last month. I'm renting a place in Sag Harbor."

"What did he do?"

She shakes her head. "Your father is a good person, a good man... Don't ever think otherwise. What's wrong between me and your father has been years in the making. I played my role in it just as he's played his."

"Yeah, right... This is on him."

"How?" she snaps. "It really does take two, Dylan."

I grit my teeth, furious with him and also angry at Mother for letting him off the hook *again*. I have no doubt there's a pretty young thing behind this split.

"It's true. I'm as guilty as he is. I looked the other way for *years*. I enabled him, allowed this deception to go on in our relationship. And I *was* angry, but I'm not anymore. Now I'm taking ownership."

"You've always deserved better, Mom."

"So did you. You deserved better. We haven't been the best role models as far as marriage goes. And I put those same ridiculous expectations on you. I'm very sorry—"

The waiter arrives with our appetizer, forcing us to take a breather for a moment as he recites the entrée specials and jots down our order. I want to tell her, to reassure her that everything good about me can be traced directly back to her. Margot Cole is the epitome of the devoted mother. But she speaks before I can gather my thoughts, and given the events of the past month, what she says leaves me temporarily speechless.

"I saw an article last year in one of my magazines. It was a reflections piece profiling successful young female entrepreneurs. That girl you once dated was featured...Kasia, remember her?"

Do I remember her? That girl I once dated?

My mood turns borderline murderous. How can my mother refer to her as if she was some folly? I was in love with her. She wasn't some girl I fucked around with before moving on without a backward glance.

"Even way back then," she rambles on, "when I was feeling generous enough to acknowledge her, I knew she was something special...motivated and independent. I think that's why I struggled to accept Kasia at first. In a way," Mom smiled wistfully, "she reminded me of a younger version of myself. Maybe I didn't like being reminded of how I'd changed, of everything I'd lost."

"I don't get it."

"I admired her and I disliked her for the very same reasons. She was strong-willed and knew her own worth. She wouldn't compromise herself—not even for you. I wasn't as courageous at her age and I regret some of the choices I've made." Swiping a piece of bread through the broth beneath the steamed mussels, she adds, "Admitting that at the time would have meant taking a good, hard look in the mirror. I guess I wasn't ready for that."

My head is spinning. All this time, and now she brings up Kasia? But she's oblivious to my inner turmoil—keeps right on talking. "I don't think I ever interfered. I mean, I don't think you would have listened to a word I said on the matter anyway. But I hope my opinion never factored into anything where she was concerned. And," she adds with a smile that seems forced, "you did wind up with a beautiful, smart and accomplished woman in the end."

"Accomplished?"

She looks down at the table as the busboy approaches to clear our appetizer plates. No, she can't look me in the eye as she makes that glowing reference to my wife. "Well, the gallery doesn't run itself."

I scoff, "It certainly doesn't."

She looks up at me, tapping her finger nervously in response to my tone. We both know that art gallery is nothing but a vanity project for Cecilia. Sure, she was into it for the first year—liked the whole busy career girl thing. But once it wasn't fun anymore, she was out. And I'm still paying a full staff to keep up this illusion that Cecilia Cole has some purpose in life. The place has never once come close to turning a profit. But I don't even have the passion or energy required to begrudge Cecilia the gallery. She deserves that and so much more. Like for instance, in this very moment she deserves for her husband to give her more than simply a passing thought. She's hardly ever on my mind, even when I'm annoyed with her.

I blurt out, "She's sick, Mom."

My mother pales. "Cecilia is sick?"

"Kasia."

"You're still in touch?"

Margot Cole, society gal, is now back on the premises and she seems a tad nervous. She might be having a mid-life kumbaya moment, but she still doesn't want to upset the natural order of life in our world.

"No, we're not in touch."

Mother nods, the relief obvious in her expression. But then she leans over and takes my hands, encouraging me to tell her more.

"I just kind of found out accidentally."

"Poor thing. What's wrong?"

"Brain cancer. She," I falter for a moment, "doesn't have much time."

"Sweet Lord," Mother whispers. "What will you do?"

I'm still not sure. "I really want to see her but I don't have a place in her life, you know? She has a family. But I want a chance to say goodbye."

"You still care about her."

"Of course I do."

Care about her, dream about her, love her.

"Then say goodbye. You'll regret it if you don't, honey. But just be careful." She looks around at the Christmas decorations, which now, two weeks past the holiday, come off as forlorn and dreary. "It must be a terrible time for them all. I imagine they're hurting."

I'm eager to change the subject, unwilling to think about the many people who most certainly are hurting, feeling the deep loss of Kasia even before she's gone.

"What's going to happen with you and Dad?"

"I honestly don't know. I can't say I'm ready to face him yet. I don't plan on moving back in with him, Dylan."

"Is there someone else?"

"For me?" She laughs, knowing it's my father I'm asking about, but her smile quickly drops. "Yes, there is someone else. And I think it's different this time."

"How old is she?" I ask through gritted teeth.

"That's not important."

I take it to mean that's she's my age or younger. "I'll talk to him, Mom."

Looking at her plate intently as she twists the fettuccini on her fork, her tone is one of conviction. "You will *not* speak to your father on my behalf." She lets the fork rest back on her plate without taking a bite. "I'm not looking for a reconciliation. I want...Well, I'm not sure what I want, but I'm taking some time to figure it out. I'm not afraid anymore."

"Afraid of what?"

"Afraid of...keeping up appearances, or concerned with what people think of me. For the first time in my life, I feel the need to be honest. When I finally get around to returning my friends' phone calls, I'm going to state the truth. I'm not afraid of the ground falling out from underneath me anymore."

"Good for you, I guess."

It comes out sounding like a question.

Chapter Ten

VERONICA

Absolutely no drinking.

That's the first rule they lay down when you're hired, and it's the rule that pretty much everyone ignores.

They ran down the list of regulations—no drinking, no taking selfies with patrons—and interspersed them with vague mandates such as: keep the guests happy. You were issued two uniforms. In my case that was two black bandage-style dresses that barely covered my ass cheeks and basically showcased my cleavage in a way that was obscene. Andy, the androgynous female manager who assessed me from head to toe that first day, summarily informed me that I would be given those two dresses and no others. I took that to mean: eat cheeseburgers and pizza at your own risk.

I nearly clobbered my friend Nell as I left the club that afternoon. "Why didn't you tell me she was going to practically molest me?"

She was doubled over laughing. "Did she tell you that waxing was a job requirement?"

"Yes! And she looked at my crotch when she said it! What the hell? I feel like I've just been hired to work the pole at Scores instead of checking coats at the Standard."

"Count yourself lucky. When I modeled the uniform, Andy literally manhandled my tits to show them to their best advantage. And you won't be knocking it when you're coming home with no less than two bills every night you work. Quickest, easiest money you'll ever make in this city."

Like Nell needed it. I don't know why she did this whole self-imposed starving artist routine. She did study art, so maybe she felt the need to suffer, but if we were stating nothing but the facts: Nell was the only child born to two very wealthy parents, she'd attended the best private schools and now attended NYU, never once wondering how she would float next semester's tuition or pay the rent. But Nell is as good as gold in my book. After Larson—after it became clear that he could no longer, um, look after me—Nell basically came to the rescue. I lived with her for months back then. It was comical. Her parents traveled so much and the apartment was so big that they weren't even aware of the situation.

Nell is a cocktail waitress at Le Bain. She has the attitude for it. It's not like I conjure up the innocence of an Iowa farm girl or anything, but I don't quite give off the experienced, street-smart vibe either. I think Andy took one look at me and decided I'd be more comfortable in the sanctuary of the coat check room, far away from the lunacy.

But not tonight. When I showed up for my shift, I was tempted when the other manager, Devon, asked if I was interested in working the floor. I said yes. And tonight I'm not abiding by the rules. In fact, I did a shot before I even stepped out of the staff room.

Between stewing over my failed reconciliation with Olivia, worrying over Kasia, and plastering on a brave face as I played with Kasia and Jake's children, holding them so close at times that I probably did more to scare them than anything else—with all of that going on I'm just about unraveling.

I need to drink, to dance, to forget about it all for a while. I need to go just a little bit wild.

"No, she doesn't need you to buy her a drink." Fixing me with a pointed look and poking me in the side, Nell teases, "In fact, we take *your* drink orders, remember?"

She's smiling—keep smiling is one of the dumb rules laid down by the all-powerful Andy—but my Nell is not her usual, playful self. Flashing an amused, mega-watt smile to the three young Goldman guys who are now flanking me, she takes my arm and firmly leads me away and back towards the staff room.

"That wasn't polite," I say, giggling.

She rounds on me as she closes the door. "What's come over you?"

I can feel myself teetering on my obnoxiously high heels and make a conscious effort to steady myself. "Nell, I'm good, really. It's just been a shitty week." I suck in a breath, knowing the tears are threatening to spill *again*. "I just need a break from my crappy reality."

She draws me in for a hug. "I'm all for that, but let's take it down a notch. Those junior analyst douchebags were all over you. Getting taken advantage of isn't going to make you feel better, you know?"

I do know better, I do. But I also like the feeling of being reckless for a change.

"No more drinks, ok?"

"I promise," I say, crossing my fingers behind my back as we make our way back out onto the floor.

Chapter Eleven

DYLAN

I was steering clear of her. Or trying to, anyway.

When I suggested the Standard Grill, it's like the words were out of my mouth before I could think it through. I was jonesing for a Veronica sighting, even though the odds of running into her were slim. I was like an addict looking for a fix, and she was my drug of choice.

I lied to myself, though. Told myself I wanted to see her just so I could check up on Kasia. And that was true to a certain extent. I needed to know.

How is Kasia?

How long does she have?

How long do *I* have to get off my ass, get over my fear and reach out to her?

Sitting alone late at night, nursing a drink long after Cecilia had gone to bed, that's when I'd admit to myself that I wanted to see Veronica for other reasons—reasons that shamed me.

And now I knew who she was. I'd no sooner think back to that first night, imagining myself pressing her up against the bar, letting her feel how hard I was for her as I let my hands roam over her body—a woman's body—before an image of her as a little girl assaulted me, a younger Veronica giggling and acting silly. It left me feeling physically ill.

So tonight we're out with two of our oldest and dearest, Tripp and Delia Parker, dining at a trendy restaurant on the ground floor of this hotel while the object of my obsession is checking coats eighteen floors up above us.

Torture.

I think Cecilia plans these nights with an ulterior motive. Does she really believe that if I'm surrounded by her version of a happily married couple, who also happen to procreate at the rate of bunny rabbits, that I'll somehow see the light?

Delia has just popped out baby number five. *Five!* Apparently, having a brood to rival the size of the Kennedys is now de rigueur among our set.

I sip my whiskey in earnest as Delia regales us with the most boring stories known to man. Even Tripp is nauseating, acting like it's no big deal, like he's not pleased as fucking punch when he casually mentions that their eldest is excelling at Collegiate. Excelling? The kid is nine.

Delia is drunk by the time our dinner plates are being cleared. That's what happens when you order seared scallops over linguini, instructing the waiter to omit the pasta and shooing him away as if he's attempting to drop a grenade on the table when he approaches with the bread basket. Have to make sacrifices if you want to keep your man interested, right? I feel like telling Delia to give up, that it doesn't matter. She might as well enjoy a big ol' plate of lasagna with garlic bread to boot, because pretty much everyone knows that Tripp is nailing his boss on the side, a slightly older, very attractive and accomplished woman. So for Cecilia to talk about them the way she does, like they're the ideal family? Makes me fucking gag. Cecilia of all people knows what Tripp is really like. Or has she conveniently suppressed the memory of spreading her own legs wide for Tripp? I know from Melanie that Saint Cecilia was always down for it back when Tripp was madly in love with his soon to be bride.

I look over at Cecilia sipping her martini and can barely conceal my hatred. In this moment I hate her for so many things—her faulty moral compass and her hypocrisy among them.

Hate, guilt and love. The three always seem to be hopelessly intertwined for me. I hate that Cecilia wants me, adores me, even though she must know deep in her heart that I do not feel the same.

She's always known she was my second choice, that she was second best to Kasia. I went to Cecilia in a moment of weakness, licking my wounds when everything fell apart. She knew, but took me in, no questions asked. Bound herself to me faster than you can say the word desperate. She ignored the fact I was irrevocably broken. Ignored my angry outbursts and reckless behavior. To this day, she has never once asked what happened between me and Kasia. Come to think of it, I don't think she's ever mentioned her name. She pretends, and I hate her for it.

She's given up her life to be Mrs. Dylan Cole, and her loyalty and devotion have always felt like a chokehold. I hate Cecilia for settling, for giving up on herself. By pursuing me, she chose to miss out on a good life with a man who truly loves her. I know I'm not a good man and I feel guilty for failing her. And as fucked up as it sounds, she is my wife and I do love her. I want what's best for her, and I'm not it.

I'm so antsy I can barely focus on the conversation. Tripp is talking nonstop, something about the ski house he's renting out west and the *epic rager* he's planning over Super Bowl weekend. I like Tripp, but sometimes he sounds like an absolute asshole. Yeah, I'll be skipping that epic rager. When one of Tripp's old college friends comes over and joins us for dessert, I see an opportunity. Studying my phone and raising my hand in silent apology to take a call, I fake a business situation. And as the elevator shoots up to the rooftop, I tell myself that I'll just get a quick look, that I won't even say hello. In and out, I won't be more than five minutes.

That sleazy fuck who's always kissing my ass—Damon, Devon? —accosts me when I breeze past the bouncers stationed like a secret service detail, turning away bachelorette parties from Bayonne and eurotrash from Brighton Beach. I give him a head nod and a look that I hope conveys my desire for him to vaporize after he hands me a shot.

I don't approach the coat check because I'm trying to be stealth about this entire operation, but stationed from twenty feet away, my spirits sink when I see an unfamiliar redhead manning the spot. I down my shot, disappointed while knowing it's for the best, and scan the dance floor before turning to go.

Maybe she quit the job. She said she hated it so I hope that's the case. She doesn't belong here, doesn't have that edge you need to survive in the clubs. And while this place might be upscale and expensive, in many ways it's seedier than a strip club.

What the fuck is he doing to her?

I'm across the room faster than I can take my next breath, but then stop myself. She's not being forced, I decide, taking in the way her fingers are fisted in his hair. But his hands, groping her ass and pressing her up against his crotch, making it so that her sad excuse for a dress is riding up to expose her—I want to choke the life out of him. Cheap Hugo Boss suit, hair gelled to within an inch of its life, square-toed shoes that are no doubt from the sale rack at Macy's. Probably some dipshit just off his first year at a private equity firm. First real taste of New York. Thinking he owns this city and can take whatever he wants. Thinking this girl is nothing but a plaything.

"Having fun?"

When her lame-ass Jamie Dimon wannabe looks up, his eyes go wide and he backs away. He knows who I am. Veronica's glassy eyes, however, take a few moments to acknowledge my presence.

She leans back into the wall for support, cocks her head to the side and shoots me a knowing smile. "Well, look who it is...Mr. Cole. One half of Mr. and Mrs. Cole." She slurs when she drags out the word misses.

Veronica is wasted.

"Maybe it's time to get you home?"

She looks around, bewildered. "I'm working."

"I hope to God this isn't part of your job description."

Meanwhile, her young suitor is wiping his nose, shifting on his feet, his jaw working overtime when he says, "Uh, I'll be back...Heading to the bathroom." Another coked-up shithead. Even on my worst nights I'll bet I never looked quite so pathetic.

"Hmm," she murmurs as she fights to keep her eyes open. "I have to get back to work."

"Damon said your shift's over...That I should take you home."

"Devon?"

"Yep, Devon. Come on, let's get you out of here."

Devon approaches when he sees me put my jacket over her shoulders. "Mr. Cole?"

Looking back as I usher her through the door, I eye him with disgust. "Consider this Veronica's resignation, asshole."

The ride down in the elevator is a slow form of torture. Veronica's body is pressing against mine as she sighs and nuzzles into the crook of my neck. At one point she slides her hand across and wraps her arm around my waist. It's probably done in an effort to hold herself up, but hell if it isn't the most sensual touch I've felt in a long time. The effort it's taking to suppress my own illicit desire leaves me short of breath. Meanwhile, my wife and friends are still in the restaurant that is inconveniently situated on the ground floor, and

I'm about to walk past them holding onto a barely conscious girl. It's like a sit-com gone wrong, or more like a horror movie.

James is waiting at the door, careful to shield me from the piece of shit paparazzi who make their living standing on the sidewalks outside of places like this all night long, all in the hopes of snapping compromising moments to sell to the highest bidder.

"Make sure she drinks some water. I'll be right back."

I literally have to wipe the sweat from my brow as I make my way back to the table.

Cecilia smiles but it does little to hide her irritation. "That took a long time."

I smile back but my tone is glacial when I say, "Unfortunately, I have responsibilities."

As instructed, James rings my phone at that very moment. While he's chirping, "Clean-up in aisle six," which I can only interpret as code for Veronica upchucking in the back seat of my new Rover, I'm carrying on an entirely different conversation. "Yes, tell them I'm flying out first thing. I'll be in Tulsa by nine."

Why Tulsa? No chance in hell Cecilia will want to accompany me there.

"Tomorrow?" she whines. "Dylan, I have that appointment scheduled for us. If I cancel, it will take weeks—"

Right, the fertility specialist.

I cut her off like the bastard that I am. "Can't be helped. And I'll make sure it doesn't take weeks to reschedule." For good measure, I slide my hand half-way up her thigh and lean over to kiss her with as much passion as I can muster. It's not much but she goes for it.

I look to Tripp. "I've gotta run to the office and straighten something out, then I'm heading to the airport...Early flight."

"Now?" Cecilia whispers, looking both embarrassed and sad.

"My team out there is a disaster," I say, playing the part of the aggrieved boss. "I have to deal with an overseas supplier now, before the close of the business day on their end. Then I'm going out there to make some changes."

She eyes me with suspicion. "You're conducting a staff meeting on a Saturday morning?"

I shoot her a look. "Yes." I pause, daring her to question me further. "I'll be home by tomorrow afternoon."

"We're going to—"

"Dinner with your parents. I know and I'll be back in time."

"You're leaving right now?" Tripp asks, looking down while raising his wrist.

The newest addition to our table laughs in an especially loud and irritating way as he gives Tripp a hard nudge to the shoulder. "Bro, you're not wearing a watch."

I met this guy, Richard Von something the Third, once before. Within two minutes of being introduced I could tell he was a complete tool. Tripp was basically a decent person in my opinion, so I could never understand their long-standing friendship. In my mind this guy would always be Dick, and I called him that tonight when he did the whole *what a coincidence*-shtick as he wedged an extra chair into our table that was clearly meant for four. He corrected me, "It's Richard," and I just smiled.

Tonight he's wearing a suit cut so slim you can practically see the outline of his ballsack, topped off with a Yale tie. Two items on the long list of things I cannot stand: men who wear college ties long after they've graduated, and grown men who address other grown men as Bro or Dude. Fucking nauseating.

I ignore Dick. "Get my girl home for me?" I ask, squeezing Cecilia's knee.

Tripp looks to his wife, who can barely keep her eyes open, and then smiles at Cecilia. "You know I will."

James is halfway down the block, incognito, leaning against the car and smiling as I approach. "There's been a bit of a situation. I don't know who this one is, but she's so beautiful she looks graceful mid-chunder."

James sounds like a proper English butler when he speaks, but my driver is anything but. A former M16 officer, the guy is tough as steel and has a wicked sense of humor. When I go to open the door, he says, "I set her all to right, she's fine. Another car's coming 'round."

The other half of my security team, Rupert, pulls up. Rupert was also M16, but unlike his garrulous co-worker, Rupert is all-business, no talk. I know it's common sense for people in my position to have security, and I understand that I'm a high profile target, but Rupert takes it to the next level—acts as if an ambush is imminent twenty-four-seven.

Veronica is curled up in the corner of the back seat. "Wake up, sleepyhead," I whisper as I pull her closer and kiss the top of her head.

The shoulder of her dress is damp, but she looks fine otherwise. James leans in to give me a helping hand. "See what I mean, Cole, she's perfect...Her vomit smells like cherry cola."

Rupert is all silent efficiency as he takes over, ushering me and Veronica into an identical black Rover. He lets himself into the driver's seat and then sits there waiting for instructions, checking his mirrors, casing our surroundings, always on alert. He borderline freaks me out, and that's why he only accompanies me and James when it's absolutely necessary.

"Veronica, where am I taking you?"

"Home," she murmurs as she turns her body and curls into mine. When I feel her breasts pressing against my chest, I throw my head up and let out an exasperated breath.

"Where is home, baby?"

She looks up at me, blinking as though it takes effort. "Take me home with you."

My damn molars are grinding. If I hadn't gotten her out of there, she would have been saying this shit to some random guy, to the guy who was mauling her upstairs. Veronica looks up at me again, this time managing to keep her eyes open as she slides her free hand down, unintentionally grazing my dick in the process. I'm now so hard that it's painful.

"Take me home, Mr. Cole."

The *mister* comment should deflate my boner on impact, but it does nothing of the sort. It makes me burn with anger and a need to own her, to press her hand right there and make her rub me raw. My chest is thumping and my hands are trembling. Fuck this girl, she's gonna kill me.

I take her by the shoulders and shake, gently at first but then with more force. "Veronica...Goddammit, just tell me where you live!"

Clean-up in aisle seven. James is close, but I peg her puke as smelling of vodka cranberry. Glad she didn't have lobster mac and cheese for dinner like I did, or else I'd be wearing that right now.

"Got any cleaning supplies up there," I yell to Rupert as I lift Veronica's hair out of the way and direct her head in the opposite direction of me.

"I'll see to that," he answers.

"No, I've got it."

Rupert hands me a roll of paper towels. There's not much I can do to clean her up with those, but I do my best. Most of it is on me anyway.

As I dry my shirt, I call out, "Ask James where he dropped her last time." When their conversation goes on a beat too long, I bark, "Put him on speaker."

"I dropped her at that flower shop on Madison, but boss, I don't think that's wise." He pauses. "I got the feeling she was dodging me, really didn't live there. She wouldn't let me walk her to the door... Shut the service gate in my face. I wouldn't take her there in her current condition."

As I rack my brain for alternatives, Veronica slumps back so that she's next to me again, her back to my front. I adjust her so that she fits in close and I wrap my arm around her. My office and my spare apartment are both off limits, for the simple reason that it's not appropriate. Do I want to strip her out of that soiled dress, rinse her off, put her in one of my shirts, comb her hair out and tuck her into bed? Hell yes, I want to take care of her. But I feel like a sick man with what's racing through my mind at the moment. I won't put myself into such a precarious position and I would never harm a hair on her head. So where to? To Jake and Kasia's? That would be fucked up on so many levels, the first being that I know exactly where they live because I've looked her up online numerous times. In one of my weaker moments, I even drove by their house.

I know where I have to go.

As we pull up outside, I feel the weight of those memories from so long ago. That night, pleading my case, being exposed as a liar and a cheat in front of a roomful of relatives. Watching impotently as she took *his* hand to reassure him while I spewed insults and tried to make him feel like the lesser man. I was the lesser man. Everyone in the room including me knew that to be true.

I tell Rupert to wait as I walk up to the front door by myself. It's after midnight so I know they're probably asleep. I ring the bell and knock on and off for a few minutes before I hear footsteps approaching the door. He's older, nearly thirteen years have passed since the last time I saw him, but he still looks like he could kick my ass.

"Dylan?"

He's gripping a wooden bat with one hand, which makes me smile for some reason. Yep, leaving Veronica passed out in the car for the moment was the right decision.

"Hello, Mr. Mazur. I'm really sorry to bother you."

He eyes me warily. "What is going on?" He's no dope, he knows this isn't a social call.

"Kind of a long story—"

"I have time for long story," he breaks in, opening the door wider and ushering me in.

I stand on the threshold, taking in their simple home. I love this house and I love Mr. Mazur's broken English. Taking in the mismatched chairs, the bold colors my own mother would never choose, and the faint smell of cabbage from tonight's home-cooked meal, I feel the weight of my own sadness. While this was the site of some of my worst memories, it also holds some of my absolute best.

"I've got your niece Veronica out in the car." I hold up my hands in defense, remembering this guy's temper. "She wasn't with me...I ran into her...She drank too much and she got sick. I just wanted to make sure she got home safe." He's still eyeing me with suspicion. "I didn't know where else to take her. Look, let's just get her inside and I'll explain."

Rupert has the car open and Veronica's limp body in his arms, walking towards the house before we're even out the front door. He has a sixth sense in terms of timing. Rupert nods and Kasia's dad backs up instinctively to let him through. Mr. Mazur is tough, but Rupert takes the whole *don't fuck with me* vibe to a whole other level. He lays her on the couch and then looks to me. It's an unspoken question: Should I stay or should I go?

Mr. Mazur's cheeks are turning a furious shade of red just as Mrs. Mazur is making her way down the stairs. The feeling of being with them again is so strange. It's so good and yet messed up in a way that I really can't make sense of. I don't want to leave, so I'll roll the dice, even though the odds of Mr. Mazur throwing a punch my way are better than good.

"Wait for me outside, Rupert."

"Dylan?"

Mrs. Mazur, still as graceful and elegant as a countess in her thick chenille robe and slippers, looks back and forth between me and Veronica.

I stammer my opening lines, struggling to explain the events of the night when she cuts me off. "What is she wearing?"

That band of fabric has ridden up again, shamefully exposing her ass. Mr. Mazur throws an afghan over her in anger.

"I'm pretty sure that's her uniform. She was at work."

"Work?" she questions me, confused. "She goes to school…She works part-time at Alex's shop and babysits for Kasia. What is that?"

She gestures to what's underneath the blanket, hurt and shame marring her features.

"I was having dinner at a restaurant and there's a club upstairs. A nice place, fancy," I add, trying to reassure her. "My group was having after-dinner drinks," I lie, "and I saw her. She'd obviously had too much to drink and some of the people there…It's not safe for a girl her age. She couldn't tell me where she lived, so I brought her here."

"Oh, my żabka," Mrs. Mazur whispers as she leans down to stroke Veronica's hair.

"She got sick in the car."

Mr. Mazur sighs. "Let's get her upstairs." He shoots his wife a look where something unspoken passes between them. "You get her cleaned up and I talk to Dylan, all right?"

"Yes."

They take her upstairs to the bathroom and Mr. Mazur makes his way back downstairs just as I hear the shower turn on.

"She is a good girl. I don't know what makes her work in a place that has her dress in that way."

"I'm sure she makes very good tips there, but I agree with you, it's not for a girl like Veronica."

He eyes me with skepticism. "You recognized her…Or is this the long story?"

I can't help but chuckle as he leads me to the kitchen and gestures to a chair. I look around, remembering mornings drinking coffee and eating babka, bullshitting with Kasia's dad in this kitchen. So out of character for me, but I always wanted his approval.

"This is the long story."

I go on to tell him about meeting her at the flower shop, not giving him any details as to why I was there, and then running into her again that day at the hospital. I have to bite back tears when I tell him that I was just comforting Veronica, someone who was practically a stranger, only to have her mention Kasia by name. That's when I put everything together.

He lowers his head, his thumb and forefinger massaging the bridge of his nose.

"I'm so sorry."

"Yes, Dylan, it's been a difficult time for the family. You know how very special she is to us all. Kasia has been through so much, and now...What the doctors tell us is not good."

The lump in my throat gives my speech a choked quality when I ask, "How much time does she have left?"

He takes my hand. "We don't know...A month, maybe two. But," he smiles in a way that is so damn sad, "you know her, she's tough. She pretends she has energy, especially when the children are about. My Kasia is always smiling, wants no one to fuss."

"Is she in pain?"

"She is but she hates the medication. Says she needs a clear head so that she can do everything she needs to do, say everything she needs to say. Still my stubborn girl."

Mrs. Mazur joins us, putting a plate of small cakes on the table, removing a bottle from the freezer and pouring me a shot of vodka. She's trying to soften the blow, preparing me for the bomb she's about to drop.

"He already knows," he says to his wife, taking her hand and rubbing his thumb over it in a gesture of comfort.

Their connection is as strong as ever. Two people who could always communicate without talking, who work together as partners, who crave each other in every way. I envy them, and back when I was young and foolish, I thought I could have that same kind of relationship with their daughter, even if I hadn't earned it.

I take her other hand. "I feel terrible for you all."

"Sometimes," she says, swallowing and holding back tears, "I wish it was over for her. She is in pain. But mostly, I'm selfish and I'm scared. Every morning when I see her, I tell myself this is good, I have one more day to care for my baby."

All three of us were mourning now, and they both joined me when I did my second shot.

"How is Jake handling it?"

"He is a wonderful husband." She pats my hand when she adds, "And that's nothing to do with you, Dylan. You know we were very fond of you as well."

I'd wager Mr. Mazur doesn't agree with that last statement, and who could blame him?

"I don't know how he's still standing. He insists on doing almost all of her care by himself. He will shoo me away, asking me to tend the children when it's time to exercise her muscles, bathe her or give her the medications. I think he wants every last minute with her he can steal."

"It is good," Mr. Mazur chimes in. "He has made a great success of the business. So now he has people who can manage the projects. He wants to be home, for Kasia and for the children. It gives Kasia comfort to know they have such a good father."

I nod. "That must be a comfort to her. How old are they?"

Mr. Mazur's eyes brighten when he talks about his grandchildren. "Jakub is eleven, Tomasz is nine, Rachel is seven and Milo is six."

"Milo? I like that name."

"Yes, they named him after my father, Milosz," she says. "And I have to say that given the situation, the children are fantastic." Her finger traces the lines of the cross that hangs around her neck. "Kasia has prepared them well. I don't know if I could be so honest with my children the way she is. But it is better, you know?" She smiles and lets out a soft laugh. "That Rachel, so like her mother. The other day she said to me, 'We will be all right, Babciu. We are lucky. We have Daddy, we have you and Dziadzia, we have Michal and Sophia, Auntie Karolina, Tomasz and Isabel, Alex and Henry.' On and on she went, naming every single person in the family."

"Kasia has been drilling that idea into their heads," her father says. "Making sure they know that they will always have people to take care of them, that they will never be alone."

Nothing about this surprises me. My girl was always brave, always selfless. "She's amazing."

"And Rachel adores Veronica," Mrs. Mazur adds as she looks towards the stairs. "The same way Veronica and Olivia adored Kasia."

"I remember that Christmas. Those two ambushed me." I laugh at the memory of the two of them climbing me like a tree. "I think they were fascinated with anyone who had anything to do with their Kasia. They idolized her."

"Oh, she loved them. The loss of my sister and Olivia still breaks her heart, but I'm thankful that we have Veronica back at least."

"They died?"

Mr. Mazur pours another shot for us two. "Might as well be dead."

"Don't say that!"

"You know I don't mean it," he says, shaking his head. "And you know I don't blame your sister for anything."

Mrs. Mazur looks back to me. "My sister and I, there's been... What's that word, a rift?"

"Veronica's father decided we were no longer family after he found out Aleksander is gay."

"Alex is gay?" Wide-eyed, I nearly choke on my shot. "I didn't see that coming."

Mr. Mazur laughs. "Neither did I!"

Kasia's mother's eyes are mournful. "I can't understand people who judge, who hate other people in that way."

Mr. Mazur looks to the stairs, lowering his voice. "Veronica's father is a foolish and ignorant man. Always was."

"Does he know that Veronica is in contact with you all?" The thought came to me. "She works for Alex. Does her father know?"

"I don't think he cares." Mr. Mazur shrugs. "He kicked her out when she was seventeen. What kind of man kicks his own flesh and blood out onto the street?"

"So where does she live?"

Mrs. Mazur doesn't look one hundred percent sure when she answers, "She lives in a spare room at Kasia's on the weekends and then she stays with a classmate during the week when she's in school."

"Oh." I decide to leave it alone.

"So tell me," Mrs. Mazur says, taking my hand, "how are you, Dylan? How has life turned out for you?"

"Good." I speak the word without happiness or conviction. And her bullshit detector is spot-on. Kasia definitely inherited that from Mama. I start rattling off stats to shield myself from her pity. "I'm married, no children yet. I still live in the city, working at Cole Industries."

"Work at Cole Industries? You're being modest," Mr. Mazur says. "I read the Times. You run the company, no?"

"My dad is still the CEO, but he's been stepping away." *Needs time to fuck his thirty-year-old nutritionist.* Bet my mother regrets getting him onto that health kick now.

"You were always a hard worker, Dylan. A great quality."

"Thanks, Mr. Mazur. That means a lot to me." I have to work myself up to asking, "Do you think she might want to see me? I...I'd like to see Kasia before..." I trail off, sorry for the way that last word came out. "I mean, can I ask Jake if it's all right?"

"Let me talk to Kasia." She looks to her husband, seeking his opinion. Whatever passes between them makes her say, "I think she would like to see you."

"Thank you." I suddenly feel awkward, like an intruder. "I guess I should go."

"Take care of yourself, Dylan."

"And thank you for bringing Veronica home," Mrs. Mazur adds. "You did the right thing bringing her here."

Chapter Twelve

VERONICA

My hair reeks of cigarette smoke and my eyes feel like they're glued shut from caked-on mascara. Someone is stroking my hair and whispering, "It's ok," and those simple, gentle words make me cry.

"Shh, little angel. You'll stay here now. Everything is all right."

I open my eyes to see my aunt looking down on me, smiling. "Good morning, my sweet."

"Ciocia?"

Oh shit, how in the hell did I get here last night?

"Take a shower and come downstairs." She wipes at a tear on my cheek. "I couldn't get all that makeup off your face last night."

"How did I get here?"

"Dylan Cole brought you here. You know each other now?"

I sit up with a start. "Mr. Cole brought me here?"

"Yes, Dylan...Kasia's old boyfriend. You and Olivia used to climb all over that poor boy. Well, that was a long time ago."

"What are you talking about?"

"Dylan brought you here last night. He said he saw you at your

107

job?" She shoots a disapproving look towards a chair in the corner of Kasia's old room that has my uniform dress laid over it. My work-issued hooker heels are on the floor nearby. "I didn't know you worked in a club."

"I—"

I was at a loss for words. Kasia's old boyfriend? Mr. Cole was Dylan?

"No, shh...We talk later. You take a shower now and I'll start breakfast. Kasia's not expecting you today."

"But it's Saturday. She needs me."

"Sophia is there with the boys. They've got it under control. We'll go there for dinner later. You'll help me cook. Yes," she says, answering for me.

When my aunt leaves, I grab my phone from the nightstand as it vibrates with an incoming text. There are no less than ten messages from Nell. I tap out a quick reply, assuring her that I'm safe and with my family. The shrill sound of her ringtone blares not a second later, a fast-paced Arctic Monkeys song that sets my head to throbbing.

"Good to know you're alive, bitch!"

"I'm sorry, Nell. Last night was a disaster."

"Devon said you left with someone. It wasn't that jerk I pulled off you earlier, was it?"

"No, a family friend spotted me. I guess he thought I was wasted, so yeah, he took me back here and now I'm completely mortified. My aunt and uncle probably think I'm in need of a twelve step program right now."

"Please, people our age do that every weekend. You *never* let loose. And I feel like a crappy friend because I didn't keep an eye on you. I hooked up with that hot guest DJ and woke up this morning at his place in a panic when I realized I'd left without even checking up on you first! I'm awful!"

She is *so* loud. I tip the phone to the side, lowering the volume.

"I'm fine, Nell, but thanks for being concerned. And don't worry, I won't be doing a repeat of last night."

"Yeah, Devon said you quit. I don't blame you."

"What?"

"You quit." She busts out laughing. "You mean you don't remember?"

"Uh, no."

"Aw honey, I'm sure they'll take you back."

I massage my scalp with my free hand as bits and pieces of last night come back to me. I close my eyes tight when an image of me dancing with two guys at once pops up. I was sandwiched between them, one at my front and one at my back.

I choke out, "No, Nell, I think it's for the best...I'll give you a call later, ok?"

Rolling over to face the wall, I let the tears fall as I think of Dylan. How much of last night's performance did he see? I can't remember anything after taking that third shot. I imagine him watching in judgement, shaking his head in disgust while I danced like a stripper, teetering on my heels in that awful dress.

I struggle to remember seeing him, talking to him—to remember *anything*—but I can't. *Please*, I pray to no one particular. It's an empty plea, born of desperation and fear. Did I go and do something shameful, or did I say anything embarrassing?

I stand under the stream of hot water until my skin is red and puckered in a failed attempt to wash the events of last night away.

* * *

Kasia and Jake's is a beehive of activity. Jake, my uncle and my cousins are busy nailing the wooden beams of what will be a pergola on the side of the house. The younger kids are playing in the back-yard, while the older ones sit in the family room listening to music that's kept at a low volume out of respect for Kasia's comfort. Sophia,

109

Karolina and Isabel are busy in the kitchen, while Rachel sits on the couch at her mother's feet, painting them a sparkly purple.

Kasia's eyes brighten when me and my aunt make our way in the front door, our arms laden with trays. I notice she does this more now, smiling or waving without talking, as if she's reserving her energy.

"I better be getting a pedicure later, Rachel. That color is fierce."

Rachel is a carbon copy of her mother, with golden blonde hair and eyes the color of pale blue sea glass. She smiles at me and winks, then turns her attention back to her task.

During the past few months, Rachel has been struggling to leave the house in the morning for school. Fearful, I think, that her mother will be gone by the time she gets home. And whenever Rachel is home she's practically plastered to Kasia's side.

I creep back into the room, watching them after I put my trays in the kitchen and say hello to the women. When Kasia catches sight of me, she asks Rachel to make her a glass of her special iced tea and then waves me over. I can tell by the look on her face that she's heard about my night. She takes my hand, smiling and then nodding as if to say: *Tell me everything*.

"I can't believe I didn't recognize him, Kasia."

"It was years ago. You were what, seven or eight the last time you saw him? How could you remember? But I have to know before Rachel comes back in, is there anything going on there?"

"Between me and him?" I am all wide-eyed innocence. "No, no, nothing! I barely know him!" She's smiling now, mocking me. Yeah, yeah...the lady doth protest too much and all that crap. "I'm serious, Kasia. Meeting him was totally random, and by the way, I think he's an ass."

She looks hurt on his behalf. "He has his faults but he's a good person."

"He's married and he tried to pick me up."

"Last night?" Now she looks alarmed.

"No," I admit. "Last night I was acting like a fool and I think he got me out of a bad situation." The smell of that anonymous guy's cologne is fresh in my senses, and the memory of him grinding against me intensifies my shame. "Dylan flirted with me a few weeks ago before he knew who I was."

She shakes her head. "He's cheating on Cecilia...How sad."

"How deceitful, how cruel...Isn't that what you mean?"

"Life's complicated," she whispers. "Dylan's complicated." She looks out the window for a moment and then turns back to me. "Enough about that, Veronica...I need you."

"I'm here! Anything you need, you know that, Kasia."

She shakes her head again, and it looks like the simple movement takes effort. "I need to know you're safe. You told me you were staying with a school friend during the week and you tell others you have an apartment at Alex and Henry's store." She holds up her hand when I go to speak. "I want you to move in here full-time. Karolina's apartment is empty. It's yours now."

"Yes."

She raises her eyebrows, amused. "No fight? No, 'I need my freedom and privacy'?"

"I think," I croak, "I think I need my family."

She blows me a kiss. "I love you."

"Love you more."

The very next day, I gather what few belongings I own and make the basement my home. I make a project out of redecorating the space, with Rachel, Milo, Tomasz and Jakub helping me out. It's more of an attempt on my part to give Jake and Kasia some quiet time without the children.

Jake knocks on the door at around eight o'clock. "Wow, it looks great in here! You guys make a good team. Getting late now, though, so let's get you guys upstairs. Mommy wants to say goodnight before we start brushing teeth and all that jazz."

"Do you need help carrying her up?" Jakub asks. Such a little man he is.

Jake flexes his muscles. "Don't insult your old man. She's already up in bed, waiting on you guys. Let's go, school tomorrow."

When Rachel frowns, I say, "Hey, I know a cool recipe for chocolate chip banana pancakes. If we get up a few minutes early we can make them in the morning. Then I'll walk you and Milo to school, all right Rachel?"

He turns to me as Milo runs past him. "We're all so glad you're here, Veronica."

I nod, knowing I'll cry if I try to speak.

Chapter Thirteen

DYLAN

The day after my very strange homecoming at Casa Mazur, I get a call from my friend, Tom Farrell. I've blown off every one of his calls and texts for the past few weeks, and I didn't show for our last monthly steak dinner. Radio silence for him and for the rest of those mother-fuckers. But now I want to hear him defend himself. If I can't see him squirm, I want to at least hear it.

"You're alive?" He goes for humor when I answer the call with a terse, *What's up?*

"I'm alive."

Silence. I won't help him out, won't do shit to fill this uncomfortable void.

He sighs. "There's something I've been wanting to tell you for a while—"

"Really," I cut in. "Can't imagine what that could be."

I can almost see him shaking his head on the other side of our connection. "From your tone, I'm assuming you already know what

I'm about to say and you're pissed that I kept it from you for so long."

"It's more than that, Tom, more than me being *pissed*." Is he serious? "I no longer think of you as a friend. So say whatever you have to say and then let's be done with this bullshit."

He sucks in a breath and then laughs like he can't believe what I just said. "You don't think of me as your friend? Fuck you. You think everything's about you, right Dylan? That was *her* wish. She only wanted a few people to know. *I* only know because I'm married to Darcy and she's been so heartbroken over the whole thing. Kasia and Jake only told their kids a few months ago, and you want to crucify *me* for not telling you?"

"What if she passed away last week, asshole? Were you going to call and give me the funeral arrangements? Or maybe not...Maybe you'd just casually mention how nice the eulogy was during our next guys' night out."

"Fuck," he says, breathing out. "I'm sorry."

"If the shoe was on the other foot, just know I never would have done that to you."

Click.

And Tom? I hope it hurts.

The day after that, I get another call. It's a banner week.

Bonnie, my new and improved, much older secretary buzzes through as I'm going through my emails. "A Mr. Wozniak is on the line. He says you're expecting his call."

I nearly choke on my coffee. He's either going to tell me to stay the fuck away or tell me to come. I send up a silent prayer that he's feeling benevolent because ever since this weekend, I've had this desperate feeling that time is running out, and I really, really need to see her.

"Put him through, Bonnie."

Deep, deep breath. "Jake?"

"Hey Dylan, how's it going?"

"I'm doing all right…How are *you* doing through all this?" Before he can answer, I blurt out, "And I really appreciate you reaching out to me. I hope you know I'd never stick my nose into the situation without talking to you first. And if you think seeing Kasia would be upsetting to her in any way…Or if she's not up to it…Or whatever—"

"Slow down, Dylan. It's gonna be all right."

Jesus, I'm babbling so hard that Jake feels the need to console *me*. "Sorry, man. I just can't seem to wrap my head around it."

"Know the feeling," he says, laughing in a way that tells me I'm speaking with a man who is anything but happy. He's a good guy, the fucker. "Listen, I talked to Kasia and she'd love to see you. Come by this week. Best if you can come by while the kids are in school, though. She's usually pretty alert at around noon."

Pretty alert at around noon. The comment makes my heart sink but makes my determination stronger. I absolutely have to see her.

"Can I come tomorrow?"

* * *

I thought I'd be nervous, but I'm feeling centered and serene as I pull onto their block in Park Slope the next day at a quarter to twelve. I give James the morning off, drive myself because I need to do this on my own.

But I don't do everything on my own. When I told Mother where I was heading, she sprang into action. She had her assistant jet around Park Slope, picking up a slew of gift certificates to the better take-out places in the neighborhood and movie gift cards for the kids. I would never have thought of that on my own.

I rap on the door lightly, afraid of disturbing her, but right away she calls out, "Come on in!"

Before hanging up yesterday, Jake warned me that Kasia looks different, and please, not to act shocked at the change in her appearance. So I'm all smiles when I walk in, concentrating on the eyes I

115

once knew better than my own, rather than focusing on her bony frame, the angles jutting out through the fabric of the blanket covering her. I ignore her sickly pallor and the breaths that are just noticeably audible.

"You don't know how good it is to see you. Get over here."

"Look at you," I say, bending down to kiss her cheek. "Leave it to you to have super chic headscarves."

"I'm the envy of cancer patients everywhere."

I'm just about to say, *You look great*, but stop myself. I know her, she'd scoff at that. "I've been wanting to come and see you for a few weeks...I was working up the balls to do it."

"Well, I'm glad you did."

I look around. "Where's Jake?"

"I forced him to take a few hours and go check on his work sites." Gesturing to herself, she adds, "He needs a breather from all of this every once in a while."

I shake my head. "When he's with you he's where he wants to be."

"That's been the hardest part. I'm not afraid, Dylan. I really do accept what's inevitable. And it's such a relief to know that my children are in good hands. He's a great father...The absolute best."

"I can believe that."

"But the thought of him grieving?" She lowers her head. "I hate the idea of his loneliness, his sadness. It breaks my heart."

"You feel guilty for leaving him?"

"Yes!" She nods, seemingly relieved to be understood.

"That's because you're selfless, Kasia. You're always looking out for everyone else."

"I have to believe he'll find happiness after I'm gone. That's the only thought that keeps me from falling apart."

I smile to lighten the mood. "Well, I'm here to give you the male perspective."

"Please," she says, laughing.

Her face might be gaunt, and some might say her beauty has faded, but her eyes still sparkle with life and her smile can still crack me wide open.

Suddenly emotional, I have to clear my throat. "You're hard to get over, for one. I can personally attest to that. And there's no way that a guy like Jake, someone who's been lucky enough to have a good, solid marriage and a family like the one you guys have...There's no way he's even thinking about moving on." I nudge her knee. "And I know you, you're a control freak, missy."

"Am not."

"Oh yes you are. And let me finish...Don't suggest anything where moving on is concerned. He doesn't want you telling him to find happiness, to remarry. I know I personally wouldn't want to listen to that."

"I've done all that and more."

"He just wants you, you and him, for every day that's left."

"I get that, I do."

"You know how much I've missed this?" I ask, moving my finger in a circle between the two of us. "How much I've missed being in our bullshit-free zone? With anyone else this visit would have been all polite talk, but with you I feel like I can kind of go anywhere."

"And in the spirit of no bullshit allowed, I want to know how you are. And please don't hold back...Tell me everything."

"Still married."

"Knew that. How is Cecilia?"

I shrug. "She's good, I guess. I don't think I'm a very good husband." When I see her go to protest, I stop her. "No, I'm not, but she knew who she was marrying."

"You're cheating on her."

"Not at the moment, but there have been more women than I can count on both hands over the years. I had the seven month itch, not the seven year variety."

"Yikes."

"I wouldn't have done that to you." We both burst out laughing at the same time. "Really," I say through tears as I keep laughing, "once we were married I wouldn't have cheated on you!"

"What makes you so sure of that?"

"I just know. And lordy, Cecilia practically encouraged it. She got me a goddamn threesome for my birthday one year."

"What the hell?"

"Right? It's like she was telling me from day one that I could pull anything…And I have."

"Do you think you two will last?"

"No."

And just like that, I know it to be true.

"So what are you waiting for?"

"Is it that easy?"

"You don't have kids, so it won't get any easier than it is now. She deserves to find love. And Dylan, *you* deserve to be happy, truly happy. I don't get that vibe from you right now."

"I'm not."

"I think you've always been caught up in seeing yourself as a bad boy, and it's grown and morphed into you actually believing you're a bad person." She squeezes my hand with her frail fingers to emphasize her next words. "You are *not* a bad person. Do *not* waste time. You have to find that one person."

"What?"

"That person." She pauses to take in a few breaths. I'm tiring her out. "The person who makes you want to be a better man." She looks over my shoulder towards the door. "Well, speak of the devil. I was just telling Dylan what a lifesaver you've been."

Veronica literally looks scared out of her wits when she catches sight of me sitting in the living room with Kasia. And now I'm a little out of breath.

"Veronica…How are you?"

Her cheeks redden but she doesn't look at me when she answers, "I'm good."

It's a little freaky being in the same room with the two of them, especially when Veronica's acting all weird and awkward. Guess seeing me is no picnic because she's gone in a flash, heading straight for the kitchen.

I turn back to Kasia and she fixes me with a knowing smile. I cock an eyebrow and shake my head. Then I whisper, "Really? She's like fifteen years younger than me."

She whispers back, "Love knows no age, killer." I smile, knowing this girl can still see into my soul.

"I almost forgot." I get up and grab the gift basket I left by the door, walking it back over to Kasia. "I'd like to take full credit, but this was all Margot's doing."

"Really?" Kasia looks touched.

"Yes. She sends her best."

"How are Vince and Margot?"

"Don't ask."

"Hmm...They were always solid."

"Solid? I think they have their own version of solid. And it worked for them, but I think Vince has gone too far this time. Margot moved out."

"Wow."

"Yep. It's kind of freaking me out and that's ridiculous...I'm not exactly a child."

"It's still your mom and dad."

I look over in the direction Veronica has gone and lower my voice. "Your parents told me about her situation. Her father sounds like a real nightmare."

She nods. "I'm glad she's living here full-time now. She needs something constant in her life. She's had it rough for a few years. And I feel terrible because for a long time, none of us knew what was really going on."

"She's a good kid."

"*She's* about to turn twenty-one," Veronica snaps as she comes back into the room with some crackers and grapes on a tray, shooting me a death glare.

"And she's feisty," Kasia teases.

Veronica places the tray down and hands Kasia a pill and a small cup of water. "Jake said to make sure you take this with some food."

When she swallows the pill down, she closes her eyes for a long moment. She's clearly exhausted.

"You tired?"

Veronica is behind Kasia, so Kasia can't see her nodding at me emphatically before walking out of the room again.

"I'm afraid so. And I like to nap before the kids get home so I'm fresh for them."

I nod, stand up and then lean down to kiss her forehead. I let my lips linger for a moment, missing her so badly already, knowing this is likely the last time I'll ever have the privilege of being near her.

What do I say to this woman? How do I say goodbye? I struggle with it for no more than a few seconds because I know I don't have to say anything. She knows. She knows how special she was and will always be to me.

I whisper the words into her skin, "Always, baby," before I break away and leave her.

Chapter Fourteen

DYLAN

I sit in the back of Church. Away from her family. Away from the friends we have in common. It's hard to be here, so hard to face the finality of the day. But I am here and I will bear this, just as everyone else who loved Kasia will.

That terrible night when I got the call from Tom, I wanted to claw and scream and rail at the world like an animal. But I didn't make a sound. I think I just nodded as he told me the arrangements. When he asked if I was all right, I muttered only, "Yeah," before hanging up on him. I laced up my sneakers and ran downtown along the West Side Highway until I reached the Staten Island Ferry terminal. I stayed there, leaning over the railing, watching the ferries and freighters make their way across the ink black water for a long while. Then I turned around and went home. I cried without shedding tears that night. I honored Kasia by replaying every memory of us that I still had. As I ran, images of her smiling at me as we joked around, gazing at me as I loved her, and images of her just being—all those times I'd just find myself staring at her—the best kind of film reel replaying over and over again in my mind's eye.

I thought I'd be stoic and steady during the ceremony, just as I'd been in the days leading up to it, but I lose it when Jakub eulogizes his mother at the end of Mass.

Through this boy I get a glimpse of the Kasia I never had the privilege to know—the woman and the mother. He is brave, recounting stories that make everyone laugh, and paying tribute to her goodness, her warmth and her determination in all things. The paper in his hands shakes when he looks up and says he knows there is a Heaven now because he can already feel his mother's strength running through him, he can feel her love, and he knows that she will be looking out for their family every day *until we're together again*.

I don't even realize I'm full-on weeping until I feel the weight of her hand on my shoulder, centering me. I reach up and lay my hand on top of hers, knowing instinctively that it's my mother sitting in the very last pew behind me.

* * *

"Hey, wait up."

My cousin Anna is chasing me, running full-speed on a pair of stilettos down Humboldt Street. If she wasn't in her third trimester I wouldn't have stopped, and that's saying a lot. I'd take a bullet for Anna any day of the week, but today I'm not feeling the least bit social.

I force a weak smile and hug Anna because words are too much of an effort.

"I'm starving," she says as she rubs her belly and leads me into a tavern a few doors down. "C'mon, the pregnant lady's gotta eat."

Because Anna is just all around awesome, she doesn't dive right in and ask how I'm feeling.

"You wanna get drunk or just take the edge off?" she asks as she peruses the wine list.

And just like that, I'm so grateful to be in the company of family.

"Pint of Guinness and a club soda for her, thanks."

The bartender nods and sets two menus down on the bar. "I'd kill for a glass of wine or a beer right now."

"You probably could have *one*. Tom's mother said she drank a small glass of Guinness every day when she was pregnant. The Irish used to swear it made the baby strong."

"I'm sure it would be fine, but I'd feel a little weird explaining that to my obstetrician, or to this guy behind the bar for that matter."

"Where were you sitting? I didn't see you."

"I came in after you. I saw Aunt Margot but…I figured I'd give you some space."

"And you figured I'd want some company now?"

"No," she says, giggling. "I saw you take off through the side door without even saying goodbye to your mother. But I know you, and sometimes you just don't know what you need."

The bartender sets our drinks on the bar, and I don't even wait the few moments it would take for the dark stout to settle before guzzling a third of it down in one draw. "That's good." I reach over and put my hand on hers. "And I am glad you're here."

Anna orders enough food for four when the bartender comes back over. "I just feel like a little bit of everything," she says in response to my raised eyebrows.

"When did you find out Kasia was sick?" I see no use in beating around the bush.

"Kate and Luke told me last week, just a few days before she passed away. I was," she pauses, shaking her head, "shocked."

My cousin is an architect working with my friend Tom's in-laws at their firm. Even though I knew Anna would never keep me in the dark like the others had, it's a relief to hear her confirm it anyway.

"You never returned my messages. I even called the house."

Anna *never* calls the house, only my cell. Not that it's so unusual, I never call landlines myself, but Anna does this in an effort to avoid any and all interaction with Cecilia.

Over the years, Anna has perfected the art of snubbing my wife. It's out of character for Anna, it isn't cool, and I've called her out on it a number of times in the past. Nothing changes, though, so I've resigned myself to the idea that it's not a priority. Cecilia doesn't care for Anna either, even though she'll never say it outright. So as long as they're relatively cordial to one another, I can't let it bother me.

"Sorry...I just didn't want to talk to anyone about Kasia."

Anna pushes a plate in front of me. "I get it."

I push it back towards her and gesture to the bartender for a refill. "Truth is, I didn't even want to come today."

"But you're glad you did, aren't you?"

"I had to come. It's like I owed it to the memory of us."

Between bites she says, "I'm not telling you anything you don't already know, Dylan, but I really loved her. I'm glad I came." Anna turns to me and smiles "And how perfect was that, listening to the Mass in Polish and English? I never got a chance to meet her family, but I feel like I understand more about Kasia now, seeing them all and experiencing where she came from."

I smile thinking about the noise, the crush of bodies, everyone happily chatting, yelling over the music, and of chairs crammed around the table whenever we were in their home. The shots of vodka passed all around, the loud laughter, the happiest Christmas I've ever had so many years ago in their tiny house. I remember Kasia's elderly Uncle Viktor, holding my shot for ransom once, refusing to hand it over until I got the pronunciation right: wódka. Then toasting me and clapping me on the back when I succeeded.

I saw them all today, with the exception of Viktor, filing into the Church as the organ boomed. They all had one thing in common: it was if you could actually see their crushed hearts just from the look in their eyes. Mr. Mazur stood proud, holding his wife with one arm around her waist and one hand on her elbow—he was holding her up. Kasia's brothers, so familiar to me, followed after with their wives, or partners as was in Alex's case. Veronica stood between Alex and his partner, the three of them holding hands. Veronica, stunningly beautiful with not a stitch of makeup on, looked straight ahead with an expression that was vacant, almost shell shocked. She seemed to physically need the support of the men flanking her. I studied them all as memories from long ago flooded my senses. But when Jake and their four children walked down the aisle today following Kasia's casket, that's when I had to look away. I couldn't bear to witness their pain. It felt too personal, like I was invading their privacy. Kasia was theirs. She hadn't been mine in a very long time.

"That's the first funeral I've been to since Will's." Lost in my own head, I need a second to process what Anna is saying. "I don't even remember Will's funeral...Not one minute of it." She looks at me apologetically. "I don't remember one word of your eulogy."

"I was so messed up back then. Tell you the truth, *I* can't even remember what I said. I'm sure I didn't do him justice."

"Young people shouldn't die."

I touch my forehead to Anna's. "No kiddo, they shouldn't."

Chapter Fifteen

DYLAN

She comes straight to me as I walk in the door from work. There's a meal cooking, the apartment smells terrific, and she's wearing a gingham print dress with an apron tied around her waist. She's smiling at me, the personification of domestic bliss when she announces, "I'm pregnant."

I suck in a breath and shoot up to a sitting position. Third night in a row I've had the same dream—same nightmare.

Cecilia is next to me in the bed, sleeping peacefully. She is beautiful. She is a good person, I remind myself. She would do anything I ask of her. She would even stop seeing Richard Von Essen if I told her to.

Cecilia is cheating on me.

The sickest part is that she *wants* me to find out. She practically leaves a trail of breadcrumbs as she makes her way to the Gramercy Park Hotel every Thursday afternoon.

Rupert handed me a manila envelope two weeks after that guy

Dick crashed our dinner party. It was the first time Rupert's expression registered any emotion. He was clearly confused to see me laughing as I leafed through the pictures.

I think Cecilia holds the misguided belief that if I find out she's fucking someone else it will unleash my inner caveman or something. Like I'll pound on my chest, beat the shit out of that pathetic loser and claim my woman.

That's how miserable she is.

Cecilia has lowered herself to sneak around town with someone who would be considered laughable by anyone from within our set, pitiful even. A guy who passes himself off as some hedge fund biggie, while in reality he's running day trades at a crappy shop that's one SEC tip away from folding. Another tidbit from Rupert's oh so thorough background check? Dick is behind on the rent for some shitty one bedroom apartment in Morningside Heights. Funny, I remember him bragging about closing on a bro-tastic bachelor pad in Tribeca as he swilled drinks that night. He's one step above a con man, a grifter. Dick has made a life out of hanging on, ingratiating himself with people who can, in fact, pay the tab. He plasters himself to people like Tripp, people who have money and influence, and then he hangs on for the ride. But unlike other guys who can turn those connections into something real and lasting, Dick just doesn't have what it takes. Schmoozing will only get you so far. You actually have to have a skill set to make it in this city. At thirty-five, he's up to his ears in debt, an abject failure.

The source of my nightmares? I'm not worried that Cecilia is pregnant with *our* child. Hell, I slap on so much spermicidal jelly disguised as lube before we do it that I'm surprised we've never slid across the bed and hit our heads against the wall. No, I'm worried that she's been careless with Dick. I am not raising Dick's child as my own—the thought of it gives me chills. But I also know that I won't throw Cecilia into the midst of an ugly scandal. After all, I've basically given her cab fare, patted her head on the way out the door, and told her to go look for love and affection elsewhere.

I have a whole speech planned out. I barely slept last night, busy plotting, thinking about how I'll do this in a way that will inflict the least amount of pain possible. But the next morning I grab the wrong tablet on my way to the office. I swipe the screen to open it, ready to enter my passcode so I can check emails as James drives. A series of texts between Cecilia and our friend Samantha Paulson fill the screen. I'm thinking that it's careless of Cecilia not to have a security code protecting her information, especially since her phone texts are shared and clearly visible on her tablet. And I probably would have ignored the exchange if I hadn't seen her name. But I did see it, and with each text I understand just how shallow and insipid and hateful my wife has become.

Sam: Did you go to Kasia's service?

CeCe: Hell no! Did you?

Sam: Of course not. Mel went.

CeCe: I'm not surprised.

Sam: Please, she hated that stuck up bitch just as much as I did. Mel actually sounded broken up about it when I spoke to her. Such a phony.

CeCe: Well, it is sad. I mean for the children and all.

Sam: Hmm...If I were you I'd be doing the cha-cha right about now.

CeCe: I do feel like dancing. Ding-dong the witch is dead, right? Seriously, we are so bad ;)

Sam: Did Dylan go?

CeCe: Yes...Little darling Anna felt the need to bring it up when the two of us had lunch with Margot yesterday.

Sam: Ouch.

CeCe: She's still the same old see you next Tuesday. She made a point of rubbing her belly every other second, trying to make me jealous I guess. I'd love to see that girl get a taste of what she dishes out. I hope her baby is buck-toothed and cross-eyed, lol.

Sam: Not likely with that hot husband of hers.

CeCe: True...I'd love to fuck him. Oh, especially if I could time it so that she walked in on us...JK ;)

Sam: Did you ask Dylan about the funeral?

CeCe: No. I've never even uttered that girl's name aloud. I'm above that.

Sam: You are.

CeCe: He had his choice between the two of us and he chose me.

Sam: Class wins out over trash every time.

CeCe: Always has and always will. So, topic change...Who is that guy you were talking to at Mel and Jon's house last weekend?

I toss the tablet to the floorboards, seething.

"Call Pete Wallace and ask him if he can get to my office sometime this morning."

My next phone call is to my wife. "Let's do lunch today."

She pauses. It's Thursday after all. She has plans with Dick that need cancelling.

"Can we do Le Coucou downtown?"

"Meet me at the office and we'll do the bistro on the corner. One o'clock," I add before hanging up.

It's not like I really need to consult with my attorney. Cecilia and I signed pre-nuptial agreements, but I want to have a good understanding of my position before I go into this.

When she walks in, I can tell she's taken extra care with her appearance. She always looks well put together, but today she's dressed to seduce: pencil skirt that nips in at her waist, silk blouse that criss-crosses over her ample cleavage, and blood red Mary Jane heels that are anything but prim. Once upon a time that would have made me feel bad for her, but not today. I have every intention of being cordial and respectful, but I'm not feeling the least bit sympathetic.

She's leaning in for a kiss and moving to sit her ass on the corner of my desk. "Hi, babe."

Before she can make contact, I gesture towards one of the chairs opposite my desk. My tone is curt when I say, "Have a seat."

Cecilia cocks her head to the side. Her forehead probably would have wrinkled in confusion if not for all the fillers and crap she religiously pays her dermatologist to stick her with.

"I'm serving you with divorce papers." Her mouth drops open but I forge on. "We've known each other a long time. I won't make this difficult for you. I'd prefer we do this as quickly and amicably as possible."

She sits stone faced for a moment before laughing. "Where the hell did this come from?"

"You're not happy, admit it. I can't possibly be making you happy, Cecilia."

She swallows, wide-eyed, shaking her head. "I love you, Dylan. I always have."

I stand, jamming my hands into my pockets. "I can't keep going on like this. I'm not happy, Cecilia."

She shakes her head again, looking away. "Is this some kind of early midlife crisis? Some fit of nostalgia about what could have been?" Her face reddens and her voice gets louder. "Is this all because of *her*?"

"Who?" I ask innocently while I silently goad, *C'mon, say it...say her name*. I can almost hear Cecilia's teeth gnashing with the effort it's taking for her to remain composed. "Who are you talking about?" I repeat.

"That girl from *Brooklyn*, Dylan!" She says the name of the borough as if one could actually contract cooties from leaving the rarefied atmosphere of Manhattan. "*You* know," she sneers, "the one you keep a *picture* of tucked between the pages of your favorite book?"

"You shouldn't snoop."

She throws her hands up. "Seriously? This is over a dead girl?"

I stare her down. "That's right...Ding-dong, Kasia's dead." Cecilia's mouth opens and closes two or three times without uttering a sound. Just for good measure, I add, "And don't worry, I won't tell Anna you want to nail her husband. I'd hate to cause a rift between the two of you."

She sinks back further into the chair, defeated. Her tears come steadily now, and although I'm disappointed and angry with her, the truth is that I've never wanted to make the girl suffer. And I have made her suffer—for years.

She whispers, "You can't do this, Dylan. You can't do this to me."

"Please, Cecilia, think about it. Can you honestly tell me we have a good marriage? That this," I gesture between us, "is good for either one of us?" She sits across from me speechless. "You deserve better than what I'm able to give you. I'm a lousy husband. I'm selfish. I really do want what's best for you. I want you to meet someone who loves you more than anything." I feel like a terrible shit when she gasps and lets out a pained cry. "I want you to have children with a good man. I want you to have a family."

She sobs, choking out her next words. "I want *your* child, Dylan. I want a family with *you*, no one else."

I come around and sit on the edge of my desk in front of her, leaning down to hold her hands. "Cecilia, I love you. I love you for all the years you were by my side, all the times you were there for me, solid as a rock. But I don't know if I'm capable of being *in* love."

"You're not in love with me."

I don't say anything and my silence speaks volumes.

She looks away from me and nods before getting up to leave.

"Cecilia?" She pauses with her hand on the doorknob. "Von Essen isn't good enough for you either. Do us both a favor and cut that guy loose."

Chapter Sixteen

VERONICA

I don't know what made me turn around at that exact moment, my focus should have been on Kasia's oldest son. But I did, and I saw him.

What is it like? To have a man love you so much that he collapses into his grief? Dylan Cole is imposing, larger than life—but not today. Today he wept openly and his shoulders slumped, making him seem much smaller and more human. And it wasn't just Dylan. Patryk was there in the church looking all heartbroken too, and it's been what, nearly twenty years since they broke up? Throughout the course of Kasia's life she's had men who have loved her with passion and devotion. You only have to hear Jake late at night in the kitchen, as I do every night, crying quietly when he thinks no one else can hear.

It's more than saying goodbye to Kasia that has me feeling so utterly alone today. It's looking at my life in comparison to hers. Yes, her family is mine, but I can't help but notice that while she was embraced by everyone she ever knew, I've been thrown away more times than I can count.

And another move is on the horizon. Jake's sister, Karolina, subtly inquired about my plans. She wants her old digs back and I can't blame her. I know she wants to be there for her brother and to be near her niece and nephews. I can live with Kasia's parents, that will be the suggested plan, but I'm dreading it. It makes me feel needy, makes me feel like an unwanted child.

I looked for them as we made our way out of the church in our long, sad procession. Maybe my father forbid them from coming. Maybe he stood blocking the doorway this morning. Maybe he slapped his wife's face hard, shaming her into submission like he'd done to me on so many occasions. Or maybe my mother had just gone about her day, convincing herself and Olivia that saying goodbye to Kasia wasn't important. The people they once knew as family long forgotten.

Their absence stings, leaves me feeling hollow and abandoned. It puts the focus on the others who have cast me aside.

It's not like I ever truly loved Larson, I understand that now, but his gentle rejection felt so terrible at the time. And I know I'm just being ridiculous and feeling sorry for myself when my very first boyfriend comes to mind. The one who got the snot beat out of him by my deranged father. He acted as if he didn't know me from that day forward, and really, who could blame him?

Family and friends are packed into every corner of Jake and Kasia's home, but today feels nothing like our usual get-togethers. The conversation is muted. There is laughter, but it's tinged with sadness. Faces are pale and drawn. The children sit in clusters in the backyard and in the living room, no running around or rough-housing the way it usually is. Rachel sits alone in her bedroom for the entirety of the afternoon, reading the letter her mother wrote to her over and over again. She answers, "No thank you," formal and polite, when I try to coax her into joining me for something to eat.

I feel out of place and unsettled, eventually giving up on any attempt to be social. Decamping to a quiet corner on the back deck, I sip a glass of club soda by my lonesome. As I drain the last drop from the glass, my aunt and my cousin Alex come out onto the deck. She's surprised to see me and looks back to Alex with a question in her expression. Standing behind her, he places both hands on her shoulders to guide her forward. "No, she should be here. She's going to be a part of this," he looks to me adding, "hopefully."

Henry follows behind with a manila envelope in his hands and a beaming smile that seems out of place on a day like today.

"Mama," Alex begins, looking over to Henry, returning his smile. "You know how you always say that angels watch over us?" She nods, her expression curious. "Well, this morning we got some news."

"Kasia *definitely* had something to do with this," Henry says as he opens the envelope and places a picture of a very pretty woman on the table.

"This is an old friend of Henry's."

"We went to school together and spent our junior year abroad together in Lyon."

Alex rolls his eyes playfully. "They dated."

"We did," Henry says, laughing. "Anyway, Nadine's family was originally from France, and she wound up moving back there after we graduated. She's a photographer."

My aunt takes Alex's hand, looking back and forth between the two of them. "What does this mean?"

Alex squeezes his mother's hand. "Nadine is having a baby."

Henry adds, "She's been back in New York for work for the past few months so we've reconnected. She was just up in Rye last week with us looking at the new house. Anyway, the pregnancy wasn't planned. The father isn't interested in Nadine *or* in being a father."

"And Nadine just accepted an assignment for a naturalist magazine that's going to be shooting in South America."

Now I am like my aunt, looking back and forth between them

like I'm at Wimbledon. I blurt out, "You're adopting her baby?" just as my uncle closes the sliding glass door behind him and joins us on the deck.

"Yes," Alex says with tears in his eyes as he looks up to his father, who is also misty eyed.

My aunt looks skeptical. "She will do this? She won't change her mind?"

"I never even brought up the idea of adoption to Nadine," Henry says. "But I was secretly harboring fantasies," he adds, looking to Alex.

Alex reaches for my hand, drawing me closer. "So this cannot be a coincidence, am I right? The other day, just hours after our Kasia passed, that's the day Nadine decides to call us out of the blue to announce that she's taken this lengthy foreign assignment—"

Henry cuts him off, excited. "And did we ever consider becoming parents? Because she can't think of any two people she'd want to raise this baby more than me and Alex!"

My uncle leans down and grabs the both of them into a crushing hug, as my aunt weeps with a smile on her face. "Yes, this sounds like the work of our angel."

I am speechless, overcome with emotion. So much love in this family, there always was.

Henry takes another picture out of the envelope. "Nadine's literally due in three weeks!"

It's the ultrasound. If this isn't a daughter they're expecting, then it's an extremely pretty boy. "It's a girl," Alex answers my unspoken question. "We're going to name her Hyacinth."

My aunt laughs. "Kasia would love that!"

"Why?" I ask. I mean, Hyacinth? I'm not sold on that name at all. If you're going for the whole, we're florists so we're naming her after a flower-thing, you could do Rose, Violet, Daisy, Lily...even Bluebell.

My uncle answers, "The first time Kasia made something on her mother's sewing machine—"

"It was awful but we pretended that it was fantastic," Alex interjects. "It was a skirt in some crazy fabric—"

My aunt laughs. "She took some old drapes that were rotting away in the basement."

"The hem was all uneven and it had a bunched up elastic waist."

"She couldn't put a zipper in when she was *nine*, Alex," my aunt chides.

"Anyway," my uncle continues, looking to me, "*Your* mother gave her a medal of Saint Hyacinth."

"Hyacinth was a *he*. And *he*," Alex says, raising his eyebrows, "is the patron saint of hopeless circumstances, among other things."

"It was a joke. Your mother was what?" my uncle asks, looking away from me to my aunt.

"Natalina was maybe seventeen?" She takes my hand, a smile playing on her lips. "Your mother *loved* Kasia but she also liked to tease her. She told Kasia that Hyacinth was the patron saint of dressmakers, and if she kept the medal in a special place, that Saint Hyacinth would watch over her and make her a famous designer someday."

"So Kasia took some of my dad's industrial strength glue and fixed it to the sewing machine they gave her that Christmas."

"I remember," my uncle pinches the tip of his thumb to his index finger, "because she also glued two of her fingers together that day."

My aunt looks up to the heavens. "It's still on that machine to this day, the little pink one that Rachel plays with."

"Hyacinth," I say to no one in particular. "I love it."

"This is," my uncle pauses to wipe his eyes, "wonderful news."

"Dad, I want to wait a little while to tell everyone else."

"Yes, yes...I know. Maybe too much on Jake and the children today. I understand."

My aunt gets up and kisses Alex on both cheeks, then does the same to Henry. "I love you both. You will make the most wonderful parents."

Henry has tears in his eyes. This must be bittersweet for him. While my aunt and uncle took basically a nanosecond to absorb the news when Alex came out, Henry's parents died in a car accident before he ever got the chance to tell them he was gay. He told me it felt like he cheated them out of knowing the real him, who he really was. And it also made him sad because he's not entirely sure they would have been accepting.

With just me, Alex and Henry left on the deck, Alex says, "So for this crazy plan to work, we need some help."

"From you," Henry adds.

"You know you two are like an old married couple, don't you? You finish each other's sentences." I gasp with a sudden realization. "Does this mean you're getting married? I could rock some awesome rainbow-themed arrangements for the reception."

"Slow down," Henry says, laughing. "And rainbow themed arrangements? Please, over my dead body...That would look awful."

"We're not getting married yet." Alex looks to Henry. "But that day will come." Settling back on me, he says, "We only have three weeks, Vee. It's going to be crazy. I can't ask Jake right now, so I'm going to be up in Rye with Michal and my father every free minute getting the house somewhat ready. We need a nursery," he says, beaming.

Henry adds, "And once Hyacinth comes home, we're going to be beyond busy."

"You need me to babysit?"

They look to one another before Henry looks back at me. "We want you to run the store for us."

"Run it, like, how?"

"You'll be managing the staff schedules, overseeing the orders, coordinating deliveries."

"Of course I'll be handling all the landscaping clients," Alex says, "but I'll need you to be my point person on that too, taking phone calls and setting up my appointments."

"Full-time?"

Alex shakes his head. "It can't interfere with school. But I know you were only taking nine credits this semester." That's all I *would* take because Kasia has been footing the bill and full-time tuition at NYU is a fortune. "If you keep that schedule then I think this can work. *If* you're willing."

Before I can answer, Henry butts in. "And one of our tenants is leaving at the end of the month. That apartment is yours."

Henry bought the building their shop is located in with an inheritance from his parents. The apartment would be right upstairs. I was already going to say yes, I'd never say no to these two, but now I was one hundred percent on board.

When I nod, Alex sweetens the pot. "And in addition to your salary, we're taking over your tuition." When I go to protest, Alex raises his palm. "That's non-negotiable."

When God shuts a door, he opens a window.

I needed a place to live and now I had one. I needed some purpose, a job that was important, and one was just handed to me. My mother, who they still spoke of with love in their hearts, abandoned me, but it no longer mattered. I was surrounded with the love and security of family.

Chapter Seventeen

One Year Later...

DYLAN

I pump in and out of Lara leisurely, appreciating her smooth skin and the way her lips part when she sighs in pleasure. She's a great lay, and a diversion that I sorely need. And best of all she's married, so she's not looking for anything more than the occasional excitement required to make her otherwise dull and predictable life bearable.

I've been to Zurich five times in the past year, which is four times more than I'd usually stop over to check in on my interests here. I need to fuck like other guys need to breathe. That's never changed. And I'm not about to be dating in New York. For one, I don't want to hear it from Cecilia if a picture of me with some other woman on my arm pops up on Page Six.

Even after separating she's still full steam ahead with her misguided plans for a reconciliation. She's begged me to try couples counseling—no thank you. She's enlisted our friends to intervene— as if a call from Tripp Parker or Samantha Paulson will help me to see her in a better light. She's even kept up her routine of lunching with my mother once a month, even though this makes Margot incredibly uncomfortable. But the primary reason I'm not looking for anything more than getting off has to do with one person in particular. She has long dark hair, a wounded heart, and a body I lust for in a way that shames me.

So I stay far away. During my last trip oversees I left Zurich for Dublin, where I have the very willing wife of a colleague who is always happy to see me, and then flew on to Paris, where basically anyone will cheat on their husband because he is most definitely cheating on her.

Life is good, I tell myself. Good enough.

Some friendships have fizzled out, but I'm all right with that. With the exception of Melanie, I've drifted away from that group. None of those people ever held a candle to my hometown friends or the close friends I made in college. And that arrangement works best for Cecilia; she has plenty of shoulders to cry on. I repaired my friendship with Tom, which took all of one phone call, and I drew closer to other old friends, the ones who weren't part of my life as a married man.

The divorce should be finalized any day now. It's uncontested, so I'm told the process is relatively quick. And while Cecilia hasn't entirely given up on her dream of us renewing our vows someday, which is downright delusional, she's given me every indication that she'll walk away quietly with her fifty-million dollar settlement.

She'd be a fool to make waves. We didn't make it close to a ten year anniversary, our union produced no children, and I have proof that she was fucking around behind my back. It's almost comical that given the number of flings I was guilty of initiating, I'd wager Cecilia didn't have one iota of proof to nail me with. My secretaries arrange my meetings with women like Lara. There's no phone trail, I don't email, I never traipse around in public with my women, and I insist on putting cell phones into my hotel suite safe the moment they walk in the door. There are no pictures or proof of any kind, only hearsay and rumors—and in a court of law that's worth less than dog shit.

At least there's only one divorce proceeding in the Cole family to entertain the masses. My father came to his senses sometime around New Year's and dropped his thirty-something-year-old plaything.

My mother didn't invite him to Christmas at her place in Sag Harbor, and maybe that was a wake up call for his stupid ass.

It was a very trippy Christmas, to say the least. My uncle Todd, my cousin Anna with Declan and their new baby, Millie Dalton and her girlfriend, and then several of Mother's new friends were gathered at her modest three-bedroom cottage out on the east end. It was a pot-luck dinner—unheard of for Margot—that had more vegan options than was necessary. Most of the guests were dressed in flowy skirts, including one of the guys who introduced himself as a performance artist. The after dinner entertainment was a live music session with people playing everything from the flute to the sitar. It was freaky and weird and pretty fantastic, seeing this independent and enlightened version of Margot Cole.

I made a point to call my dad when the wine had kicked in for most of the partygoers. His house sounded like a mausoleum in the background, while Margot's home was filled with people and laughter. He paused mid-sentence when he heard a man strumming on a guitar call out, "Get back in here, Margot, it's time for a duet!" I'm sure my father was thinking the same thing that I was at that moment: *Margot sings?*

"Wait a second," my father stalled when I was looking to end the call. And I couldn't make a sound then, because I was transfixed listening to my mother sing *Leaving on a Jet Plane* in perfect harmony with her new friend Manny. Her voice was clear and pure. She was confident singing and *so* damn good. This was a woman I didn't know. And the words, I imagine they were hitting my dad like a freight train. You could interpret the lyrics as a final goodbye or a wish to have someone's love back again. *Hold me like you'll never let me go*—was she singing to Vince or to this new guy? I'm sure my father was wondering just that when he broke into my bliss and asked, "Who is she singing with?" When I didn't answer, he barked, "What's his name?"

"I don't know, Ma—"

My father cut in. "Is it Jesse?"

"No, Manny I think."

Who's Jesse?

When he heard Anna start to whoop in the background, he asked, "What's happening?"

I couldn't pass up the opportunity to tease the old man. "Oh, so *now* you want a play by play?" In awe, I looked over at my mother. Her chords were simple, but hell, I'd never seen the woman even pick up an instrument. "She's, uh, playing guitar."

"Hmm."

As she sang the closing words, *Oh Babe I hate to go*, I got angry on her behalf and decided to twist the knife. "What are you and what's her name doing today?"

"I'm home by myself, Dylan."

Serves you right, asshole, was my initial reaction, but I did sort of feel bad for him. It was hard to envision him in that big house all alone. He was probably sitting in his office sipping on a glass of scotch, silent except for the crackling fire and the ice cubes rattling in the crystal tumbler. Don't get me wrong, the place is special to me, but it's huge. Back in the day, I loved it when my parents went out of town and left me on my own. I threw so many rowdy parties in that house that I'm surprised it's still standing. But I imagine that for my father, closing in on sixty-two and being hit with the reality that he might very well have lost my mother, his partner for over thirty-five years, that day was hard.

He deserved to feel lonely, it served him right, but I did love the man. And I think there's a kid in all of us, one who will always want his parents to be together—happily ever after and all that crap.

"Did you even bother to put up a tree?"

He cleared his throat. "The housekeepers do all that."

"If Mom knew you were alone, I'm sure she would have included you."

In a rare show of weakness, he countered, "I did drop a few hints."

"You can push a person too far sometimes, Dad. I should know."

There was silence on his end for a few moments before he said, "Enjoy the rest of the holiday, Dylan. I love you."

"Love you too, Dad."

"Tell your mother I said Merry Christmas."

"Hang on, you can tell her yourself, she's right here," I said as I passed the phone to my mother. She shot me a death glare as she took the phone. She took a breath and then pasted a smile on her face when she said hello. My father must have had his A-game going, because Margot was smiling wistfully within a minute, sinking into an armchair in a room off to the side of the kitchen.

"Who's on the phone with Margot?"

Anna had Mason on her hip, and when his hands reached out for me to take him, I'm sure my smile stretched a mile. This pudgy, drooling little pile of poop was my favorite person on the planet. I never realized how a simple smile from a baby could magically turn a person from moody to ecstatic within the blink of an eye.

"Earth to Dylan."

"Come here, young Dylan."

"It's Mason, you tool. You're gonna confuse him."

I sighed, teasing, "He's going to have to rise above that name."

In truth, I liked the name Mason Banks. It was formidable. I could already see this kid dressed in a pint-sized suit, barking orders into the phone, his desk next to mine as he's being groomed to take over Cole Industries.

I looked back to Anna, rolling my eyes. "I think Vince is trying to win back his woman."

Anna clapped her hands and smiled. "Really? I mean, I still want to damage his face but," she paused, scrunching up her nose as she looked over to Mother's duet partner, who was now twisting his long gray hair up into a man-bun, "I do really love Margot and Vince together."

"Not if he's just looking to go back to the way things were."

"You're right. But I'm kind of thinking he's learned his lesson."

"Have you spoken to my dad?"

She nodded and smiled. "I took Mason by the house last weekend when I was up in Connecticut to see my mom. He *loves* babies. I could barely pry Mason out of his arms when it was time to go." She took a sip of her wine, the smile now faded. "He's really sad, Dylan. I was angry at him for a long time, especially after I met that bitch." She winced, holding her hands over Mason's ears one syllable too late.

"You met her?"

"It's not like I got a formal introduction or anything, it was more like an ambush on my part. Declan and I were out for dinner...It was right around the time your mom left." Shaking her head, she said, "Vince is such a dumbass sometimes...Can you believe he took her to that tapas place right down the block from their apartment? I mean, your mom could have walked in to see the two of them cozied up in that back booth!"

"Yeah, he's getting careless in his old age."

Anna's dad came over and took Mason, telling us there were rabbits in the backyard. Which was a good thing, as Anna was about to let it fly. She wasn't even listening to me as I tried to change the subject. I didn't want to hear about my dad's mistress, otherwise known as Allison. The name alone gave me heartburn. But Anna's face was twisted, like she was fully back in that moment.

"Do you know that stupid twat introduced herself to me, calling me by name? How the fuck did she know my name? It's like Vince had showed her family pictures or something."

Oh, this ought to be good. I could picture Anna. The girl was not stuck-up or haughty, but damn, she could cut someone down with just one look—no different than if she was wielding a sharp axe. "What did you do?"

She laughed. "I looked her up and down, made a face like I smelled some bad fish, and then I told Vince he was a colossal disappointment."

I high-fived her. "Holy crap! You used those words?"

She nodded, offended. "He is! Aunt Margot is the best woman I know and he's acting like a fool, falling all over himself for some girl my age. And she's not even that good looking."

"I think that's the worst part."

"What do you mean?"

"He's got a type. He likes them young, blonde," raising my eyebrows I added, "great assets. This woman is plain in comparison to what he normally goes for. My mother knows it wasn't just sex."

Anna bit her lip, mulling that over as she studied my mother. "So she thinks Vince really has feelings for this one." After another pause she looked across the room at her husband and added, "That hurts."

I've caused so much pain for the women in my life over the years. Why is it that when I'm the one doing it, that I don't even seem to notice or care? But witnessing another person hurting because of what some other guy has done can crush me, make me feel like my heart's breaking for them.

"I mean, he's calling your mom...Do you think maybe he's done with this girl?"

I had Rupert keeping tabs on him since all this began. I practically knew the exact time my dad took a crap every morning. "She flew out to Napa with him last month but flew home alone on a commercial flight."

Anna raised her glass of wine halfheartedly. "Here's hoping."

I shook my head because I wasn't entirely sure my parents belonged together anymore. "It'll work out the way it's supposed to.

As long as I know my mother can be happy without him in her life, then I'm okay with however this plays out."

"What about Vince?"

"I hope he's happy." I really did. "And I don't mean that to sound bitter, because I'm not. I mean, if they get married there's *no* fucking way I'm attending the wedding, and I'm never, ever speaking to the bitch—"

"Noooo, you're not bitter," Anna teased, laughing.

I shrugged. "My allegiance lies with Margot."

With that, my mother walked over and handed me my phone. "All good?" I asked.

She tilted her head to the side, considering my question. "We had a nice conversation, but," she shrugged, her expression now pained, "I feel bad he's alone on Christmas."

"That's on him. Actions have consequences."

"They do."

"Mom, who's Jesse?"

Her eyes were saucers. "What?"

I turned to grab a chocolate-chip cookie from a tray on the table marked gluten free. Taking a bite, stalling, I conceded that it actually tasted good.

My mother knew what I was doing, so she was laughing as she poked me in the ribs and asked, "Where did you hear the name Jesse?"

Anna's eyes were bright with mischief now. "Is he an old flame, Margot?"

"Dylan," she pleaded with me for an explanation.

"Dad heard you singing that duet and he wanted to know who the guy was. He actually sounded like a jealous lunatic for a second there." I did an imitation of my dad in frantic mode. "Who is it, is his name Jesse?" My mom was actually giggling. "And kudos, by the way...I never knew you could sing like that, or play the freaking guitar? I kind of feel cheated right now."

"I don't sing all that well," she demurred. "And my guitar skills are amateur at best. But," she smiled, looking around at the odd cast of characters assembled in her living room, "I do enjoy it."

Anna shook her head. "No, Margot, your voice is really beautiful."

"Thanks. I started singing in the choir out here."

"That's great," we said in unison.

"It is." Taking in her surroundings, she said, "I needed this. I needed to get away from that life...the society luncheons, the charity event hypocrisy, the servants—"

"You clean this place yourself?" I was legitimately stunned.

"Yes!" she nodded emphatically. "And I actually enjoy doing it. It's cathartic. And I appreciate that everything in this house isn't perfect. I like the imperfections in the wood flooring, the outdated kitchen, the rickety door on the screen porch. Life is simpler here. I bike to the farmer's market, I host yoga classes in my backyard, I eat dinner among friends...I'm not lonely."

"Do you miss Dad at all?"

I guess I sounded like a forlorn little kid when I said that because she looked at me with sympathy and squeezed my hand. "Of course I do, Dylan." She nodded in the direction of her guests but kept her gaze on me. "These people are my friends, but your father is my life." Before the next question left my lips, she cut me off. "And no, I don't know what the future holds for us."

Anna nudged her. "And I guess you won't be telling us who Jesse is?"

She smiled over her shoulder as she walked away from us. "Nope."

I stuck around for a few days because, well, because I had nothing better to do before Caleb and Rene's annual New Year's Eve bash. Sunday morning I even tagged along to twelve-o'clock Mass at St. Andrew's. I guess I wasn't entirely surprised to see Vince slide into the pew next to me a few minutes before the offertory hymn began. Mom noticed him, I'm sure, and I was at a fist-pumping level of happiness when the Mass ended and the guitarist in the small folk group choir was practically falling all over Margot, complimenting her solo rendition of *Here I Am, Lord*. For once, Margot was the main attraction and Vince stood by as an outsider. I was lovin' it. Dad invited us to lunch afterwards, but I declined. My mother knew I was lying when I said I had to get back to the city pronto, but she didn't say anything. I think she wanted to be alone with him. It was time.

* * *

Sitting in first class on my way back to New York, I'm still thinking about my parents. Still wondering if I'm destined to be just like him, if it's in my blood.

I picture Veronica, conjure up this crazy fairy tale where she's mine. I come home to her at night, wake up with her in my arms every morning. *Never*, I tell her, *I'll never hurt you.*

I take a sip of my drink and close my eyes. My heart is heavy wondering if I'm even capable of keeping a promise like that.

Chapter Eighteen

VERONICA

To My Darling Wife.

There are three arrangements I'm responsible for making each week with that same tired message, all delivered to the swankiest buildings on the Upper East Side. It used to be four. The one that went to the West Side, to the San Remo? That order was cancelled nearly a year ago, the weekly residential delivery dropped.

Same week that Kasia died.

It's impossible to believe that one event didn't precede the other. Just thinking back to the look on his face that day, his body language —he was gutted. Not one month later, I read about it in the paper. It was one of those blind items. The ones that say things like: Which tech mogul can't keep his hands to himself? This one read: *Word on Park Avenue is that the honeymoon's over...She's one of the most high-profile socialites in Gotham and the toast of the downtown art scene, and he's the bad boy of the boardroom, once named Forbes' wealthiest bachelor.*

I see him all the time, and it's not like I'm even looking for the guy. He's impossible to miss. They all want his picture. It's like they're on a vigil and ready to pounce, bloodthirsty for that first picture of him with his arm around another woman. How awful it must be to have throngs of opportunistic bottom feeders snapping away at you, invading your personal space—the man can't have dinner with his mother without a photo appearing in the paper the next morning. I'd ask why they don't get bored of Dylan Cole, but I know the answer to that one myself. He's as close to physically perfect as a man can get, he exudes power, and to me, his eyes are a window to the sad, tortured soul he doesn't do a very good job of hiding.

Every time I get a glimpse of him I remember that kiss. I'm sure he doesn't, but I still can feel his arms wrapped around me in the hospital lobby, and the way he kissed my hair, huddling me in close as if I were precious to him.

I'm not and I know that. It's just a fantasy. I seem to have a thing for older guys, a need to feel like I'm under some man's solid, protective wing.

Thanks Dad.

I guess being thrown out the door and being branded a whore while in the midst of one's formative years can leave you more than just a little bit screwed up.

Daddy issues aside, I remind myself that my life is pretty freaking great right now. I am managing a business—H&A Florist and Landscape Design has been thriving, thank you very much. I am no longer reliant on the kindness of friends and classmates, as I have a small but gorgeous one bedroom apartment overlooking Madison Avenue that I can call my very own. I am surrounded by close family that, in the face of enormous tragedy, has pulled together and is muddling through pretty freaking well.

And speaking of family, I am an aunt. Aunt Veronica. Technically, Hyacinth is my first cousin once removed, but that doesn't roll off the tongue very well. At this point she only calls me Bee, mimicking her daddies as they bark orders at their gal Friday, Veronica shortened to Vee. Oh, she is a beauty, with wisps of auburn hair on her sweet little head and the bluest eyes. She couldn't possibly be loved any more.

Rachel can't get enough of her, to the point where she begged her father to let her skip tennis camp this past summer so that she could spend two uninterrupted weeks playing mommy. When I see Rachel holding Hyacinth, or Cinthy as she nicknamed her, I imagine it's the way Kasia looked cherishing me as a baby.

Done.

I make all three of the *My Darling Wife* arrangements the same, every single week. This week I go with densely packed yellow calla lilies. It's March, springs-a-coming, and these arrangements, though not the ones I put my heart and soul into, are awesome.

Since Dylan Cole stormed in here fuming last year, I make a habit of looking up some of the customers online. Among this group, one is a really lovely looking older couple. I'm sure the husband wouldn't mind if I personalized his note some, but I took a solemn vow not to be a butt-insky ever again. I peg the other two as Wall Street titan, Dylan Cole types. I secretly hope their wives socialize with one another. I imagine one Park Avenue princess walking into the other's sprawling penthouse, only to see the same arrangement with the same exact note, coming face to face with the cookie cutter nature of her husband's weak gesture. Ah, a girl can dream.

As I put the last arrangement into the cooler, my phone pings with an incoming text. I can't help but smile.

Introduction to Business Statistics is mind numbing but Professor Phillip French is not. He's actually pretty perfect. He's newly divorced, stumbling his way through shared custody, not currently using his best judgement, and looking for love in all the wrong places. I think he's hovering at around age forty, maybe a little younger. I could ask him but I'm not really all that interested. Just like Larson, I had him pegged the minute we met, and I went after him the same way a shark hunts a surfer with a skinned knee.

He was weak and I was hungry.

The first night of class we had to sign up for a one-on-one meeting because he would also be serving as the freshman advisor for business majors. We would be making a final choice in terms of major concentration by the end of the school year.

Yes, I'm in my fourth semester but am still a quasi-freshman. I'm part-time, and at the rate I'm going I'll have my undergraduate degree by the time I hit thirty. The entire process is disheartening, especially because I'm still not convinced this whole college degree-thing is necessary, or something I believe is worth the toll it's taking on me to achieve it. Practically every minute of every day is taken up between my job, school and family obligations. And the hours spent in class feel like my least productive and enriching. I know the basics of accounting from keeping the store's books, I had a major hand in designing our website, so there goes marketing and IT, and business management? I have that down cold—ask any one of our employees who've dared to slack off on my watch.

So I purposely chose the last slot of the evening: nine-forty-five. And while I did plan to discuss the merits of slogging through this program as opposed to dropping out, I went into the meeting focused on getting to know Phillip French.

I arrived a few minutes late, hoping to avoid the student who would be on their way out. I was dressed in tight black crushed velvet pants, a gray heather cashmere sweater that hugged my shape up top but draped out in a slight trapeze along the asymmetrical hem, and black suede open-toe shoe booties that were a gift from Henry. He has great taste. The open-toe was pushing it for late March in New York, but as long as there was no snow on the ground Professor French was getting a glimpse of my glossy, dark red toenails.

Nothing happened that night, except for the fact that we talked in his office until ten-thirty before he suggested we grab coffee at a place down the block. I'm assuming he knew this place morphed into a wine bar at night, because really, coffee at nearly eleven p.m.? French was adorable, trying his darndest to get me to see the light about sticking it out and earning my degree. As I drained the last drop of my Malbec, I licked my lips and told him that everything was riding on him. I'd make my decision at the end of the semester so, "You better give me everything you've got." I hoped *he* got it. I don't often use the words *ride* and *give me* within the span of two sentences. If he needed more of a roadmap than that to realize I wanted to get laid, then maybe French wasn't up for the job.

French: Can you meet me tonight?
I'm closing up at six. Come over?
French: I'll bring dinner. Anything special you want?
Dumplings from that place on 23rd would be awesome.
French: Done. See you later.

We danced around each other for another two weeks before I wound up straddling him in his office chair and unbuttoning my blouse as he struggled to explain regression models. Once he saw me topless he was done for, and we've been fucking like bunnies ever since.

Lately he's been saying weird things that make me think he's getting too attached. I don't have serious feelings for French, but there are things he gives me that I need. He tells me I'm beautiful and he seems genuinely impressed with my intellect—French lets me know in so many ways that I'm special. I realize that needing that kind of affirmation on a regular basis is pathetic and unhealthy, but I don't care. Every time he gazes at me as we lie in bed naked together, it's like he's giving water and sunshine to a seedling.

And I've come to understand something about myself: I enjoy sex and I need it. With Larson we were both so inexperienced it was comical, but I knew I liked it even then, the feeling of his hand caressing my body, the surprise of being filled by him, watching in wonder as he moved in and out of me. And with French it's entirely different...better. He's older, knows what he's doing, and seems to enjoy getting me off more than he needs his own release.

I thank the stars above that I'm naturally good at math, because as I sit across from him in class every Tuesday and Thursday evening, I can concentrate on nothing besides my overwhelming desire to crawl across the classroom floor on my hands and knees to suck French's dick while every other student watches.

Growing up in a home like mine was soul *and* libido crushing. Especially for a girl like me, one who sprouted full breasts by the age of thirteen. I garnered unwanted attention on the street, hiding myself under baggy sweatshirts when grown men began to whistle and leer at me on a regular basis, and I scored looks of derision in my own home, the place that was supposed to be my safe haven.

Once when I was fifteen, I remember being at a holiday party thrown by one of my father's business associates. I knew when I was getting dressed that the hem on my dress was short, but I just chalked it up to a growth spurt, making a mental note to tell my mother I needed to go shopping. He didn't see what I was wearing under my wool coat until we got to the party, and then it was too late. We all knew on the car ride home that something was not right. My father gripped the steering wheel tight and muttered to himself the entire way. No one dared to ask him what was wrong because for one, he had a violent temper, and two, he was driving drunk—you didn't want to rock the boat under those circumstances.

He waited until we were inside the house and then turned on me and pushed me into a wall as he wrestled the coat off my shoulders. Olivia was crying and my mother was yelling at him to calm down, but her appeals were weak—we all knew she wouldn't intervene on my behalf in any way that was meaningful. Once I was standing there in my dress, he slapped at my thighs, left then right, again and again, so hard he left marks. "Is this what you wanted them all to see? All those men, you want them to look at you? Are you a whore now that you have these?" He sneered as he grabbed at one breast and squeezed until I cried out. "Get out of my sight!" he roared after slapping my face.

It's hard to wash that kind of upbringing off. No amount of soap or hot water will do the job.

Chapter Nineteen

VERONICA

As it turns out, French is forty-one. He offers that up when I mention in passing that Henry and Alex gave me a car for my twenty-second birthday, so I can drive us to the North Fork vineyards when we both agree that we need a day away from the city.

It's absolutely ridiculous to have a car when you live in Manhattan. They did get me a very small car, so I haven't had much trouble finding spots as I move it from one side of the street to the other to avoid getting parking tickets. Basically, the alternate side parking rules have been the only reason for me to drive the thing since I got it. But once we're on the Long Island Expressway heading east with the sun shining on a beautiful July morning, I'll admit, I'm loving my sweet ride.

He's a little hesitant before he drops the number, like he has to brace me for the news that I'm with a man nearly twenty years my senior.

"You act like I'm going to crash the car or something. I'm not exactly shocked, French. You're a tenured professor at NYU," I say, shrugging. "I guessed you were somewhere between thirty five and forty-five."

"It doesn't bother you at all?"

"No," I say without taking my eyes off the road.

It *doesn't* bother me. I like that he's older; the lack of bullshit is refreshing. What *does* bother me is the way he's been looking at me lately. He looks at me like he wants more. He drops hints about meeting my family, wanting to tag along when I head up to Rye on Sundays or when I pop out to Brooklyn after work some nights. When French ups the ante today and asks me if I want to join him when he takes his daughters on vacation to Maine this summer, I have the urge to scream, "No fucking way, I'm not marrying you!" because I begin to understand that's where he imagines this whole thing is heading.

After I politely dodge that invitation, I pull off to refuel. French, gentleman that he is, goes inside to pay and then comes out to pump the gas. I have a sudden urge to buy a pack of cigarettes, even though I've never smoked one in my life. I'm seriously nervous that we're about to have one of those, *Where is this relationship going?* conversations, and I have no experience in that area.

We've been sleeping together for just over a year. Our conversations are deep, but that's just because it's in his nature to be open. He tells me about his ex-wife and explains what he thinks went wrong in their marriage. He cheated, but I don't tell him I'm pretty sure *that's* the one and only thing that went wrong. He tells me about the struggles and guilt that come with co-parenting. I feel for him and do my best to be supportive by listening. He doesn't ask me to reveal my inner self in return, and I have no compulsion to do so. I'm thinking that maybe the urge to dig around and regurgitate the inner workings of one's own psyche doesn't hit until middle age. French can talk for hours. He is also good in bed, so the endless yammering is something I just have to deal with. It's actually not a bad trade-off.

Disaster averted for now. French and I arrive at a quaint little winery that specializes in Rosé. This place is far, far away from the behemoth-type wineries that host stretch limos filled with tiara-wearing bachelorette parties from the outer boroughs—no thank you. And I'm from Brooklyn, so I'm allowed to say that.

Taking it all in, I decide that it's perfect. There are no more than twenty or so people walking about, sipping wine in this spectacularly beautiful garden. There's an old barn painted red with the doors wide open. Inside, the husband and wife team who operate the winery are preparing cheese plates and fresh baked bread for sale. French settles me at a small table and then sets off to get us something to eat. The sun is warming my skin, I've got my aviators on, and I've sunken down into a comfortable Adirondack chair as I sip a cool, crisp glass of this awesome deliciousness.

"Are you old enough to be drinking wine?"

Even with my sunglasses on, I have to shield my eyes with my hands to make out the very large creature looming over me. I know who it is, but I have to see him with my very own eyes to believe it.

He crouches down so that we're at eye level. "Hey, I thought that was you. How are you, Veronica?" When I don't answer, he adds, "It's great to see you."

There's no snarky tone to his voice, no look that could be construed as the least bit sexual, no tension in his demeanor. The man looks relaxed and happy, which for some reason makes me angry. Has it gone unnoticed that I'm wearing a short sundress that exposes a hella lotta leg, or that my cleavage looks fantastic in this get-up? Doesn't he notice that I've cut my hair in a pathetic attempt to look more grown-up? Suddenly I want to cry, and I'm not clear as to what's driving this emotional meltdown.

Tongue-tied, I stammer when I say, "I'm g-good, how are you?" and then wince when I notice what's-his-name heading back our way balancing a plate and a wineglass in one hand, while wielding a baguette in the other like it's a light saber. I always found his Star

Wars obsession goofy and adorable, but right now I want to banish his absurd ass to the outer limits of the galaxy.

Fuckity-fuck-fuck-fuck. Right about now I'd give a pint of platelets to be on one of those limo busses wearing a dildo necklace and a tiara. I don't want to introduce Dylan Cole to—what? To my boyfriend? I suddenly realize that it's been a year and I've never referred to French as my boyfriend. He's just...French.

He puts the plate down and looks between me, Dylan and his lady friend, confused when I continue to sit there mute. "I'm Phillip."

Dylan takes French's outstretched hand while looking him over. "Dylan." Looking behind him as if he suddenly remembers he's on a date, Dylan introduces the woman as Gia.

I choke on my wine, laughing uncontrollably when he says her name, realizing too late that I now look like an idiot, a child among this group of adults. "Sorry, I—"

He turns to his date, smiling as he reassures her, "It's an inside joke...I'll explain later." He looks to me then shaking his head, but there's a hint of mischief there. "How's your family doing, Veronica?" I know that's his way of asking how it's been since we lost Kasia.

And for some reason, knowing how special Kasia was to him, I want to comfort him. But curling up and hugging him close as I nuzzle into his soft, worn t-shirt wouldn't be appropriate right now. "It's been a tough year," I say instead. "But everyone has been pulling through. Jake and the kids are doing pretty well, I guess, and you know Alex and Henry adopted a baby, right?"

"No, I didn't know...That's great!"

"A girl...Hyacinth."

Dylan actually doubles over laughing. "Hyacinth?" He can barely get the word out. "Are you serious? That's priceless!"

"You know about that?"

"Saint Hyacinth of Poland, patron saint of shitty seamstresses? Kasia would love that!"

Then I'm laughing too, the both of us laughing so hard we have tears streaming down our cheeks. As I try to suck in some air and calm myself, I notice that French and Gia are both looking on as if they're evaluating us for spots in the psych ward.

Dylan turns to his date, but before he can get the words out, she interjects, "I know, inside joke." She is not amused. Dylan clears his throat and smiles at her—a winning smile that could turn any woman into an obedient pile of goo. He's better at making small talk than I am, so while he smoothes things over by steering the conversation towards wine, engaging both French and Gia, I stay off to the side observing.

Gia is a good decade older than me and very attractive, with golden blonde hair pinned up in that expert way so that it looks effortlessly casual but neat. She's trim with an athletic build; I can picture her in equestrian gear or tennis whites. I can't place her accent but it's not from the New York I was born and raised in. It's not like I order "cawfee" in the morning or "axe" questions or anything—I speak eloquently, thank you very much, as do most New Yorkers. That fuggedaboutit bullshit is just that, made for TV, Tony Soprano bullshit. But Gia was either from that rarefied Manhattan prep school environment, or she's from somewhere else entirely.

"Veronica?" French prompts me, rousing me from my stupor. "Gia just asked what you do for a living."

I answer absently, never taking my eyes off Gia's hand as she interlaces her fingers with Dylan's. "Oh, I manage a flower shop."

"She's being modest." French apparently feels the need to override me. "She's very talented...Makes the most exquisite flower arrangements I've ever seen."

I look to French as if he's sprouted horns. Exquisite? Laying it on a bit thick, no? And who *are* you right now using that word, the Lord of the Manor?

Gia cocks her head, smiling in a way that is at once cutting and sympathetic—if that's even possible. "That's so darling."

Dylan clears his throat again. He either has a bad case of strep coming on or he's just as uncomfortable as I am. "She *is* talented," he adds quietly.

"And what about you, Gia?" I ask in an effort to sound at least somewhat confident. Up until now, I'm sure I've been doing a spot-on impersonation of an easily rattled imbecile. "What do you do for a living?"

She licks her lips, pausing for effect. Ugh, cue the damn drumroll. "I'm the global marketing director for Spectra." When I didn't ooh and ahh, she says, "Dylan and I are direct competitors." And with a sly smile Gia adds, "Guess Cole Industries is looking to get in bed with the enemy." I cringe and Dylan cringes, because that statement is just...cringe-worthy.

French, on the other hand, is now a little starstruck and that's just downright embarrassing. "Wait, you're Dylan Cole? Cole Industries?"

Dylan looks away as he nods, a clear indication to most human beings that he doesn't want to get into it. French, usually a master at reading nonverbal cues, is oblivious. He starts in on some inane yarn about how he used Cole Industries sales data in his most recent Advanced Statistical Reasoning and Data Mining course. He stops blathering a few moments later when he finally catches on to the fact that no one is joining in or contributing to this oh so interesting topic of conversation.

I suddenly feel small, ridiculous and awkward. I'm now ten minutes past being ready to bail.

"Hey French?" I say, raising my eyebrows, trying to telepathically communicate my immediate need to get the hell out of here. "Before we leave I want to buy a few bottles of this wine for Henry, he'll love it." Looking to Dylan, I take a deep breath and say, "It was really good to see you again." I don't say anything to Gia because what is there to say? It hasn't been even remotely nice to meet her, nor did I hope to see her again soon. None of those parting words fit this situation and it wouldn't be appropriate to say what's really on my mind: *Please stay the fuck away from Dylan.*

"Good to see you too," he says, looking down at our full cheese plate and the bread that's untouched. "Actually we're heading out now...Already have a case of this stuff in my trunk."

He shakes French's hand, but before letting go, Dylan cocks his head and says, "I keep thinking that we've met somewhere before. Your face is so familiar."

French smiles as he shakes his head, doubtful. "I don't think so. I never forget a face. And I've read your professional bio, so I know you never studied at NYU."

Dylan's eyes widen in surprise as one corner of his mouth ticks up in a triumphant smile. "NYU?" he asks, casting a sideways glance my way.

"I chair the Information and Operations Management Department in the business program."

Dylan ignores him then, stepping closer to me. When he leans down to kiss me on the cheek, he whispers, "You're a bad girl."

I shiver and suck in a breath when his lips touch my skin, and damn if he doesn't notice. Gia's caught on now too, locking elbows with Dylan in a show of ownership as she nudges him and they turn to leave.

I collapse back into my chair once they're out of sight and proceed to drain my wine glass. I'm focused on subduing the ache between my legs and my staggered breathing, so I barely register French's voice when he says, "He seems like a nice guy. Where did you two meet?"

My response is automatic. "Dylan was Kasia's boyfriend...He was in love with her."

Chapter Twenty

DYLAN

I slap Gia's ass once, then twice more as I ride her hard from behind.

So, you fuck guys who are older than me? You fuck your teacher?

This is my inner dialogue, punishing Veronica for pushing me away, for letting me think I wasn't good for her, that I was too old for her. Out loud I groan Gia's name on my release. I'm not afraid I'd yell out the wrong name because in a way, Veronica will always be Gia to me.

I could scarcely focus on a word this Corporate Barbie version of Gia was saying on the drive back from the winery to her place. She's in a rented beachside cottage in Amagansett, that while tiny, probably set her back more than a quarter million for the season. Cecilia and I had a place in Southampton, but I gladly threw that in to sweeten the pot during the divorce proceedings. Cecilia was pleased and I wasn't much for the Hamptons anyway—to me it just didn't compare to the Vineyard.

Gia is the first woman I've been seen out in public with since the divorce was finalized three months ago. Are we dating? I don't really know. I was trying my best to be into Gia, into anyone for that matter, but I'm quick to find something wrong with every woman I meet. Dylan Cole, appointed New York's most eligible bachelor once again, has no shortage of women to choose from, but lately I've become exceedingly choosey. And now as Gia rolls over with a sated look and reaches for her cigarettes, I'm overcome with disgust.

"Didn't know you were a smoker," I say, making no effort to hide my distaste. "Don't expect me to kiss that filthy mouth of yours."

"I hardly ever smoke!" Wide-eyed, she tosses the pack back into the nightstand drawer.

"Sorry," I say, realizing I must sound like a dick. "I just can't stand the taste or smell of it."

"Understood." She smiles, adding, "You'll be good for my health. Come on, Dylan, you feel like a swim?"

I watch her walk naked from the room to the plunge pool that sits just outside the bedroom on a private patio. She's perfect, if you're grading Gia on her body alone. Anyone else in their right mind would also say her face is flawless, but her smile, her eyes—she just doesn't do it for me.

"Sure," I answer as she looks over her shoulder, beckoning me. But I really want to tell her not to change any bad habits on my account. It's already Sunday afternoon and Gia won't be seeing me again once I hit the road back to Manhattan before dawn tomorrow. Thankfully, she's based in Los Angeles. Not that I really care, but it's a plus knowing that avoiding her won't be much of a problem.

* * *

"All right, don't laugh, but I'm just throwing this out there."

I groan, certain that whatever Tom is proposing is going to make me want to hurl.

"Darcy booked our Cape May week for mid-August. She

thought you might want to go." In response to my hearty laugh, he says, "Wait, asshole, let me finish."

"You could tell me that the house next door was chock full of centerfolds and I still wouldn't want to be trapped on vacation with five happy couples and the, what, thirty kids they have between them? I'd have a better time at the Branch Davidian complex."

"It's only four couples this year and you know you're grossly exaggerating the number of children we have."

"Jake and the kids aren't coming?"

"No, he thought it was too soon for the kids. The place would remind them of Kasia too much, and not in a good way."

"What do you and Darcy think about that?"

"I totally get it but Darcy's upset. She's concerned that our kids will lose touch. But she also understands that it's his call and he knows what's best for them. Jake planned a family trip with their cousins instead."

"How are they doing?"

"I was out with Jake a few weeks ago. Caleb and I met up with him in Brooklyn for a few beers. I gotta say, he looks like hell. He's always been fit but he's lost ten or fifteen pounds…Looks like he's got the weight of the world on his shoulders. He's been getting back to work, though, and I think that's good for him."

"Are they all right financially?"

"Oh yeah," he says, dismissing the idea in a way that makes me feel relieved. "His business basically runs itself now and he's done very well. And Kasia…Her net worth alone will make it so that her children won't ever have to work a day in their lives if they don't want to."

I feel proud of my girl all over again. She really did it—started something from nothing and turned it into a brand that was a household name, if you had any fashion sense.

I laugh when I say, "I can't imagine Mazur-Wozniak offspring thinking it's acceptable to live a life of leisure."

"True. When Jakub and little Tomasz were around eight and six, they set themselves up with a lemonade stand on the sidewalk outside the Cape May house. No one even told them how to do it, it's like it was second nature to those kids."

"I can believe it."

"So before you shoot me down cold again, just consider it. Mick and Caitlin are coming—no kids there—and Rene is bringing one of her producer friends down from the network. She's single and Caleb said she's hot."

"Tempting, but it's still a no."

"All right."

"Thanks for asking, though."

"Want me to see if Caleb can set something casual up? Maybe you can meet this girl over drinks at their house?"

"Not looking for a set-up. Just not looking right now, period."

"I saw a picture of you online with that woman from Spectra."

"Nice, stalker."

"In your dreams, dickwad. It was on a business blog. Something about," Tom paused, gagging like he was choking on a dick, "a merger of some sort?"

"Yeah. I merged, I came, I conquered—or whatever that saying is."

"She seems like an interesting person. That's a pretty big position for someone in their early thirties."

"Gia's no joke. She's attractive and she's got balls the size of Texas in her professional life. She's just not for me."

"Are you missing Cecilia?"

"No." I don't even need to consider the question. I didn't miss her at all. "It sounds terrible to admit this, but I never missed her, even early on in our marriage when she was away or I was traveling. I was never in love with her. The day the divorce papers were delivered, I felt nothing but relief."

"There's someone out there waiting for you, Dylan. I know that."

"There definitely is."

And now that I know Veronica is fair game, I'm not wasting any more time. I'm going after what I want.

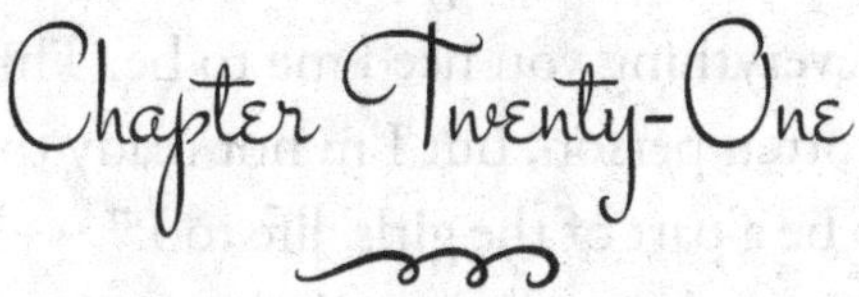

Chapter Twenty-One

VERONICA

No one stays in the city during the month of August.

Let me amend that statement: No one with scads of cash to throw down on obscenely expensive flower arrangements stays in town during the month of August. So it made sense and it was well known among our customers that H&A closed shop for a few weeks every summer.

I decide on spending the break in Rye with Alex, Henry and Hyacinth. The property is on Long Island Sound, and it has a pool and a tennis court. In other words, it's a five-star resort in my book. And I want to spend the break with *my* family, not French and his daughters.

We met a few nights before he was set to leave for Maine with the girls, and he knew what I was going to say before the waiter even set the menus down.

"You're thinking it's time for us to part ways?"

"Am I that obvious?" I shook my head, feeling awful. "Have I been terrible to be around these past few weeks?"

"No. I just knew you were having some serious second thoughts." When I went to speak, he held up his hand. "I'm a lot older than you are, Veronica. I knew it would be a problem for you at some point."

"No! It's really not about age, French. It's more like I'm not ready to take on everything you need me to be. This probably makes me sound like a rotten person, but I'm not ready to be a part of your life as a parent, to be a part of the girls' life too."

"If that was the only issue, then I'd try to reassure you, tell you I'm prepared to keep that part of my life separate from what we have. But I can tell it's more than that. This has run its course for you, hasn't it?"

"I care about you."

"I know you do," he said, squeezing my hands when he reached across the table. "And I'll be here waiting if you change your mind."

"No, you'll be scooped up by someone else in no time. And I have a feeling that person will be a lot better for you than I am." Now it was my turn to silence him when he went to protest. "No, French, you're a good father. Eventually that whole keeping your life compartmentalized thing wouldn't work for you."

When the waiter came back to take our order, we looked at one another and smiled. "Just a check for the wine," French said. "I think we're going to call it a night."

* * *

"Look at you go, girl!"

Hyacinth took her first steps a month ago, and just a few weeks later she's now boogying across the great big lawn in their backyard. She looks over her shoulder every few moments and flashes a crazy smile, like she still can't believe how awesome this new trick is.

Mama hen Rachel is never more than a few paces behind. It's overkill, but I understand her need to believe that everyone around her is safe, is going to be all right—is going to live. So rather than remind Rachel that Henry and Alex have basically baby-proofed every square inch of this three-acre property, I let her hover.

This is a girls' weekend. I'm technically in charge, even though Rachel is doing all the heavy work, while the daddies get a much needed night away from diapers and baby food. Jake is off fishing with his boys.

The best thing about this weekend? I love Hyacinth, truly, but every time Hyacinth goes down for a nap or when she settles into bed nice and early at seven, I get some quality time with Rachel. And while I came armed with no shortage of fun activities that would keep her mind off of her troubles, it turns out she wants no part of baking brownies, painting each other's nails, or applying some very believable looking temporary tattoos—thought Jake would get a good scare when he saw those. No, Rachel only wants to curl up next to me and hear stories about her mother.

"Tell me *everything* you remember, Veronica," she says. "I want to know what my mother was like when she was younger."

"Well, you have to understand, Rachel, I was much younger than your mom. It's almost like she was my aunt instead of my cousin."

"Kind of like how you and me are?"

Huddling in close and giving her a squeeze, I say, "Yes, exactly like how we are."

So I tell Rachel everything I remember. I tell her about going to Broadway plays with Kasia, feeling so grown up sipping Shirley Temples and eating tea sandwiches at the Carlyle afterwards. Kasia never took us to hokey tourist traps like the ones cluttering the streets of the theater district. No, New York with Kasia was an adventure because she knew all the best little secret places. After outings in Central Park, she'd take us to a nearby restaurant that made the best gnocci and had bocce courts in the back where old men played this unusual game while razzing each other in Italian. On cold winter days we hit her favorite fondue restaurant. The interior was the closest I've ever come to being inside a Swiss chalet, and the menus were written in French. Kasia would encourage us to order in French as she pointed the items out on the menu to the baffled waitress. I remember they had these plush round banquets and I loved sliding into those booths. On the chilly walk there, Kasia would take one of my hands and one of Olivia's, sticking them into her coat pockets, warming our hands in hers—the anticipation of the last course, a chocolate fondue with bananas and pound cake for dipping already on my mind.

I do *not* tell Rachel that I went there this past winter on my own one day. I walked back and forth that stretch of Fifty-fifth Street, wondering if I had the wrong address when I couldn't find it. I stood outside a Five Guys as I searched the address online, sadness weighing me down like a bag of bricks when I discovered our special place had boarded up its alpine shutters more than a decade ago. Instead, we make fondue ourselves. Rachel and I dip our strawberries, bananas and marshmallows into a pot of melted chocolate, laughing ourselves silly as we watch our favorite movie, *Elf,* in the middle of the summer.

I can't give Rachel her mother back, but I can dedicate myself to becoming an awesome aunt-cousin. I'll surround her with the same goodness and love that her mother once showered on me.

Chapter Twenty-Two

DYLAN

Closed for the month of August.

Seriously?

I stand on the sidewalk outside the shop for a good five minutes taking this setback in. I came here without knowing what I was going to say to her, how I'd explain this casual pop-in. I wanted to come in that first Monday after our awkward encounter at the winery, but I held back. She wants me—I'm sure of it—but I need to play this right.

Hell yes, honey, I saw the way you shifted in your seat, practically collapsing into it after I inhaled the skin on your neck. And I nearly reached down to give you some relief, desperate to touch the skin on your thighs exposed in that short sundress. I saw the way you looked at Gia's hand when she latched onto me like a spider—you wanted to slap her hand away just like I wanted to slap that jerk's face when he smiled at you like you were the best thing on the planet—possessive. And I almost laughed out loud taking in your face when your man fawned over me. You wanted to scold him like you would a child. You felt just like I did, wanted those two annoying pests to fade away into the background so that we could be together.

That's what I hoped, anyway.

Veronica Petrov.

It took some effort just to track down her last name, which is saying a lot, given that I assigned the task to my man Rupert. And once I had the name, I didn't have much else. No social media accounts—not one. Veronica is the antithesis of everything society attributes to Millennials. No publicly posted selfies, no blogs recording her every night out or her feelings on inane subjects. And she certainly isn't entitled or lazy, given that she's been known to work three jobs at once.

I was starved for the woman, for any information I could get. The only thing Rupert came up with was that her credit card was used once in the past month, at a craft store in Westchester County.

Her anonymity is something I envy. If you want to get the latest on me, all you have to do is type my name into a search engine and no less than ten very recent posts with pictures will pop up. Veronica is off the grid and I want to exist there—with her.

* * *

"How are you doing?"

"What are you asking me, Melanie?"

She laughs, taking me in. "I'm asking you how you're doing," she repeats. When I don't answer, she says, "Like are you lonely? I mean, you've hardly left the city this entire summer. Should I alert our friends that you're on suicide watch or something?"

Handing her a vodka rocks, I answer, "Yep, let Samantha Paulson know that I need a shoulder to cry on."

Melanie throws her head back, shaking it from side to side. "That traitorous bitch would cream herself and drop your weepy ex-wife in a heartbeat."

"How is Cecilia?"

"Managing, I guess. But you and I both know she's only ever wanted you. Her world's been rocked off its axis."

"Is she seeing anyone?"

She raises a brow and frowns. "Are you looking to reconnect?"

"No," I say without a nanosecond's hesitation. "But *you* wouldn't be happy about that?"

"My feelings are irrelevant here, Dylan. I just don't think you were ever truly happy with her. I love the girl like a sister, but her happiness shouldn't cost you your own. Know what I mean?"

"We won't be getting back together." I knew that as fact.

"Are you still seeing that skinny bitch from California?" I smile, shaking my head. "Nice try, by the way." In answer to my confused look, she says, "Blonde hair, tall, killer body."

"Think I was going for a Kasia look alike? I wasn't."

"No one would blame you." She stands and makes her way over to the window, looking down on the peons below. "Her funeral was really sad. That crap usually doesn't faze me."

"You were there?"

She nods. "I saw you but I left you alone. I figured listening to me talk about how fuckable her brothers are would grate on your nerves."

Melanie is as genuine as they come. An acquired taste? Yes. But no matter what, no matter how furious she can make me sometimes, I've always been grateful to have her in my life—grateful to have someone who knows me so well and who is honest with me to a fault.

"You're no longer appreciating the ladies, Mel?"

"I've always preferred dick, you know that," she says, shooting me an annoyed look. She turns and sinks back into her chair then, a dreamy look on her face. "But yes, every single member of that family is delectable. What a gene pool."

"What are you doing in town? Isn't everyone we know in the Vineyard?"

"Yes, but I kind of hate them all, including my husband. He's on a mission to get me with child, and I...I—"

"Don't want kids?"

"No, I can't say that with conviction." She's about to go on but then stops. "Forget it, it's dumb."

"Tell me."

"I miss Christian."

Christian was Mel's college boyfriend and is still a close friend of mine. Now I get to see him no more than twice a year, those rare times when I'm out west and not bogged down with work. Melanie never asked about those trips though, so I'm surprised.

"I know it's ridiculous to waste my time thinking about him, and I haven't been. It's just that lately...I keep hoping to run into him."

We both know the man now lives in San Diego, happily married to a very beautiful and sweet-natured girl. Cora and Christian have three boys, all athletes—confident little shits like their dad. From my vantage point, Christian is living the dream.

Melanie takes in my doubtful look. "I know I won't run into him, stupid. It's just that lately I've been feeling unsettled and it's horrible. My husband is a good person. He tolerates me with a freaking smile on his face. But I regret what I did because I know I threw away my chance at happiness. Christian was it for me."

"So having a child with Jon—"

"Closes the door on that chapter of my life. And that's fine. I mean, I know Christian isn't even thinking about me. From what I hear, he's deliriously happy." I don't answer because she doesn't need me confirming the fact and pouring salt in her paper cut. She drains her glass and looks down as she spins the ice cubes in the crystal tumbler. "Who needs him anyway? Kind of a baby, don't you think?" She looks up at me smiling. "It's not like I fucked his father."

"Yeah," I deadpan, "he totally overreacted."

"And his stepfather was hot. I kind of blame Christian for the whole thing."

I nod and stand up. "Absolutely." She knows I have a conference call scheduled, so I'm not being rude showing her the door. "Can we grab dinner one night next week?"

"No can do. I have to head up to the Vineyard sometime in the next few days. Jon's parents are going to start bitching and putting ideas into his head if I stay here. I don't think his mother likes me," Mel says as she salutes her mother-in-law with her middle finger.

"We'll set something up next month."

Walking towards the door, she turns back to me and says, "I'll see you at Margot's event, right?"

Oh yeah, my mother's new pet project.

My mother is back living on the Upper East Side and back with my father, but she hasn't fallen back into her old ways. Now she volunteers her time teaching yoga at a youth center in Chelsea, and this event she's hosting is a pared down version of the lavish fundraisers she used to organize. She's developed a bond with a group of teenage girls who attend the center, and according to Anna, she has a religious following at her Tuesday and Thursday afternoon classes. Some of the girls' mothers have even started crashing the youth center, coming to Mom's class. Mom told me they sit after class and talk about goals, obstacles they face in the form of race or class or gender, empowering yourself as a woman, and just life in general. It energizes my mother and it's given her a renewed sense of purpose.

"Your mother told me this is the first *real* fundraiser she's ever thrown. And it's true, isn't it? All of those galas where people like us used to get drunk and high and hook up, then we'd cut a fat check to orphans starving in Timbuktu?" Melanie smiles, adding, "This is the first time I'll actually be contributing directly to improve someone's life. Margot is inspiring me to be a better person."

"Thinking of volunteering at the youth center with her?"

"I don't think she'd let me through the door. I'd corrupt those little bitches."

Yep, Melanie imparting her version of female empowerment to the next generation had disaster written all over it. Speaking of disasters, I *have* to attend this event to support my mother, but it will mean running into my ex and her parents.

"I hope the venue is big enough for me to avoid the Tates."

"I honestly don't even know if they're invited."

"Say what?"

"Yeah," Melanie says, shrugging her shoulders, "your mother and Bunny aren't overtly at war or anything, but they're no longer besties."

"That sucks."

"It was inevitable. I think your mom was developing an ulcer leading up to those monthly lunch dates. Cecilia and Bunny were obviously plotting when they still thought there was a chance she could win you back. Your mom dragged me to a few of those lunches just to have a buffer and they were painful. Cecilia would wind up dabbing at her eyes at some point, acting like she was holding back tears...Fucking nauseating. Then your mom got wind that Bunny was making your father's affair public knowledge."

"Really?" That surprises me. It's not like my mother kept it a secret, she did tell her closest friends about their split at the time, but it wasn't in the tabloids or anything. And Bunny was a good person, like a sister to my mom. That kind of betrayal would have felt like a knife in the back.

"Yes, really. My mother shut Bunny down one day when she heard her laughing with a few other women, totally at your mother's expense, describing in detail how your mother found out about your dad and his," she added air quotes, "Pippa Middleton look-alike."

Ouch. "I never thought Bunny was that low. I'm kind of shocked."

"I'm not. Bunny doesn't know her place in the world anymore.

Her only daughter is *divorced*. That's like...I don't know, death to people in our parents' circle. And on top of that, her best friend is changing, evolving. I mean, my mother tolerates Margot's new age nonsense, and they're still tight, but even she's dropped a few comments about the new wardrobe, new interests. She stayed with your mother out in Sag Harbor for a few days last year and was a little horrified. She described your mother's yoga friends as homeless vagabonds." We both laugh at that one. I could totally imagine Melanie's mother, cross eyed and appalled, breaking naan with that rag-tag group. Melanie mimics the closing yoga pose, palms together over the heart. "But I'm digging the new Margot."

"So is my father, thank the Lord."

"That burns Bunny's toast too. Here she is, making sport of your parents' marriage issues, while it's plain to see that whatever's gone down between them has made them stronger. I think a lot of those ladies are jealous. They're too scared to throw their cheating husbands to the curb like your mother did. Margot didn't cave in, she wasn't afraid...She dropped his ass! *And* he crawled back!"

I was back in time, back to the night I crawled to *her* with my tail between my legs. Not above begging when I realized I was in danger of losing the one person who meant everything to me.

I didn't get a second chance. My father was lucky.

Melanie leans in to plant a kiss on my cheek. "I'll see you."

Chapter Twenty-Three

DYLAN

"How was Tom and Darcy's party?" Mom asks as she pours me a glass of wine.

"The Labor Day bash was good…A little heavy on the munchkins, but good."

My dad turns and looks up, smiling at my mother affectionately as she pours him a glass. "One day your munchkin will be running around on that beach and you'll feel like the luckiest man on the planet."

There are times when I have to rein in the smart-ass comments that sit on the tip of my tongue, listening to this new, loving husband version of Vince Cole. I take a breath and remind myself that he's happy—I want that—and more importantly, my mother is happy.

My mother's brow creases in concern when she glances my way. The woman will always worry about me. "Was every person there married with children?"

"No. Caleb's wife Rene had a few of her friends from the network down and Darcy's cousin was in from Chicago too." I roll my eyes. "Both of them were looking to set me up...I felt like a contestant on some lame reality TV show."

"Anyone interesting?"

I sit on that one for a moment, looking out into the distance. All four of the single women at the party were good-looking, going somewhere in life, and not one had a dull personality. Still, I didn't feel so much as a hint of interest towards any of them. "Nice women, but no."

"How is Rene doing?" My mother asks. "I saw her on the Sunday morning program a few weeks ago."

My father adds, "Times have changed. They'd never have an obviously pregnant woman on camera anchoring the news when I was your age."

I smile thinking about Rene, my shock at seeing a very pregnant woman wearing a bikini for the first time. And it's not like I'm hot for my friend's wife or anything, but I thought she looked oddly sexy like that. "It's weird. She doesn't look pregnant until she turns to the side and then you're like...Whoa, she's huge!"

"She must be due soon."

"Middle of next month."

Disappointed, my mother says, "That's too bad."

"Why's that?"

"I was planning on inviting all of those girls to the benefit. I'm sending my final list to the engravers today."

"Invite her anyway. Rene's always up for anything as long as the timing works out."

Mom takes a sip of her wine, studying me before she speaks. "There's something I wanted to run by you, Dylan. You know how the benefit is going to be like an upscale consignment shop model, right?"

I nod, because she probably told me all this already but obviously I wasn't paying attention. My father chuckles, taking in my expression. "Neither Dylan nor I have any idea what an upscale consignment shop model is."

"Well, a consignment shop is a place where women of means can sell their clothing, items that are couture level quality. The store pays you, taking a percentage for themselves after the item sells."

My father looks as if he's just gotten a whiff of something foul. "Have you ever sold your clothes?"

"No," my mother answers, as if the very notion is ridiculous. "I donate my clothes. But people fall on hard times, Vince, and consignment shops can come in very handy when you're in need of fast cash." My mother takes a hearty sip before adding, "I know that when my father's gambling problem was at its worst, my mother unloaded suitcases full of her clothing at those shops, along with my favorite riding boots."

I know my grandfather was no angel, but I have only good memories of the man. He taught me to play Texas Hold'em, helping me to amass my version of a small fortune while I was still in middle school. So I'm only into reminiscing about him when it's on a positive note. Changing the subject, I ask, "So how does it work for the benefit?"

"I've called on all the ladies, along with my favorite designers, to donate their very gently used formal wear. The designers are donating items that have been worn in their runway shows. The guests at the benefit will bid on the items and the proceeds will go to the scholarship fund." She smiles, adding, "Simple."

"Your friends won't turn their nose up at bidding on used clothing?" my father asks.

"I've invited *all* my friends, new and old." Her face sours. "Some of them would die before they wore a used item, you're right. But it's for a worthy cause, so they'll bid, even if they just turn around and dump the items in the trash afterwards." She brightens when she says, "I've invited a diverse group with a lot of young blood, and the response I've gotten so far has been great."

"I'm assuming you're taking cash donations too, right? I won't be bidding on any dresses."

"Of course, Dylan. And I'm expecting a nice fat check from both you and your father."

"How many scholarships are you sponsoring the first year?" Dad asks.

"Just two. One of the girls from the center is graduating from high school with a near perfect GPA, but I'm most excited about the other recipient—her mother. Her name is Cheryl Hart. The scholarship will enable Cheryl to take a leave of absence from work so she can be a full-time student. She's had a tough life but she's never lost her motivation to better herself. And she's so excited about this opportunity. Cheryl and her daughter Skylar will be attending classes on different campuses, but they'll be experiencing college at the same time. Isn't that wild?"

My father squeezes her hand. "I think it's great, and I think you're amazing."

Following a look that goes on a beat too long between the two of them, I'm just about to get up and excuse myself from the lovebirds when my mother stops me. "Wait Dylan, I wanted to ask you something. I reached out to Jake Wozniak to see if he was okay with me donating a few of Kasia's earlier original pieces for the auction. I hope you're all right with that."

"What was Jake's reaction?" I don't know the guy well, so I'm not entirely sure how he'll take my mother's gesture. Would he see it as a compliment or as an intrusion?

"He seemed really happy about it. In fact, he asked if his daughter could attend."

"So he's bringing his daughter?"

I toss that around, and can't say that I feel easy about it. There's definitely no ill will between us, it's not that. I'd come to realize years ago, even before I knew Kasia was sick, that Jake was never the villain our story. I didn't begrudge Jake as much as I regretted the behavior of my twenty-two-year-old self. But hanging out with Jake for an evening like he's my buddy? Not sure how I feel about that.

"I told Jake he's welcome, but that it would be mostly women." She points at me and then my father. "But you two *will* be sitting at my table to support the cause." She adds, "I reached out to Kasia's mother as well, so she'll be bringing Rachel."

"Can I have one of the invitations, Mom?"

"You have someone you want to invite?"

"Maybe."

She smiles, knowing I won't divulge anything more. "I'm going to bring us out some snacks. Be right back."

When she closes the sliding glass door behind her, my father turns to me. "Your mother wants to sign the Vineyard house over to you."

"Why?"

"I think she found the last two weeks insufferable. Same tired old crowd, same parties."

"She doesn't feel like a part of that world anymore?" Dad nods. "I get it. Did you run into the Tates?"

"Only when it was inevitable. We managed, it wasn't entirely awful. They aren't the reason she wants to unload the house. She—"

I stare him down, cutting him off before he tries to spin some bullshit excuse. "Mom knows you brought *her* there, doesn't she?" He lowers his eyes to the floor. "Sell it," I say as I get up to go back inside. "I don't want anything that stinks of her either."

Chapter Twenty-Four

VERONICA

"Ouch!" Rachel looks up at me with a puzzled expression as she wriggles her hand free from my tight grasp.

"I'm sorry, Rachel," I say, smoothing her hair.

I'm on edge. Waiting on the short line to check our coats, I take in the space. I know from reading the Style section of the Times that this downtown tap room sometimes hosts small concerts, but it's more of a hip date spot known for its trendy craft beer pairing menus and Sunday jazz brunch. I've never been here before but imagine it's been transformed for this evening's event. Tonight it looks like an extremely fancy flea market, and women are already walking the perimeter, scrutinizing the dresses that are hung up and backlit with a write-up about the designer posted next to each garment.

"I wonder where Mommy's dresses are," Rachel says as she looks around in wonder.

"We'll find them," I assure her.

Getting dressed for this thing was a nightmare. The thought of being overdressed or too casual had me trying on outfit after outfit, discarding every castoff onto a pile on my bedroom floor. I settled on a short, moss green sleeveless dress paired with my favorite peep-toe heels. Inspecting myself in the mirror, I knew I wouldn't look as well-heeled as the other women at this event, but I was satisfied, thinking it looked good enough.

I was mad at myself for even caring.

Ever since July, since that whispered near-kiss he laid on me when he scolded me, I couldn't get Dylan Cole out of my mind. I hated the knowing look he shot me, as if he suddenly had some kind of window into my screwed up psyche once he found out I was nailing my professor. And all summer long I had that glamazon's face in my head, refusing to admit that I was green with jealousy at the thought of him so much as touching her.

Hate, jealousy and then tenderness. My feelings are all over the map when it comes to him. When he showed up at the flower shop a few weeks ago to drop off an invite to this fundraiser, he was a different man. He seemed unsure of himself, hopeful that I might attend—even pointing out Kasia's name among the featured designers listed on the invitation to entice me when I didn't automatically commit. When my aunt called to ask if I'd take Rachel, I was grateful to have her as a buffer, as my reason for going.

Looking around, the women here range in age from what I'd estimate to be early thirties up through their seventies. Although most are no doubt part of the socialite, ladies who lunch crew, the crowd is a mixed bag. Definitely a few artist types, and the designers are easy to spot, fussing over their favorite clients.

"That's Mommy's!" Rachel skips ahead, making her way towards a confection of a dress, the top a strapless bodice covered in beads that catches the subtle light in the room, the bottom a tulle skirt that makes it look like a dream to dance in.

"Are you sure?" This doesn't look like one of hers. Kasia never did whimsy as far as I knew.

"Yes, it's hers." I breathe in deep at the sound of his voice. "She made it for my cousin Anna years ago. Anna treasured that dress and everything else Kasia made for her." I can barely make out what he's saying because he smells so freaking good. "She was happy to donate it for tonight, though. This is a great cause."

Rachel pipes up, tapping Dylan on the arm. "Hi."

"Hey," he says, crouching down to her level. "I know you must be Rachel Wozniak because you look so much like your mom."

Rachel beams whenever someone makes a comparison between her and Kasia, so she's a fan of Dylan's from the start. "You knew my mother?"

"We were really good friends back in college."

"Oh. Do you know my father too?"

He nods and smiles. "Yes, I know Jake too. Your dad is a really great guy."

Getting right down to business, Rachel gestures towards the bid sheet and asks him, "How does this work?"

"Well, people write their name here and then write down how much they're willing to spend on the dress. Then they either get to keep the dress for that amount, or someone else can come along and write down a bigger amount, and then that person gets to keep it."

"I bet someone is going to spend a lot for this dress. Look! Someone wrote down one thousand dollars and then someone else, M.C....Who's that?" Before getting an answer, Rachel exclaims, "That person wrote three thousand!"

Guess I'll be buying the modestly priced raffle tickets instead. I lean down and kiss Rachel's cheek. "Everyone loves you mom's designs."

Looking back to Dylan again, she asks, "Are you here to bid on the dresses?"

He bites back a smile. "No, I'm here because my mother is the one running this party, so I'm kind of helping her out." Turning to me, he says, "I don't think I'd look so hot in that number."

"No, you should stick to suits." And he looks damned delicious in the black suit he's wearing tonight, a black button down shirt open at the neck completing the look.

"So how's the flower business, Veronica?"

"It's good." I breathe in deep again, trying to collect myself. I can't help it, he unnerves me. "I'm managing the store now."

"Manager," he says, nodding in approval. "So I trust you're now making a habit of being fully dressed when the store opens in the morning?"

Such a wiseass. "I'm working on that."

"The display windows are really great. You design them yourself." It wasn't a question.

"I do, thank you."

"It's sort of on my way to work." *No, it's most certainly not. I know where you live and I know where you work.* He catches my curious look and clears his throat. "Once every so often I see you in the window wrestling with some branches or bales of hay. I like the giant crows this week."

The fact that he went out of his way to see me quickens my pulse and makes me smile. I decide to let him off the hook. "They're ravens, doofus. It's Halloween season and I put a lot of thought into the whole Sleepy Hollow theme."

"Rachel, did you hear that? She called me a doofus! No one has called me that since I was in the third grade."

Rachel giggles and then gasps when the lights flicker on and off.

A woman's voice announces, "Ladies and gentlemen, please take your seats so we can begin tonight's program and then get back to shopping."

"Rachel, let's go look for our—"

Dylan swallows, looking tentative and...shy? "Um, you and Rachel are sitting at our table up front. I hope that's all right." Rachel beams as she takes Dylan's outstretched hand as I follow behind the two of them speechless.

I still can't get a good read on what's happening here. How does he see me? Is this just a game to him or is he trying to draw me in? I can't help this growing sense of longing, and my emotions leave me feeling both confused and irritated.

Dylan pulls Rachel's chair out for her and then turns to me, placing his hand on the small of my back as he guides me to the chair next to hers. His hand burns hot onto my skin through the fabric of my dress, grazing just above the curve of my lower spine. As he pushes my chair into the table, he leans down and whispers, "You look beautiful tonight, Veronica." I take in a shaky breath, unable to reply. I'm relieved when the lights dim and the spotlight fixes on the podium.

"Good evening everyone, and thank you so much for supporting this very worthwhile cause. My name is Skylar Hart and tonight I have a lot to be thankful for.

"Last year I signed up for an after-school yoga class, not expecting much from it. I certainly wasn't expecting it to change my life, but it has. The sisterhood that developed in that class is something that took all of us by surprise. And as word spread, more girls started showing up. Within a few weeks, some of our older sisters and even our mothers were looking to downward dog."

After the laughter dies down, her tone changes. "Those classes never ended on time. Margot...I mean Mrs. Cole, always brought treats to share after class." Looking towards a beautiful older woman at the head of our table, she points and says, "I'm counting on one or two care packages next year. I don't know if I can live without those cinnamon scones." They share a smile before she goes on. "Not one of us was in a rush to leave after class because that time turned into something very special. We sat as a group of women sharing our experiences about growing up and living in this city, the good and the bad. We shared our dreams, our disappointments, and talked about things we saw as barriers to our success.

"This city is so strange, you know? On any day of the week you can be standing on a subway platform wedged between a homeless person and a stock broker. In so many ways, we're a city divided. And when you're from the projects, success can seem like no more than a pipe dream, even when you work your butt off to get straight A's.

"For as long as I can remember, my mother has worked two jobs. But even with all that she's sacrificed, college could still be out of reach. She always says, 'College is important. It's like a calling card that says: Treat me with respect.' Well, I have the utmost respect for my mother and for all of the women in our group. We will all make it, pulling each other up and supporting each other along our journey.

"And although I consider my mother to be one of the smartest women I know, college degree or not, I cannot tell you how proud and excited I am right now. Thanks to all of you for supporting this scholarship program, my mother will be attending Hunter College right here in New York City while I'll be studying at Cornell this fall. It's a journey we'll be taking together."

The crowd erupts into applause as the girl's mother joins her on stage. And when her mom says, "Margot, get up here with us," the room gives the group a standing ovation.

I lean over to Dylan without thinking and say, "Your mother is awesome."

"She really is," he answers.

But my heart is sinking at the same time. I am now officially a college drop out. Just two years under my belt before I gave up, feeling lost and without direction. Meanwhile, so many people in this city dream of something I took for granted. I study Rachel for a moment, wondering what kind of example I'm setting for her.

"What's up?" Dylan asks, nudging my knee with his.

I shake my head. "I'm good. Just thinking it's time I got my life together and finally finished my degree."

"Don't beat yourself up. Juggling work and classes at the same time can be difficult."

"No...I dropped out."

"And now you regret it?"

"Yeah, I'm thinking that I do regret it."

The woman I now know to be Margot Cole comes over and approaches Rachel. "Did I hear that you're Kasia's daughter?" When Rachel nods, she says, "Can I introduce you to my niece, Anna? She was a friend of your mother's and she's standing over by a dress your mom made that's my absolute favorite. C'mon." Rachel leaves with Mrs. Cole without a glance backward.

"Applications are probably due next month for the spring semester, Veronica. Make sure you get on that." Resting his hand on top of mine, he adds, "You're too smart and accomplished not to see it through."

"Stop being so nice to me."

He laughs. "Come again?"

"I just...Ugh! You're sweet and nice one minute, dark and nasty the next."

"Dark, nasty...Who, moi?" he jokes, gesturing to himself.

"I guess you've conveniently forgotten that crap you muttered in my ear at the winery?"

His eyes darken. "That, sweet Veronica, was born of anger, pure and simple." He leans in closer, so close that his hard chest is pressed against my shoulder and his breath warms my neck. "I'll be honest, I'm jealous of that lame dick professor. You made me so mad I wanted to toss you over my lap and spank your ass red."

"French is a great—"

He cuts me off. "He's not a great lay. Don't even try to sell me on that bullshit."

My eyes are saucers. I was just about to say he's a great *person*, but now I have to go with it. And no way am I telling this cocky bastard that I haven't seen or spoken to French in months. "Matter of fact, he is."

"Just proves to me that no one's ever given it to you good." He looks down at my body as he says that. His eyes fix on my tits, my hard nipples so painful that I want to press into him to ease the ache. "What's that they say about teachers? Yeah, I remember…Those who can't do, teach. I *can* do, Veronica. I'll do you so good you won't remember your own name. And," he adds, raising my chin so that I have no choice but to look at him, "I'll *be* good to you." His eyes soften. "Let me be good to you."

"I—I don't understand any of this. What do you want from me?"

"I want everything…But you already know that."

Okay…*What*?

I breathe a sigh of relief when Rachel comes back and crashes our very odd party of two.

"Dylan, I won the dress and I didn't even write on the paper! Someone wrote my name next to the winning number! And it was a *lot* of money." She leans over me to whisper in his ear, "*Five* thousand dollars!"

Even though my head is basically still spinning from our bizarre little exchange, without thinking I look to Dylan mouthing the words: your mother. He holds my gaze for a moment before nodding. Then looking at Rachel in a way that melts my heart, he says, "That's great, Rachel! Which dress? The red one, or is it the white one that looks like a princess dress?"

"The white one," she says, spinning in a circle as if she's already imagining herself in that dreamy cloud of a dress.

Mrs. Cole makes her way back over with a tall, glamorous young woman by her side. And while Dylan's mother fixes me with a warm and welcoming look, the other one makes no effort to conceal the fact that she's appraising me from top to bottom.

"Hello, I'm Margot Cole. Thank you so much for coming and for bringing Rachel. She's an absolute treasure."

I stand and take her outstretched hands. "It's so nice to meet you. I'm Veronica Petrov. And thank you for inviting us. Tonight was very…inspirational."

The younger woman makes her way around the other side of the table and taps Dylan on the shoulder as she nods her head towards me. "Dylan, aren't you going to introduce me to your friend?"

"Hey, Mel," he says, bending down to kiss her.

She eyes me playfully while his lips are on her cheek. She's perfectly groomed—glossy hair, a tailored pants suit cut with precision for her body alone, and perfectly arched brows that give her face a severe quality. Something about her sets me on edge. Maybe it's the simple fact that someone so beautiful is obviously well acquainted with Dylan.

"Melanie, this is my friend, Veronica—"

"Petrov," she finishes for him. "My, my, Dylan," she muses, "another beautiful eastern European. You always go for the exotic ones."

She extends her hand, and forget shaking it, I want to spit on it. I turn away from her and tap Rachel's shoulder.

"Sweetie, it's getting late and I promised your dad we'd be home by ten o'clock. We'd better go."

"Okay," Rachel says with a smile, and in this moment I am thanking God that she is such an easy-going child.

Looking to Mrs. Cole, who is now joined by her husband, I add, "Thank you both for everything. It really was a wonderful evening."

Mrs. Cole flashes me another warm smile and then reaches down to hug Rachel. "Goodbye, sweetheart. I'll make sure the dress you won is sent to your house, okay? Be on the lookout for a special package this week."

Dylan is by our side a few moments later as we're making our way back towards the coat check near the exit. He grasps my wrist when he catches up and his look is apologetic when he says, "That's just Melanie. Don't pay any attention to her." When I don't look his way, he adds, "She was rude back there."

"And obviously doesn't know her geography very well. Let her know that Poland is in central Europe so she doesn't go around sounding like such a dumbass." Looking down to make sure Rachel is still paying attention to the jazz quartet playing near the bar area, I whisper, "Because she *was* referring to Kasia, wasn't she? And we *are* the same type...We're cousins after all."

I can tell from his clenched jaw that my comment hit a nerve, but he still acts calm, ignoring me as he takes the coats from the attendant while tapping Rachel on the shoulder. "Let's go, ladies. I have a special car waiting out front to take you home."

"I called for an Uber already."

"Really, without taking your phone out of your bag? You must be a magician," he teases.

I want to kick him in the shins, and might have if Rachel wasn't with me.

"Hop in," he says to Rachel, handing her a pastry box. "My mother wants you to bring this home for you and your brothers... Some extra dessert."

"Thank you, Dylan," she says demurely. Jeez, she's already under his spell.

"Give me a minute with Veronica, ok? I have to ask her something."

"Okay," she chirps, while I simultaneously snap, "We have to get going."

He closes the door halfway and then places both hands on my shoulders, moving me away so that we're out of earshot. "What's really wrong?"

I cross my arms over my chest and purse my lips. What can I possibly say right now? That I'm hurt? That I don't know what's going on, that I feel young and naïve in your presence, that I want you to really want *me*—not some version of a woman you were devoted to once upon a time?

"I can't read your mind, Veronica, but I know what was said back there hurt you."

I whisper, biting back tears and hating myself for being so affected. "I'm not Kasia."

He shakes his head, never once taking his eyes off me. "You're not. You're entirely different, Veronica, and I want to get to know *you*."

"You're still in love with her. I knew it when I saw you together."

He steps back, jamming his hands into his pockets as he looks up to the stars. "She was the first girl I ever loved. And yes, it was epic... One of the best experiences in my life." Looking back at me, he says, "And yes, there's a part of me that will always love her. But that's very different from being *in* love with a woman. It took a while for me to get over Kasia, but I did...A *long* time ago. I may be an idiot but I'm not fool enough to waste my life pining away for a happily married woman with four children." When I give him nothing, he moves in closer and asks softly, "Have you ever been in love?"

"I have to go," I say, pushing past him to get into the car, closing the door right behind me.

He raps on the roof of the car twice, the driver's signal to pull away. Rachel busies herself eating pastel colored macarons as I sit there drowning in sorrow. *Have I ever been in love?* The word *no* sprang to mind the moment he posed the question. A high school boyfriend that I dated for the blink of an eye—he didn't count. Larson and French? That wasn't love. Both of those relationships were born of my own greed. I was in it for the conquest, for my need to be taken care of and to be wanted.

No, I've never been in love.

The realization leaves me feeling hollow.

Chapter Twenty-Five

DYLAN

She might have closed the door in my face, but this isn't anywhere near close to over. I don't back down that easily.

I want that woman.

I'm going to have her.

So I'm leaning on the hood of my car, waiting outside the flower shop drinking coffee that very next morning, hoping she isn't the kind of girl who sleeps in late on Sundays. When eight turns to nine and then nine turns to nine-thirty, I'm on the verge of ringing her buzzer. That would mean ringing every one of the six buzzers in the building's vestibule, as none of them are marked with names. Thankfully the door swings open as I'm contemplating the pros and cons of waking her up on her day off. Dressed in a snug sports top and leggings, her hair pulled up into a simple ponytail, she takes my breath away.

"It's a little cold for that outfit, no?"

"Well, well, well," she says, looking down at one of those ridiculous sports gadgets on her wrist, "if it isn't my favorite stalker."

"I'm satisfied with being your favorite anything."

"What are you doing here?"

"Just wanted to see you. We left things unfinished last night."

"Um, I'm taking a run, so…"

I'm in step right beside her. "You think that's wise for your long-term breast health?"

"What the hell are you talking about?" she asks, laughing as she looks down at her chest.

Getting her to laugh was my goal so I stick with it. "You've got beautiful, ample breasts. All that bouncing around can't be good for them, right? Take a walk with me instead." I unzip my hoodie as she looks at me wide-eyed. "Here," I say, placing the jacket over her shoulders. "You won't be working up a sweat and I don't want you to get cold."

She looks away from me as she considers my offer. At least I hope she's considering it. She adjusts the sweatshirt then, sliding her arms into the sleeves and rolling the cuffs up two or three times until it fits her.

"If I'm going to walk with you, I'd like a coffee of my very own." Shaking her head, she asks, "Who shows up to someone's apartment on a Sunday morning and only buys a coffee for himself? That's just rude."

I poke her in the ribs as we begin walking in the direction of Central Park. "I've been on a stake-out for the last hour and a half. I'll gladly buy you a coffee now that you've finally rolled your lazy ass out of bed."

"Tea," she says when we pass a small pastry shop.

"I pegged you as a plain black coffee girl."

"No sugar because I'm not sweet, right?" She's smiling but there's hurt there too.

"Not at all." I think the world of her and still she questions me every step of the way. "I guess I just see you as sort of fierce…Able to tackle the world on your own. Forget it, now I'm going to put two sugars in your tea."

She smiles, shaking her head. "No sugar, just a little milk."

We enter the park at Sixty-ninth Street, sipping our drinks, both lost in our own thoughts. In my case I'm trying to come up with words to broach the topic that looms large over us. She beats me to it when we reach the pond. "Kasia used to take us here."

I take her hand and lead her to a bench overlooking the water. "Tell me about it."

Veronica looks to me, unsure. "It's not just this place...She took me and Olivia all over the city. She was a lot more fun than my parents were."

"You're good to Rachel the same way Kasia was good to you."

"I want Kasia to look down and be happy about that," she says, nodding. "I also love spending time with her boys. They're just...I just love them so much. When I was seventeen, when my life wasn't going very well," she bites her lip before going on. "I used to think I'd never want children."

"Why's that?" I had a good idea why, but I want her to open up to me.

"My parents," she shrugs and then shakes her head. "They're not like my aunt and uncle. Kasia and her brothers grew up very differently from me and Olivia. My mother took a back seat and my father was strict...punishing. He used me for target practice whenever he was in a bad mood."

My hand stiffens in hers. "He hit you?"

She considers my question before answering, "Um, no." *What the fuck does that mean?* She sips her tea, thinking, and then says, "He could be rough but he typically laid into you with words. He made a habit out of cutting me down." She looks to me cautiously. "I hate him, Dylan. And my mother never stood between us, never defended me. I'm pretty sure that someone who can't feel love for her parents isn't the best candidate to be a parent herself."

"That's crap. I see how you are with Rachel. Believe me, you're a natural. I'm the one who probably won't ever be receiving a coffee mug with Number One Dad emblazoned on it."

She bumps my shoulder. "Why would you say that?"

I stare out over the water because I can't say what I'm going to say and face her at the same time. "I was married for nearly eight years. She wanted children and I put her off, lied to her...Did everything in my power to make sure she wouldn't get pregnant." I look to Veronica, wanting to see her reaction but wary at the same time. "I was a rotten husband."

She looks at me with sympathy and then fixes her gaze on a father rowing his two daughters in the small pond. "Tell me about your wife."

"Her name's Cecilia. I've known her since I was a kid. I kind of went running back to her after Kasia dropped my ass." I see her crack a smile at that. "It was a bad decision on my part. A rebound relationship I could never extricate myself from."

"You weren't in love with her?"

"I tried to convince myself of it, but I don't think I ever was." Shaking my head, I add, "That sounds so shitty."

"I feel bad for both of you. And you split up right around the time Kasia died?"

"I was already heading in that direction, but yes, Kasia actually gave me the kick in the ass that I needed."

"What?"

"The day I went to visit her. You were there."

"I remember."

"She told me to stop wasting time. Told me to find happiness."

Veronica looks at me with one eyebrow raised. "And the first stop on the road to happiness is getting a divorce?"

I can't help but smile when I nod. "For both of us."

"So you're happier being alone?"

"I don't want to be alone, no. But I'm happier today than I was when I was with CeCe. I'm sure of that."

"What's she like?"

"Like most people...She's a lot of things. She's caring, but she dismisses certain people in a way that can be cruel. She's beautiful but she can act pretty ugly sometimes. Loyal in some ways, unfaithful in others. I really can't fault her, though. Everything that went wrong in our marriage, starting with me even proposing in the first place, is on me."

"So what's next for you?"

"Like today, or what's next on my list of life goals?"

She turns and nails the equivalent of a three-pointer, banking her cup off the lip of a trash can a good ten feet away. "I don't want to know your life goals just yet. I do want to know what your game is, though...with me."

"No game. I just want to take you out for dinner sometime... Sometime soon. Will you let me take you out next weekend?"

"What if I say I have plans?"

"To *say* you have plans implies you'd be lying. You don't strike me as dishonest."

"You make me feel..." She stops short, shaking her head. "I don't know what it is you see in me." She looks embarrassed at the admission.

"I'm drawn to you, Veronica. I don't know how else to explain it. I was drawn to you that first night in the club," I need to emphasize the next words, "*before* I had any idea who you were."

She doesn't respond. A minute passes before she looks at me and says, "Come on, let's head back. I'm driving up to Rye in a few hours."

"Alex and Henry's place?"

"Yeah, I need to talk to them about my schedule...About going back to school part-time."

"That's good," I offer as we make our way back towards Madison.

"First I have to take a good look at NYU's course catalog. I don't want to be a business major anymore." Looking down at her feet, she adds, "They're footing the bill so I don't want to waste any more of their money."

"Are you floating any ideas?"

"Yes and no. I want to keep running the store and maybe have a shop of my own someday. And yes, that's business, but those classes feel like a waste of my time. I want to study design or, I don't know, maybe foreign language. I speak Polish and Russian, but I can't read or write." She looks uncomfortable, jamming her hands into the pockets of my sweatshirt. "I'm all over the place right now."

When we reach her door a few minutes later, she says, "That wasn't so bad."

I'm about to hit her with some obnoxious comeback but stop myself. I don't want to play around or waste time, so I just put it out there. "I like spending time with you."

She bites her lip before saying, "I'll go out with you this weekend."

I breathe a sigh of relief as I hand her my phone to enter her number. "Friday at around seven sound good?"

She looks up at me with what looks like hope mixed with some measure of fear. "I'll see you then," she says before standing up on her toes and kissing me on the cheek.

That kiss, I feel it down to the soles of my feet. She wrecks me. I want to take her face in my hands and kiss her deep, I want her in my bed, I want to take up space in her heart—I want it all. But nothing about this girl is easy. She's like a skittish cat, prone to run off at the first sign of danger.

Chapter Twenty-Six

VERONICA

"Dammit!"

"Here, let me see," Henry says as he takes my thumb in his hands, inspecting the gash. "Doesn't look too bad." Wrapping some paper towel around it, he raises my arm up in the air. "Keep it elevated, I'll run to the back and get some bandages."

My breathing is uneven as he holds my thumb under a stream of icy cold water at one of the prep sinks. "Sorry Henry, I'm kind of a mess today."

"Noticed that. What's going on?"

"I have a date tonight."

"All righty!" he says with an ear to ear grin.

"But I don't know if I can be with this guy. He's older—"

"That's your specialty."

"Don't be an ass."

He steps back, surprised. "You're never this touchy and your hands are literally shaking." He turns the water off and leads me to a chair, lifting my arm up over my head again. "Relax, take a breath, and tell Uncle Henry *all* about it."

I laugh. "You know it sounds really creepy when you say that, right?"

"If I was straight it would sound creepy. Come on, stop stalling. What's his name?"

"That's kind of the issue. It's one of Kasia's old boyfriends."

From behind me I hear, "You're going out with Dylan Cole?"

I turn to see Alex with Hyacinth on his hip. Shock registers on his face, but not disgust or anger.

"This is going to sting," Henry warns as he dabs some antiseptic on my cut. I don't even feel it.

"Alex, I don't know...It just happened." Shaking my head, I correct myself. "I mean, nothing's happened yet. He just asked me to dinner, that's all."

I see Henry shoot Alex a warning look. "I'm putting a butterfly on this. You definitely don't need stiches. But you won't be making any arrangements today. No scissors for you in your current mental state," he jokes, leaning down to kiss my cheek when he's done. "So, tell us the whole story."

"Not much to tell. I met him randomly one night and then I ran into him at the hospital when I was visiting Kasia. Apparently that's how he found out she was sick." I leave out the drunken details of our next run-in because I honestly don't remember most of that night. "Then he invited me to a benefit his mother was hosting and... I don't know, he asked me out." I look to my cousin. "Is he a good person, Alex?"

"My brother will tell you no...Tomasz basically hates the guy. I'm on the fence, though. He cared about my sister, that was obvious, but he was young, immature, and came off like a bit of an entitled ass back then. I don't know the man he is today, but I like to give everyone the benefit of the doubt."

Henry takes Hyacinth from Alex's arms, waggling his eyebrows.

"I noticed him at the funeral." Looking to Alex, he adds, "C'mon, the man is spectacular." Smiling at the annoyed look Alex is trying to play off, he says, "Anyway, he looked devastated and I was devastated that day too, so I felt some sense of solidarity with the guy. Alex told me who he was after the service."

"I just keep asking myself, 'Why me?'"

Alex comes over and turns me so that I'm facing the mirror. "I'd say take a good, long look at yourself for starters." Meeting my eyes in the mirror, he adds, "But there's so much more to you than this. If Dylan has spent just a few minutes in your presence, then he's already gotten a sense of what we all know about you. You're truly special." I look away from my reflection and he turns my chin so that I'm forced to look back. "You're a good person, you're intelligent and you're independent. You are every man's dream woman."

Henry chimes in from behind us, "Now that we're clear on that, let's talk about what you're wearing tonight. At the Mass, Dylan was sporting a custom made suit and shoes that probably cost more than mine, which is saying a lot. I think we need to up our game."

"Ugh, I don't even know where we're going!"

"Text him right now," Henry insists. "We need time to shop and to primp."

Chapter Twenty-Seven

DYLAN

I was proud of myself as I pulled away from her apartment on Sunday. When she mentioned NYU, my first instinct was to ask about her professor. Was she still seeing him? My intuition told me no, and really, I was too proud to give her the impression that I was even the slightest bit troubled where he was concerned. But I *was* uneasy. I didn't want anyone standing in my way. I did do an internal fist pump when she said she was no longer pursuing a business degree, though. That would limit the chances she'd be running into him on campus.

As the week wore on, I busied myself with the pressing issues that came with my position—another potential strike in the Midwest, political unrest in a country that housed one of our smaller manufacturing plants—but my focus was never far from Veronica.

I had a lot riding on this date. I weighed my options, trying to decide what would please her most. I was invited to a party at Rene and Caleb's home, but that was definitely out—too many people closely associated with Kasia. I was also expected at a dinner hosted by Melanie and her husband, celebrating Samantha Paulson on her engagement to some poor sucker. Obviously that wasn't an option, as my ex would be there along with several other people I no longer cared to associate with. What I really wanted to do was cook for her at my apartment, but I thought that might seem a little too forward, like I wanted her in close proximity to my bedroom—which I did. I decided on dinner at a cozy spot in her neighborhood. I'd just have to wait and see how the evening unfolded.

When I got her text Friday morning asking me what to wear, I texted back to dress casual but then questioned my plan. Was I better off treating her to a night that was more upscale? I dreaded the idea of shielding my face as I walked past the photographers stationed outside of spots like Daniel or Momfuko. I was used to the circus, but she might be turned off by that kind of attention. And while I was proud to have her on my arm, I wanted privacy. I wanted to protect her from all that bullshit. I stuck with my plan to take her to Eli's. It was going to be a fairly warm night for mid-October and it was within walking distance from her place.

* * *

Stepping out of the car, I tell James he's off for the night, that I'll catch a cab back to the West Side later on. He doesn't move the car immediately, and when I turn around I see what's holding his attention. Veronica is coming out of the building's front door and she waves to James before fixing her eyes on me.

"Have a good evening, Miss Veronica."

"Thanks, James."

He chuckles when I snap, "You can pull away now, James."

Who can blame him, though? Veronica stands taller than her natural five-eight in a pair of high heeled brown boots. She's wearing dark jeans tucked into them, which showcases her long legs. Her top is a cream colored cashmere sweater that hugs her tits. She's wearing more makeup tonight than she usually does, but it's still minimal. And her hair, now grown back to its longer length, falls in soft waves.

"God, Veronica, you look great."

She looks down at her outfit and then takes me in. "Is this all right? Casual can mean just about anything so I didn't know what to expect. I have a feeling that casual for you means you've decided not to wear a tie."

I take her hand, smiling. "It kind of does, but we're both perfect for where we're going. Are you all right to walk a few blocks in those boots? I picked a restaurant on eightieth and third."

"That's fine. It's so warm out tonight."

"Do you even own a coat? You always seem like you're dressed for weather that's twenty degrees warmer than it actually is."

She looks at me and winks. "I'm hot blooded."

I give her a little hip check because I know she's screwing with me. "You know, I was all prepared to do the whole come in and wait while you finish getting ready-thing. You didn't need to come out and meet me on the street. I wanted to make a good first impression."

"I'm not like that, Dylan. I don't expect hearts and flowers and all that. Believe me, in my business you get to see first-hand what a crock of bullshit that usually is." She winces. "Sorry."

"No, it's okay. And in my case, you were right."

"I put my foot in my mouth a lot."

"I'll get used to it."

I spy one photographer snapping a picture from across the street as I hold the door open for Veronica. Part of me is grateful for it. For one, the guy isn't up in my face or asking me who I'm with in a way that's intrusive, and also, I'm not into hiding this. I want people to know I'm with Veronica. Have to convince Veronica of that first I suppose, but still.

"You choose, Dylan. Something red but I'm only having one glass."

Pointing the sommelier to an Australian cabernet and then turning back to Veronica, I ask, "One glass?"

She cocks her head to the side and gives me a weak smile. "I haven't had anything to drink since that night you brought me home from work."

"Really?"

She nods. "I felt...wretched the next day. I was sick, I was embarrassed, and I was really worried that I couldn't remember much of what went down that night."

I hold both hands up in defense. "Nothing happened with me... You know that, right?"

"My aunt told me you took me home. I pieced together from what my friend Nell told me that you sort of came to the rescue. I put myself in a bad position that night."

"You were definitely attracting attention from the wrong sort of guys."

"I don't normally drink much at all, but that night? It's like I was on a mission to get destroyed."

"I was about to say I'm glad the night turned out the way it did, because you were safe, but I wouldn't want a replay of knocking on your uncle's door late-night again like that. He greeted me with a bat in his hands."

"I'm so sorry," she says, covering her face in embarrassment but laughing. "I can totally picture him doing that." When she looks up again, I can tell she's uneasy. "I don't want you to think that I'm like that...That I'm reckless, that I hook up with strangers."

"I'd never judge you, but for the record, you don't strike me as a one time hook-up kind of girl. I know the type, and you're not it."

"You know the type?" she asks with a raised eyebrow.

"Sadly, yes. And please don't ever ask me my *number*. Personally, I hate that crap. And I also think you'd go running for the hills if you ever found out. I'm definitely no saint, so you should know that up front."

"Duly noted." She watches me as I sample the wine, gesturing for the sommelier to pour. "Seriously, Dylan, do you even know what you're doing when you roll it around the glass and then stick your schnozz in it?"

I nod solemnly. "My schnozz does, in fact, know wine."

She rolls her eyes. "Right...I bet you went to some snooty boarding school in London where you took ballroom dancing, business etiquette for future masters of the universe, and wine tasting for uppity snobs."

"I went to public school, thank you very much. And I never required training on how to become a master of the universe...Comes naturally to me." She's practically snorting she's laughing so hard, and I feel like a champ for making this girl smile again. "But I did take a wine tasting class while on vacation in Bordeaux, which does sound like an uppity snob move."

"We come from very different places, Dylan."

"I don't think that's important, do you?"

"I don't know...Haven't been in enough relationships to know the difference."

"There had to have been obvious differences between you and the professor."

She grabs a piece of bread and leisurely drags it through the dipping oil. "You just *love* referring to him as the professor, don't you?"

"Seriously, I don't even remember the guy's name. But yes, I am teasing you."

Veronica looks up at me. "I'll tell you my number, even though you didn't ask. It's two."

"The professor—"

"French," she corrects me, "and Larson."

When I don't respond, she says, "Larson was older too."

I sense I'm not going to like the direction this conversation is taking, but I'm hungry for any insight I can gain when it comes to her. "Tell me about him."

"He was my high school tennis coach." In response to my clenched jaw and fist, she says, "Easy now. I certainly wasn't taken advantage of. If anything, it was me who lured him in."

"I don't think you can rationalize a teacher-student relationship. French is different...You're a consenting adult."

"I was eighteen when I slept with Larson."

"Still, that's fucked up." Grabbing her hand and shaking my head, I add, "Wrong on *his* part, not yours."

"Have you ever read Lolita?" She doesn't wait for me to answer before saying, "I was the living, breathing version."

"I don't buy it."

"I'm not perfect. Don't delude yourself."

"Never said you were, but I doubt this tennis coach of yours was anything close to innocent."

Over the course of our entrée and dessert, Veronica goes on to explain how this guy *was*, in her eyes, totally innocent at the start of the whole affair. In training to become a priest, no less.

"He was Deacon Pete to everyone else, but I called him Larson. It started out as a joke because he called all of us girls by our last names during practice. He was twenty-five, assigned to our school teaching Theology while doing his doctoral studies, and took on the role of tennis coach because he played in college. I think he felt the need to look out for me after seeing my father in action at a few of my matches."

"Overbearing?"

"Critical, demeaning, degrading...You name it. One particularly mortifying day, he screamed obscenities at a line judge when I had clearly double faulted. He was actually banned from school grounds for the duration of the year. I was a junior then and that ban," she breaks into a wide grin, "was sweet relief. So Larson had some inkling of what my life was like. Little by little I shared more with him, but never the entire story. He knew I was saving up to leave home, so he went out of his way to get me a job teaching rich kids at Midtown Tennis. He'd even pick me up after work and drive me back to Brooklyn on his way home after his own night classes. With a college scholarship and that extra money, I knew I'd never have to spend so much as a Christmas break in that house again, so I was very grateful."

"He cashed in on your gratitude?"

"No! Larson's intentions—I'll swear it on my deathbed—were innocent. I was the one growing restless. I had a boyfriend, a guy who turned out to be a bit of a jerk." She pauses and her shoulders drop. "But really, I was no better. I used him to torture Larson. I'd sit in his lap on the bleachers and make out with him when I knew Larson was around and might see. And during practice I'd purposely touch Larson's hand when I could, hike up my tennis skirt when I knew he was watching, bounce a little on my toes while I wore training shirts so tight that my breasts strained against the fabric. God, I was awful," she adds, shaking her head. "Biting my lip when I spoke, smiling sweetly at him when I'd catch him looking my way...Doing anything I could to break him. But he was pretty solid in his faith at the time, so it was no more than just a game to me."

"So senior year?"

She nods. "One night Larson was driving me home and my father was outside, throwing all of my things out onto the curb. Apparently he found my diary, and aside from writing hateful things about him, I also wrote about letting my boyfriend kiss my tits for the first time."

"Oh shit."

"Oh shit is right," she says, nodding. "Meanwhile, half of the girls my age were already having sex. So as of that night, I was literally thrown out of my house and disowned."

"Are you serious?"

"Serious as a heart attack."

The waiter comes and drops the check. I prompt her to pick up where the story left off during the walk back to her place.

"I'm not boring you? I feel like I've been monopolizing the conversation all night."

"This is some pretty compelling stuff, Veronica. I'm totally engrossed so continue, please."

She looks at me, unsure, and then sighs in resignation. "We went back and forth. He wanted to call the police on my father, I argued that I'd be put into foster care because I was still under age. He wanted to go to the school authorities, again I argued that social workers would inevitably get involved and I could be removed from the school...Yada, yada, yada."

"So he took you in?"

"Yes. I stayed in his bedroom and he took the couch. It was only for three months. I had a job at a sleep-away tennis camp lined up, so I guess he figured he could stay strong." Looking to me with a sad expression, she says, "I ruined him."

"How do you figure?"

"I was like a cat rubbing up against a scratch pole. I'd watch movies with him on the couch, moving closer any chance I got, I dressed in pajamas that covered me but did little to hide what was underneath, and I took advantage the one night poor Larson had anything to drink."

"Did he serve *you* alcohol?"

"No! Listen to what I'm trying to tell you." She shakes her head in frustration. "He's a *good* person. That night he came home from his end term dinner. He was out with a bunch of other soon-to-be priests."

"They like their wine," I say dryly.

"I wouldn't know," she says shrugging. "That was the first and only time I ever saw Larson buzzed. Anyway, I was on the couch in short shorts and a tank top without a bra on, watching a movie that started out innocent enough but turned out to have some heavy love scenes. He went to turn it off at one point but I grabbed his hand, stopping him. I turned to face him and begged him to kiss me. I didn't even wait for him to bridge the gap. I was kissing Larson and leading his hand to my chest, moaning like a porn star when I straddled him."

I'm about to blow just listening to this story. And now we're at her door. Am I coming in? She looks behind her. "I want to ask you up but my apartment's a mess. I basically ransacked my room getting ready for tonight."

"Up to you...I don't want to push you, Veronica."

"I think it's me who's trying to push you." She looks away, swallowing as she crosses her arms over her chest. "I think I'm telling you all of this because I need to know what you think of me...Now that you know the worst." She stops me when I go to speak, fixing me with a hard, intent look. "My family is so screwed up. Growing up, my father constantly referred to me as a whore. And now look at me —I crave sex, I'll do horrible things to lure a man in, so I feel like maybe I am a whore." Covering her face as I pull her close, she says, "I don't know who I am. I feel undeserving, but then at the same time I know he's wrong, that what my father said and did to me was wrong."

"You were a kid acting out a role with Larson. You were a woman having a fling with an older guy with your professor. You've been with two men. At nearly twenty-two in this day and age, that hardly makes you a sinner...Kind of makes you a saint."

She nuzzles into my chest, seeking protection or comfort or some kind of connection. I want to slap the shit out of her father for creating this, for making her doubt her own worth. Tipping her chin up, I say, "Veronica, if you want to know how I see you, I see you as someone who endured a lot and still came out on the other side, strong and positive. I see you as a beautiful, intelligent and capable woman... And I want you like I've never wanted anyone before."

She holds my gaze for a moment, maybe to sort out if she can trust in what I'm saying. She tugs on my hand then and gestures towards the door before fishing her keys out of her bag. When she leads us into her apartment, she points me towards her couch and then proceeds to sit astride me the moment I make contact with the cushions. This is happening too fast and she suddenly seems removed, far away. I try to hit the brakes, needing to make certain she's really here with me and wanting this. "Are you sure, Veronica?"

She nods with hooded eyes but something is off; it's as if she's flipped a switch. Pressing herself down onto my lap as she goes to raise her top over her head, she says, "I don't want to talk anymore. I just really, really need you to fuck me."

That poor sap Larson didn't stand a chance faced with the eighteen-year-old version of this. I actually find myself feeling bad for the guy because I'm no better. I know taking Veronica to bed tonight is a bad idea, but damn if I'm not balls deep, screaming out her name as she rakes her nails down the length of my back not ten minutes later.

Chapter Twenty-Eight

VERONICA

A hand is skimming up and down the length of my side, down to the curve of my hip and then back up again until fingers stroke the sensitive side of my breast. It takes a few seconds for it all to register. Dylan Cole is the man holding me in his embrace, his body curled around mine, my back to his front.

He must feel my body tense, and rolls me onto my back a moment later so that I have to face him. "Good morning." He's smiling but then his expression grows concerned. "You feeling all right?"

"Um, yeah," I hedge, pulling the top sheet out from beneath the quilt to cover myself as I make my way towards the bathroom.

I splash cold water on my face and then look at myself in the mirror, angry at the person before me. I had next to nothing to drink at dinner, so I can't blame last night's lust induced haze on alcohol. What must he think of me? He was fending me off, telling me we should take things slow, but I wouldn't be deterred from my mission.

No, I had his cock out and in my mouth within five minutes of luring him into my apartment.

After another splash of cold water, some toothpaste and a swipe of deodorant, I'm ready. I have my game face back on. I kick the sheet aside and come out of the bathroom, sauntering back to bed. Glancing at my phone on the nightstand, I make an attempt to be playful. "Seven o'clock on a Saturday morning? Do you ever sleep in?"

He doesn't even crack a smile. He's looking squarely at my face, not once glancing down to my naked body. He's not going for it, so I up the ante, climbing onto the bed next to him and sitting on my heels with my knees parted. My breasts are heavy with wanting him, nipples tight to the point of pain, and I'm wet. His dick is hard, his rigid length obvious even though he's covered by a quilt. So what's stopping him?

"Don't you want me, Cole?" I cringe at the sound of my own voice. I sound pathetic. But I keep at it, sliding one hand across my breasts, down my abdomen and resting it between my legs before touching myself.

He looks down for a moment, watches the performance I'm putting on, and then slowly rakes his eyes back up to my face. His look communicates pity and then disappointment. It's as if he's pleading with me silently—for what I don't know. I only know how to tempt a man, how to seduce.

"C'mon Cole, do you want me?" I let out on a breathy exhale.

"I've got a better question, Veronica," he says as he turns away from me and gets up off the bed, grabbing his pants from the floor. He looks back to me as he puts his pants on without underwear and then throws his sweater over his head in a hurry, like the place is on fire. "Do you want *me*?" In response to my confused expression, he says, "I'm not gonna be your casual fuck. And I'm sure as hell not some needy older dude who'll be rendered stupid just because you've got a nice rack and you're willing...I can get that any day of the week, sweetheart." Slipping his feet into his shoes and grabbing his keys and wallet off my dresser, he lands his parting shot. "I'm not Larson and I'm not French. So that shit you pulled just now? Your little vixen act? It's old and it's tired and it won't work on me."

My shock turns to fury within seconds. "Then go," I bite out. It's as if I'm sixteen again, in my childhood home being judged harshly, feeling ashamed and burning with anger. He hesitates. Feeling stupid and exposed, I reach for a t-shirt and the panties I discarded last night. He isn't moving and I can't bear to look at him. I'm humiliated enough without seeing that look on his face again. "Get out of my apartment, Cole...Now."

"Is this what you do, Veronica?" Grabbing my upper arm and turning me to face him, he asks, "Is this how you keep your distance, how you keep the upper hand? Yesterday I was Dylan and now that we've fucked I'm suddenly Cole? You never called those other guys by their first names, did you?" He lets go of my arm, shaking his head. "You keep asking me what my game is, but it's you who's playing the game."

I basically revert to a fetal position for the next two hours. His words were like a hard slap to my face. Not just because they were words of rejection, but because everything he said was dead on.

At quarter to ten I have to drag my sorry ass out of bed, quickly wash the smell of sex off my skin, and head downstairs to open the store. Unless we're booked for a wedding, Saturdays are typically quiet. You get a few people coming in for cash and carry bouquets, but the bulk of our business is made up of corporate accounts and regular customers with set preorders in place. I busy myself making the few deliveries that are set to go out, but spend most of the day running Dylan's words over in my mind.

I never had the urge to call Larson or French by their first names. And it didn't take a rocket scientist—or Freud for that matter—to see that I was pretty skilled at keeping both men at arm's length. A man I knew was on his way to becoming a priest and a newly divorced man desperate for some rebound affection—even my choice in men showed a deliberate desire to maintain my distance. But I didn't want that kind of relationship with Cole...I mean Dylan. I was ashamed to admit this even in the quiet of my own mind, but I wanted to be his girlfriend. I wanted to be someone very special to him. That day we sat in Central Park looking out over the pond, my mind had even conjured up the image of a strong and protective Dylan rowing our own children in one of those boats, doting on them.

Waiting for the delivery guy to take the arrangements out to the truck, I stand back for a moment to look over my day's work. Each piece has a haunted, dark quality to it. I toy with the idea of changing the Happy Birthday arrangement to something more colorful and upbeat, but decide against it. They're pretty awesome, if not a bit on the stark side. Fusion lilies interspersed with barren branches stained black. Golden Zebra irises mixed with white orchids. Birds of Paradise making up an arrangement that stands nearly three feet tall.

I decide on a whim to make a fourth arrangement. A short, square glass container packed with nothing but Snow Fire tulips. The fluttery, fringed white petals are stained with red streaks that resemble blood. His words had cut deep, so it seems fitting. Cueing up his address in the database, I load this one onto the truck myself.

Nothing.

Not a word since he stormed out of my place Saturday morning, and the ache in my chest gets heavier with each passing hour.

I'm glad I have Hyacinth to keep me busy on Sunday. Otherwise, I might have been fool enough to keep chasing after Dylan, to beg him for another chance. I have little to my name other than my pride, so I'm not willing to sacrifice any more than I already have.

"Cinthy!"

It's Rachel bounding into the house, making a beeline for her favorite baby. The three boys and Jake follow behind, holding trays and cake boxes.

"Way-way," Hyacinth answers happily, holding her arms open in anticipation of being picked up. I love witnessing the bond forming between the two of them.

"Bet that's how Kasia was with you when you were a baby," Jake says, smiling down at me.

The smile I return to him is laced with sadness. "I was just thinking the same thing."

He squeezes my shoulder. "Mama and Tata are right behind me and I wanted to talk to you." Looking back to the boys, he says, "Guys, just give a quick look around the lawn for goose poop, ok? Last time we played soccer out there I had to wash everyone's sneakers afterwards."

"What's up, Jake?"

He rolls his eyes, smiling. "I had to hear all about Dylan, Dylan, Dylan last week after that fundraiser. He made quite an impression on Rachel."

My cheeks heat at the mere mention of his name. "Um, yeah, but I think his mom was the one who wowed Rachel with that dress."

"It's swimming on her but she puts that dress on every day after school and dances in front of the mirror in it." He looks out the window to where the kids are chasing after one another and adds absently, "It makes me smile and breaks my heart at the same time."

"You should have seen her that night, Jake. She was so happy and," I try and fail to hold back my own tears, "Rachel was so proud. Everyone...All of those important people knew Kasia and they were talking about her, about her work. Rachel was drinking it all in. So was I."

He draws in a shaky breath. "God...Sometimes I don't know how they can wake up each day and go on. They talk about her all the time, repeating something she once said or something silly...Like the time she made minion costumes for all of us one Halloween. We looked like six giant, yellow marshmallows." When I laugh, he looks at me and says, "I don't know when I'll get there. Anytime a good memory pops up, I want to fucking die myself, crawl into the ground...Anything to be with her." He takes in my shocked expression and shakes his head. "I'm just rambling...Of course I'm committed to them, Vee. My life is about making their lives good and helping them to be everything they're destined to be."

"Jake, I don't know what to say."

"I started going to a group therapy thing...A grief group."

"I think that's great."

"We'll see...Anyway, I wanted to tell you that whatever's going on with you and Dylan Cole?" He smiles at me, a knowing smile. "Alex told me. So I just wanted you to know that Kasia would be good with it. I used to hate the guy...Used to fear Kasia would wake up one day and realize she'd picked the wrong man. But she did pick me and I know he's lived a good part of his life hurting because of that. Never once did she have a bad thing to say about him. I think he's a good person, and more importantly, I think he's grown up."

"Well, I'm not sure anything *is* going on."

I shoot Jake a look when my aunt and uncle come inside. I'm not ready to talk about Dylan with anyone. In fact, even the mention of his name causes me pain. It's the first time I've ever come completely clean with another person—about my childhood, about the way I am with men, revealing my shame—and Dylan obviously decided that I wasn't worth the trouble. I turn my phone off when we sit down to Sunday dinner, angry at myself for checking it like a pathetic loser every half hour since he left me Saturday morning.

Lesson learned.

Monday morning I'm dragging ass. I think I managed to sleep a total of one hour the entire night, two tops. I don't even have the energy to blow dry my hair, making my way downstairs right at ten o'clock dressed in a pair of sweats and flip flops with my hair up in a wet ponytail.

I barely have a moment to turn on the register before she comes through the door.

"Loyola Tennis? I played for Spence. We always wiped the courts with you guys."

I'm confused for a moment before looking down to see my high school's logo on the hip of my sweatpants. "Oh," I say, but I think it came out like a question. I'm not running on full speed this morning.

"You must be Veronica."

Now my back is up because this woman is fixing me with a glare that's borderline murderous.

"Cat got your tongue?" She advances a few feet closer. "I asked if you were Veronica, the slut who fucked my husband." She laughs before saying, "I know you are because you're just like her. You know that's why he wants you, right? You know he's daydreaming about sticking his dick in *her* when he's with you, don't you?"

"Wh-wh-why are you here?"

She tosses the card I wrote for Dylan onto the counter and waits. My breath hitches at the sight of it. "Do you know why she left him?" She doesn't wait for me to respond before snatching the card back and saying, "It's because he can't be satisfied. He was fucking both me and my best friend while he was supposedly in love with Kasia." She grits her teeth when she says my cousin's name. "He likes that, screwing two girls at once. And he also likes to invite one of his buddies to join in and tag team his girl. Has he asked you for that yet? If he hasn't, he will. Nothing's off limits for Dylan Cole." Cocking her head to the side, she asks, "Can you handle all that, little girl?"

I can't help my voice from shaking when I say, "I want you to leave."

She smiles, admiring her perfectly manicured nails painted a candy apple shade of red. "I let him get us both off last night when he came crawling back to me—nostalgia and all that—but I'm done with him. My advice to you? Stay far away from Dylan Cole."

The woman I now knew to be Cecilia Cole turned on her heel and sauntered out the door.

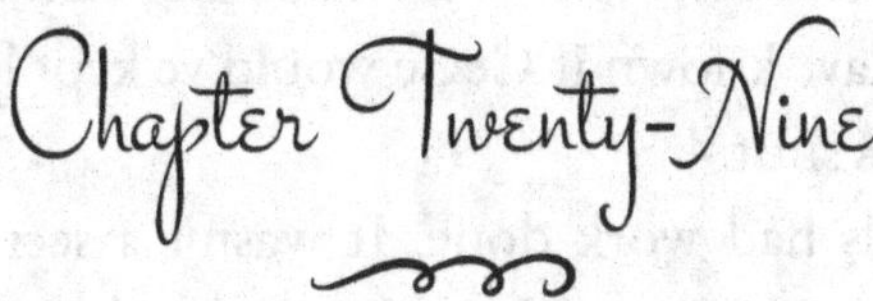

Chapter Twenty-Nine

DYLAN

My secretary buzzes through right after I settle into my chair on Monday morning. I'm in a foul mood so I'm sure I snap when I say, "What is it?"

"Mr. Cole, Mrs. Melanie Sheffield is here to see you."

What the fuck is she doing here? It's all I can do not to say those words out loud so she can hear me through the intercom. "Send her in," I say, doing nothing to soften my clipped tone.

"I'd say it's a pleasure to see you, but it's early in the morning and I'm already up to my ears in shit." Exasperated, I ask, "What can I do for you?"

"I came to say I'm sorry."

That gets my attention because Melanie never apologizes. Like, she could run a red light and mow you down with her car and still manage to find you at fault.

"That sour bitch made a crack about me in front of the other girls, in my own *home* no less, and she expects me not to hit back?"

"What are you talking about?"

Mel's eyes are wide. "Cecilia hasn't stormed the castle since my party Friday night?"

"Please explain yourself. I'm losing my patience."

"I got a little work done, all right?" Tipping her chin up to show me her profile, she adds, "And I look fucking fantastic. Point is, no one ever would have known if CeCe would've kept her big, fat, artificially-injected lips shut."

All those girls had work done. It wasn't a secret, but still, you didn't out anyone. So I nod. "Yeah, that's a low blow."

She looks up at me wide-eyed. "So I may have mentioned your new hot girlfriend to the others loud enough for CeCe to overhear."

"Go on," I say through clenched teeth.

"And I *may* have mentioned that Veronica is related to Kasia." She murmurs, "Might have added something like, 'He never got over her, so this comes as no big surprise.'"

"Mel, that was mean, even for you...And I just don't need the headache."

"The former Mrs. Cole had it coming, Dylan, so save your breath." Fixing her ass on the corner of my desk, she waggles her eyebrows. "By the way, how's the new romance going?"

"Think I'm giving you any more ammunition?"

"You're no fun anymore."

* * *

The former Mrs. Cole barges into my office not three hours later, pushing past my secretary.

"Did your driver bring you here?" I ask, taking in the blouse tucked only halfway into her skirt, the mussed hair and the glassy-eyed scowl. Cecilia is drunk.

"Fuck you!" She collapses onto the leather chair opposite my desk and murmurs, "You're seeing someone." When I don't answer immediately, she raises her head and snaps, "You're *not* seeing anyone? Melanie was lying?" Now she stands up on wobbly legs, pointing at me. "You haven't been fucking your dead ex-girlfriend's niece?" Sneering, she adds, "Do you know how pathetic you are?"

I'm about to correct her—tell her that Veronica is Kasia's cousin —but I refrain.

"*I'm* pathetic?" I ask, referring to her drunken tirade routine. "Why are you here, Cecilia?"

"Can you imagine how humiliated I was, hearing about my husband's love life at an engagement party in front of everyone we know?" *Ex-husband*, I want to correct her, but again I think better of it. "And the stupid little slut is sending you flowers?" Shrieking now, she adds, "Sending them to *our* apartment?"

With that, she stands and flings a small card onto my desk. I turn it over to see the gold embossed letters of H&A Florist with a hand-written message underneath.

I'm really sorry, Dylan.
I do want you, more than anything.
—Veronica

I do everything in my power to school my expression, and it's hard because an atomic bomb blast level of joy is threatening to burst from my every pore. But I know Cecilia must have been truly hurt by this and—deep, cleansing breath—I never intentionally want to cause her pain.

"I'm sorry you had to see this. And I'm sorry you heard about Veronica from someone else."

"Just how old is Veronica?" she asks, slurring her name. "She looks like she's seventeen. Are you into *that* now?"

"Jesus, Cecilia, let it go." She's still standing there with her arms crossed, and I'm growing more impatient by the second.

"Does she remind you of *her*? Is that what this is all about?"

"No. I didn't know who Veronica was when I met her."

"Did you meet her while we were still married?"

"Yes," I say, raising my hands to placate her, "but nothing happened, Cecilia...Not until very recently."

She flops back down onto the chair, defeated, holding her head in her hands. "I never stood a chance against her, did I? The entire time we were dating, when we were married...You wanted her back."

I could have countered because it wasn't entirely true. I'd honestly given up on the idea of me and Kasia a while ago. But she'd never believe that, so what would be the point?

She stands up, smoothing her skirt down as she teeters on her heels. She doesn't look at me as she strides to the door, taking care to steady herself when she grips the doorknob. "I hope you burn in hell, Dylan."

On any other day I would have laughed in her face, because seriously, was she gunning for the lead on a daytime soap with that line? But today I happily let her have the last word. I just want Cecilia gone so that I can get to Veronica.

Chapter Thirty

VERONICA

"You are officially a Manhattanite," my cousin Alex quips, rubbing behind Chuck's ears as he leans into him. "You have every impractical amenity. You have a car—"

"Never wanted a car. You and Henry bought that."

"You have a stove and a fridge but you'd starve without GrubHub."

I hold my thumb and index finger close. "My kitchen is like a shoebox."

"You have a dog—"

"I am a woman living alone in the city. I need him for protection."

Looking down at my Cavalier King Charles Spaniel's droopy ears and sweet smile, Alex says, "My money's on the intruder if this is your watchdog."

"You'll protect me, won't you Chuck?"

Yes, I'm officially baby-talking to my dog.

I asked Henry to cover for me Monday afternoon. After the

unexpected visit from Dylan's disgruntled ex-wife, I felt jumpy and scatterbrained. I set out for a long walk to process everything she'd said. It hurt to hear Dylan described as a heartless cheater, even though I already knew that to be true. But she also made him out to be uncaring, depraved and vulgar, as if he'd take anything he wanted without regard for anyone else. The one line that kept replaying in my mind, tormenting me, was one of her parting shots: *You think you can handle all that, little girl?* I knew the answer to that question was most definitely no.

Stumbling across the mobile pet adoption fair near Charles Shurz Park was divine intervention as far as I was concerned. I probably had a pouty face to match my new pup's as I entered the wide trailer, but my spirits lifted in response to the sounds of all the dogs' happy yapping. My little guy was in a corner cage, his head cocked to the side in a way that made him look vulnerable and sad. His hair, snowy white on most of his body and a rich dark brown just around the eyes and ears, looked soft to the touch and I was desperately in need of a cuddle. It was love at first sight. And the name was easy. King Charles discovered at Charles Shurz Park—how could I go with anything else?

Alex sighs, conceding, "He is pretty freaking cute."

"Cinthy's going to love him."

"Henry already does. He bought some pricey organic dog biscuits and told me we have to get one of those in-ground perimeter fences so the damn dog doesn't get lost when you bring him up."

"I have to thank him again. I felt like I was up for a job at the CIA with the background check they did on me. Henry hooked me up letting me take off yesterday, too."

"I think it's good they have a twenty-four hour waiting period."

"Definitely. Hey, maybe you guys should consider getting a dog. That way Chuck will have a friend to visit."

"Do *not* put that idea in Henry's head."

"Did you hear that, Chuck?" I tease. "Uncle Henry's gonna get you a friend! And the two of you are going to have a big, giant patch of grass to play on, and you can go out on the rowboat with me, and you're gonna wuv, wuv, wuv chasing all the rabbits and squirrels, aren't you?"

The bell above the store's door tinkles in the middle of my babbling, but I don't stop loving on my puppy until I hear Alex clear his throat and say, "Dylan…It's good to see you."

I freeze, my body hidden by the service counter.

"You too, Alex. It's been a long time. Oh, and congratulations…I hear you're a father. How's parenthood so far?"

Alex beams. "Best thing that's ever happened to me and Henry. She'll be two in April."

"Hyacinth, right? Veronica told me her name." Louder, he asks, "Isn't that right, Veronica?"

Straightening up, I hold Chuck in front of me like a shield. "Hello, Dylan." My speech sounds stiff and formal. But how in the freak am I supposed to act? For the past forty-eight hours I haven't been able to think of Dylan without picturing him standing at the foot of an ornately carved four-poster bed with me tied to the posts, him watching on and directing the action as some other insanely hot guy does dirty things to me. A blistering hot fantasy? Hell yes. But in real life I know that's not exactly my bag.

"You're a hard lady to track down. I came by the store on Monday and again yesterday."

I lie. "First I'm hearing of it." Henry did tell me, both times. I just wasn't ready to face him.

"Hey Vee, King Chuck's tail's a twitching." Alex hands me the leash. "Better take him out for a walk."

I shoot Alex a scowl over my shoulder as I make my way towards the door. Traitor.

Dylan follows along even though I didn't invite him to come with. So freaking awkward.

He breaks the silence. "You're avoiding me."

When I look at him with hands jammed in his pants pockets and a pained look on his face, I soften. "I'm sorry. It's just that things ended on such a bad note on Saturday, and then when I didn't hear from you the rest of the weekend...I thought..."

I can't finish the sentence because my head is all over the place.

"I was worried about you, Veronica. I didn't know what to think after we spent the night together. You seemed like you didn't want to be with me...*Really* be with me."

"I—"

I shake my head in frustration, unable to verbalize what's in my heart.

"What did you think? That after you told me everything then I wouldn't be interested in a relationship, in something pure and good with someone like you? Did you tell me about your past in the hopes of pushing me away?"

"No, I wanted you to know me."

"I do know you, Veronica. And everything I know makes me want to get closer to you, to be with you."

He's advancing on me, and it feels good and suffocating at the same time. I blurt out, "Cecilia came to see me the other day."

Dylan's face pales. "I'm so sorry."

Pain shoots through me. Dylan looks stunned, he looks sorrowful, he looks maybe guilty even. "You're sorry? Why, because you *did* go running back to her?" I want to kick Dylan in the shins and run, but Chuck is in the middle of dropping a deuce so I'm stuck. "Stupid me...I thought your crazy ex-wife was lying."

"What? No!" Dylan grabs my arm and spins me to face him. "What are you talking about? I wasn't with her. She's just hurt and angry...She found out about you. Mel told her and then," shaking his head, he adds, "you sent the flowers to her apartment, not mine. She got the apartment in the divorce settlement. She came by my office drunk and spewing nonsense on Monday afternoon."

"After she came to see me. She had the card I sent you. I felt like a fool."

"Well, you do screw up the deliveries a fair amount." His attempt at humor falls flat. He runs his hands through his hair in frustration. "But that card, Veronica...It gave me hope. I practically sprinted over here right after, but you were gone. Same thing yesterday. And if you weren't here today, I would have been at your place tomorrow and the day after that. I'm not giving up."

"I meant what I wrote but," I pause, shaking my head, "I need some time to think, Dylan."

"I want you to think it through *with* me. Can you get away from work today?"

"No chance of that...I took off two days in a row. Alex is heading up to Fairfield for a job as soon as I get back."

"If it's all right, I'll hang out at the store with you today." Before I can tell him no, he pushes. "You can boss me around, I'll sweep, I'll fetch your tea."

"Right...I'd pay to see that."

He smiles, knowing he's warming me up. "I mean it, Veronica... I'm your bitch today."

The half-smile that's taking shape falls. "I can't, Dylan."

"You mean you won't." Backing up a step, he fixes me with a hard stare. "Did Cecilia say anything to you that..." He trails off, frustrated. "If there's anything you want to know, I'd rather you just ask me straight out."

I can't even fathom how to form those questions. *So, you're into orgies?* But I do want to know what his deal is, and what the hell, no time like the present. I gesture in the direction of the store and Dylan follows a step behind me and Chuck.

Our conversation stops and starts three separate times, with customers walking in, phones ringing and shipment arrivals interrupting us. "Let's work now, talk later," Dylan offers. And he's true to his word.

He rolls up the sleeves of his tailored shirt and dons an H&A apron. He carries stock in as it's delivered, sweeps discarded stems off the floor in the prep area and fetches items from the cooler for me—smart bastard actually knows which flowers I'm referring to, even when I try to stump him.

At six o'clock I turn the key in the lock. Taking in his wide grin, I ask, "What is it?"

"Nothing...Just that I actually enjoyed today. It's pretty nice working in a place like this," he adds, gesturing around at all the flowers. "I can see why you like your job."

"I kind of love it."

"Why do you sound apologetic when you say that?"

I shrug. "Maybe because a lot of people in my family are over-achievers. It's expected that you breeze through school with a perfect GPA, get a college scholarship, go onto graduate school and then do impressive things."

"You're referring to your cousins."

I nod. "Everyone's a lawyer, an executive, a business owner. Me? I lost that college scholarship my first semester."

"But you run this place," he says, looking around the store and then back to me.

"I'm a glorified shop clerk, Dylan."

"Well then I'm a glorified plumber, because I'm up to my ears in crap all day long." When I smile, he asks, "Can I make you dinner tonight at my place?" When I hesitate, he says, "We're talking, nothing else. We need to talk. And I know my ex...I think the questions you want to ask me shouldn't be said aloud in a public place."

"Okay."

He unties his apron and lays it on the counter. His hopeful look and sweet smile melt my heart. "All right, I'll send James for you in an hour? I need to head back and get started on dinner."

"Can I bring anything?"

Chuck leans into Dylan when he kneels down to scratch behind his ears. "Just bring this little guy. I have a feeling you have lots of questions. We might be a while."

* * *

I pull the sleeves of my sweater down over my hands during the drive over to the West Side, so on edge that I'm in danger of gnawing my own fingernails off.

"Miss Veronica," James says, "is something wrong?"

"Hmm?"

I'm so lost in my own head that I don't realize James has pulled over and is now standing with my door open and his hand extended.

"No James, I'm fine," I say, recovering as he helps me out of the car. "Just daydreaming. Thanks for the ride."

"It's my pleasure. Have a good night." Looking down at Chuck he says, "Don't you waz on Cole's floor now, you hear? He's a bit of a neatnik."

Dylan lives in one of those buildings that has serious security. The doorman isn't wearing the standard topcoat and hat ensemble that you see at most high-end residences. No, this guy is dressed like an investment banker but looks more like a secret service agent. Another employee mans a desk viewing surveillance camera footage. Even though I've never been here before, I'm greeted as Miss Petrov when I enter the lobby and then I'm directed to an elevator separate from the others. The doorman presses the only button in the elevator and then bids me goodnight, exiting before the door closes. It's not creepy but it's not quite normal either.

The elevator door opens to a vestibule done in wood paneling that had a sleek, modern look. It's minimalist and masculine. The glass door, which spans from floor to ceiling, was left ajar. I realize this when King Charles breaks free from me and scampers in on his own, yapping away. I follow, calling out to Dylan but I get no answer. Looking around, I note the modern art prints dotting the walls, but the first large piece stops me in my tracks.

I'm suddenly nine years old again.

There's an oversized, goofy portrait of a nerdy guy with a toothy grin hanging in the Metropolitan. I was amazed at the time to realize that it wasn't a photograph because the detail is just so realistic. I remember standing in front of it that day, transfixed. Kasia turned me around at one point, put her glasses on me and snapped a picture—totally against the rules in the museum. I had a wide-eyed look of surprise because I couldn't believe Kasia would take a chance like that, and I was laughing. With her big glasses on and the offbeat clothes she liked to dress me up in, I looked like the subject of the painting's wacky kid. We laughed ourselves silly when she had the picture developed.

I wonder where that picture is now.

I focus on the piece before me, swallowing back the emotion because I don't want to be missing her so badly in this moment. My life, and this situation in particular, is bizarre—to be wanting a man who was so intimately and utterly in love with Kasia once upon a time. I'm still not entirely comfortable with the idea of me and Dylan.

This piece is different, but it's another one by Chuck Close, a self-portrait made up entirely of a series of dots. I stand close to see the detail and then back up several feet to take in the image in its entirety. It's amazing, and I realize as I move in close a second time that it's an original.

Holy shitcakes.

I draw in another breath, acknowledging that Dylan's wealth is another thing that throws me off balance. It's not like I grew up destitute. My father, while he wasn't as successful as others in the family, earned a good income from his rental properties. I know my aunt and uncle's real estate holdings are very valuable, and Kasia was an extremely wealthy woman in her own right, but still, we were a family of immigrants at heart. My people came from economic hardship, political unrest and suffering. Even when you made your fortune, maybe you were still wary of the floor dropping out from beneath your feet. So you invested in what was tangible—real estate, gold bars. I don't ever recall my mother or father writing a check or swiping a credit card. No, they dealt in cash. I bet that to this day, my father doesn't even have a bank account. The gun in his nightstand and the safe in his bedroom closet offer more security. And while the second generation is different, people like me still don't spend money impulsively, indulging in whims.

"You like this one?"

"Mmm," I murmur incoherently, nodding as I stand before what is probably a high seven-figure indulgence.

He moves in closer, placing his hands on my shoulders and giving them a light squeeze, the heat of his body and his scent rendering me lightheaded. "Some people hate it. I guess he does kind of look like a wild man. Cecilia had this one banished to my home office when we lived together, so now that I'm on my own I decided to bust him out of captivity. Every night when I walk in, it's that look on his face...It's like he's saying, 'What's up?' like he actually cares."

I nod, taking in the cigarette dangling from the subject's lips, the scruff on his face, and the way he's looking down on you, but not in a way that's critical. "Yeah, I can imagine that too. This one's an early self-portrait, right?"

The intercom buzzes. He walks towards the door, looking over his shoulder when he says, "You know your art, Veronica." Opening a concealed panel to retrieve a phone, he says absently, "Yes, have it sent up with Rupert."

"That surprises you?"

He raises his hands in a gesture of defeat, closing his eyes for a moment and shaking his head. "Easy, killer...That wasn't meant as an insult." He asks, "Why are you always prone to assume the worst when it comes to me?"

"I don't assume the worst. I just...don't know how to be around you sometimes."

He goes to speak when he's interrupted by a knock on the door. A tall, imposing hottie dressed in a dark fitted suit stands on the other side of the glass door holding two large bags.

"Thank you, Rupert. I'll take those."

"Anything else, Mr. Cole?"

"No, we're good."

"Have a good evening then." Looking to me, he adds, "Goodnight, Miss Petrov."

Taking in my confused expression, Dylan says, "You, um, met Rupert the night I took you to your aunt and uncle's house."

"He's—"

"My driver...One of my drivers."

"Oh."

He calls out from the kitchen over the sound of paper bags being opened and unloaded. "I'm actually a decent cook, Veronica, but I had to take care of some emails and phone calls when I got back here before. I know my good intentions don't amount to shit and all, but I was planning on blowing you away with my maple glazed salmon."

"Hey." He's behind me again now, his hands back on my shoulders, his voice uncertain. "I really did want to put some effort into tonight, to impress you."

"I don't care about the food." Raising a hand up to cover one of his, I add, "Whatever you ordered actually smells great."

"Then what's up? You seem unsettled."

"Is this an original?"

"An original what? Are we still talking about this painting?"

"Yeah," I say, turning around to face him. It's not just the painting. The art is a symbol of the differences between us: our upbringing, our lineage, every facet of our lives. I mean, I don't view us on the level of some Pygmalion type mismatch, but maybe I do see something of Eliza in me and Higgins in Dylan. And even though

I've made an odd habit out of choosing older men, everything in me bristles against being schooled, taught—being told what to do in any way, shape or form.

He cocks his head to the side, challenging me. "It is, but why is that important to you? Does it give you more ammo to use against me?"

"It's just weird, that's all."

"Define weird."

"When you walk into my apartment, there's a crappy table that needs refinishing, an uncomfortable couch, mismatched chairs, and posters...tiny replicas of art, not—"

"The Lovers."

Shitfuckdammit.

This man is always one step ahead of me. Why did I even mention my place? The "artwork" affixed to my walls with two-sided tape is a window into my screwed up soul. A barren barn out in the middle of nowhere by O'Keefe, Wyeth's rendering of a paralyzed girl sitting on the grass reaching for home in the far-off distance, a golden haired beauty cradling her infant by Klimt. Every picture speaks of loneliness, longing or feeling deserted. I might as well have had a giant mural of a rudderless ship painted on my wall, because that's what I am.

The print he's referring to though, that's the one that reveals the worst of me. And like a cornered alley cat, I'm getting ready to sharpen my claws. He doesn't have to say anything else because now I know how he sees me.

"I always knew you were special...unlike anyone else I'd ever met, Veronica. And from the moment I saw you," he looks down, shaking his head as if he's in pain, "acting like you had it all under control, wearing that skimpy dress those assholes put you in your first night working in that shitty club...I wanted to shield you. But the other night when I saw that print, I had this feeling that overwhelmed me. It still kind of doesn't make sense, but it was as if you were the one protecting me. It's like I imagined in that moment that you already knew my bullshit, all the fucking awful things I've tried to bury and hide about myself, and you still wanted me, flaws and all."

Sucking in a breath, I stand there speechless. He sees himself in that picture? Yes, he does. He's the one kissing me. Just like me, his face is wrapped tight, hidden behind a veil.

"I picked that up at a flea market one day for three bucks. It was right after I started up with French. I didn't give it much thought that day...Just knew I wanted it. But it is about hiding, being close without letting the other person really see you. I get angry when I look at it now." Looking away, I busy myself fiddling with a loose thread on my sweater. "I thought you were about to call me out on it."

"That would be pretty hypocritical on my part, don't you think? I've been an imposter in every romantic relationship I've ever had. It was always like that...Even with her."

"You *can* say Kasia's name in my presence."

"But it's another one of those things that's weird for you, right?"

My shoulders sag, no fight left in me. "It is, but then it's not." I walk around Dylan and take a seat, suddenly exhausted. "Pour me some of that wine please, and give me a spring roll."

He stands on the other side of the kitchen island, studying me as I eat.

"God, I love spring rolls," I gush, in desperate need of a topic change. "The greasier the better. And duck sauce? I could put it on everything."

But he's not having it. "Ask me."

"What?" I ask with a full mouth, feigning ignorance. He fixes me with a pointed look. "Ask me."

I take a healthy sip of wine in an effort to stall and to fortify myself. "You cheated."

"Every time." He chews on his lip to the point where it looks painful. "Never...I've never been completely faithful."

"Why?"

"First, let me say that I've only been in two relationships I'd consider serious."

"Kasia and your wife." He nods. "So, the woman at the vineyard?"

"Nothing...A fling."

"She was beautiful."

He shrugs. "Lots of women are beautiful."

"From where I was sitting it looked like you two were pretty close."

"Then I'd say you need glasses." He pours himself a glass of wine and takes a sip. "She was a business associate. I know it makes me sound crude, but she was there to scratch an itch, nothing more."

"Crude? Makes you sound like a bastard."

"I grew up understanding that people wanted to be around me for different reasons. When *you* made a friend at school, it was because the other kid genuinely liked you, right? But I never knew if the kids liked me because of me, or they liked me because I had the tricked out house, the best video games, tickets to the playoff games, or because I threw the craziest parties. And with girls it was worse. You tend to start using people before they can use you."

"That's a rotten perspective to take."

"Veronica, I had friends, *real* friends, but I also had my share of bootlickers. People who'd laugh when my jokes weren't funny, people who were just along for the ride. It makes you guarded. In my case, it made me...I don't know, maybe a little mean spirited."

"And I bet you loved Kasia because she didn't care about your money."

"Not only did she not care about my name or my money," he smiles, waving a hand towards what's likely a fraction of his vast art collection, "it's like she found me and my whole situation repulsive."

Knowing Kasia, I totally get it. "Oh, I hated guys like you when I was in high school."

"Why?"

I can't help but roll my eyes. Guess I do need to spell this out for Little Lord Fauntleroy. "You have to understand what it's like. Families like ours, new to the country and speaking a foreign language... We're different. Our parents are viewed as second class citizens sometimes and it riles you up. As a child you view them from inside the bubble of your little world...You love them, you're proud of your parents. Then you grow up and see that in the world outside of the bubble, they get treated like they're ignorant because they aren't fluent in English, because they work menial jobs, because they have to ask questions about things that are second nature to people born in this country."

"I get it," Dylan says, but he so does *not* get it.

I shake my head with vehemence, that feeling of being on the outside running through my veins like it used to. "My parents and others like them dream of better for their children. So with good intentions they thrust us into the upwardly mobile stratosphere of prep schools, violin lessons, tennis academies...All that crap. And you come to want that life and hate it at the same time, because those kids at school? They look at you the same way the uppity shopkeeper looked at your mother. You're a gatecrasher, a wannabe. And you come to despise those people."

He reaches over and puts his hand on top of mine. "Does it still hurt you so much?"

"I didn't have a lot of friends growing up."

"A scholarship kid...Like Kasia."

Yes, but if I leave it at that then I'm not telling the whole truth. "Dylan, that's not the big, defining experience that shaped me. If it was just a class warfare thing I don't think I'd be so screwed up." I can feel the heaviness coming over me, the feeling of shame like a weight on my back. "I didn't have *any* friends growing up. I only had Olivia. No one could come to my house after school because my father was...unpredictable, and he was so controlling that I basically wasn't allowed to go anywhere. So at school I was an outsider and at home I was isolated."

"He sounds like—"

"An asshole? He is."

It's not fair to lump them together because I don't think my father is half the man Dylan is, but I can't help myself. "He cheats on my mother...Such a pig that he makes no effort to hide it."

Dylan's look is pleading. "I don't see myself as a monster, Veronica. And I don't want to do that to another person ever again...I won't." He shakes his head, defeated. "But if you want to stop this right now, I get it."

"You're not like him, Dylan. But I am curious...If you loved Kasia so much, then why were you even tempted?"

"I can only chalk it up to being young, incredibly stupid, being high on drugs and definitely being drunk on power for the first time in my life."

"How did she find out?"

He groans. "Tomasz officially outed me, but I think deep down she knew." He spoons food onto our plates and hands me a pair of those cheap wooden chopsticks. "I went into a tailspin after that. And Cecilia? She was collateral damage."

"You cheated on her right away?"

He pauses before answering. "I wouldn't call it cheating in the beginning because she was in on it. And before we were married, she was part of my drug fueled, sex crazed youth. The party never stopped, you know?"

"She condoned it?"

"We didn't have an open marriage or anything, but she was on board for a lot of, um, mischief."

"Can you be a little more specific?"

He pushes his plate away and runs his hands through his hair. "Ask me."

"Threesomes?"

"Yes."

"Foursomes?"

He nods. "We switched partners."

"Sex with men?"

"No. Maybe crossed swords in the act a few times, but I'm hetero."

"Anal?"

He cocks his head to the side, narrowing his eyes. "Is that even considered out of bounds?" I think I make a sound that's half gasp, half squeak. Dylan smiles, nodding to himself as if he's taking notes on me. "Hmm."

"Did you ever sleep with one of her friends?"

"Not when we were a couple, no. Cecilia did sleep with a good buddy of mine, though. Pretty sad, but I didn't really even care that much." He gestures to pour me some more wine but I decline. He pours a bit more for himself. "Keep going...You can ask me anything."

"I-I think that's it."

He takes a sip, studying me over the rim of his glass. "Can I ask you a few questions?"

I shift in my seat. "Sure."

"Did you ever tell French or the priest that you loved them?"

"Just Larson. But now I know that I wasn't in love with him...I was just grateful. When my father kicked me out, I didn't even cry. I guess a part of me was glad to be away from him, but it was scary, you know? I don't think I've ever really acknowledged how scared I was back then."

"Larson took care of you."

"He did...He saved me." I look at Dylan with a warning. "And he took me in out of kindness and with purely good intentions. I was the one who screwed that up."

"Why didn't you go to your aunt and uncle instead?"

"I was ten years old when everything happened between our

families. I would hear my mother crying nearly every day after my father left for work, but she wouldn't talk about it. At night I'd hear my father yelling at her, threatening her. Lots of talk about sinning and filthy faggots." I let go of my water glass when I look down to see that I've got an angry, white knuckle grip going. "We were never allowed in their home again. He changed our telephone number and my mother was too afraid to reach out to her sister." Looking to Dylan, I add, "My father can be really intimidating."

"And this was all because of Alex coming out?"

"That was his excuse, and my father is a hateful bigot, that's for sure. But I think he envied my aunt and uncle's success, and blamed them for not giving him the head's up when good properties were available. He basically blamed someone else whenever he failed. And he's a manipulative, abusive man. He needed to isolate my mother, make her dependent. He hated how much we loved our family, and in one fell swoop he took them away. And over the years, maybe you start to believe all the lies. You never see them, they aren't looking for you, so maybe you are *dead to them*, as my father loved to say."

Shaking his head, he says, "I just...Kasia wouldn't have done that. I can't imagine her giving up. She loved you and your sister so much."

"Do you know how hard it was for me to show up on their doorstep?"

The shame I felt that day was strangling me right now as if I was back in the moment.

"You must have been in a pretty bad place."

"Dire straits." I try and fail to crack a smile. "I told Larson I had a place to stay when I left, but that wasn't really true. I have one friend in the world, Nell, and after a year of couch surfing on and off at her place I just couldn't do it anymore. I couldn't concentrate in class, so I lost my scholarship. I was working two or three shitty jobs at a time, barely making enough to eat. I was just so...tired."

Dylan leads me over to the couch. He guides me down next to

him so that my back is resting on his chest. He kisses my head and wraps his arms around me. Words cannot describe how good the simple gesture makes me feel.

"It was a Sunday of all days, so you can imagine the scene at the Mazurs."

"Half the neighborhood was there, right?" I can feel the smile in his words.

"Just about. It was so loud compared to my house, but in a good way."

"That's how I used to think of it."

Chuck hops up into my lap then, licking my face like he knows I need some love. "The entire room fell silent when my uncle opened the door. Seeing them all for the first time in so long...Seeing Kasia holding Milo," I stop, unable to hold back my tears. Dylan pulls me closer when I begin to shake with sobs. "I'm sorry, I shouldn't be telling you all this...I know this must hurt you too."

"Shhh," he whispers. "It's ok, baby."

"It overwhelmed me. There were so many children there and I didn't know one of them. Years had gone by...So many years."

"They must have been so happy to see you."

"They were, no questions asked."

"Figured that."

"Jake took the kids home and Kasia and I stayed up that entire night, talking and crying. She told me they tried to reach out so many times, but my mother wouldn't disobey my father. Kasia's parents believed at a certain point that they were putting my mother in danger by pushing it. And I also know my aunt and uncle were hurt. My mother never apologized for my father, and she agreed with him on some things. Kasia told me my mother started spewing her own toned-down version of gay bashing, so eventually they wrote my parents off." Using Dylan's words, I add, "Me and Olivia were collateral damage."

Chapter Thirty-One

DYLAN

I wanted her to spend the night but I didn't offer. Tonight was a lot. After all that heavy soul searching, I wasn't sure that jumping into bed with Veronica was a great idea. Couldn't get a read on what she wanted either.

She let out a big yawn after telling me about her reunion with Kasia and the rest of the Mazurs, laughing when she remarked that telling the truth takes a lot out of you. I felt the same. What she probably long suspected about me she now knew as truth. What would she do with all that?

I wanted to reassure her that I didn't need any of that bullshit anymore, didn't want that kind of life—and that was the truth. But saying things like, "If I never see the inside of a sex club again it will be too soon," probably wouldn't go over big. So instead of taking her to bed, I took Veronica and Chuck back to her place, gave her a chaste kiss, listened for the lock to click behind me and then made the lonely drive back across town. I knew it was the right thing to do, but it sucked nonetheless.

Tomorrow I was heading out of town, and the realization of how much I was going to miss Veronica struck me suddenly. When her name flashed on my phone screen, I sent up a silent prayer that she was feeling this thing between us as much as I was.

"Hey, can't sleep?"

"My furry little monster is convinced that this bed is actually his. He just curled up next to me and his butt is practically in my face."

"You're spoiling him."

"Probably." She sighs. "But I didn't really want to sleep alone tonight."

I turn over onto my back and began stroking myself gently, my dick painfully hard at just the thought of her lying in bed—even with the damn dog. "I wanted you to stay but I didn't know…"

"Yeah," she says on a breathy exhale. "It was better that I didn't stay…But now…"

"Now you miss me?"

"I do."

"So everything you know about me?"

"Scares me and…turns me on."

Fuck, is that good or bad?

"I'm not the same person, Veronica. I don't want that life. I'd never share you, never let another man touch you. I couldn't." Just the thought of anyone but me touching her sends a rush of pure rage through me.

"I don't want another man touching me, Dylan." She lets out a soft, breathy gasp. "Just you."

"You're touching yourself now."

"I…Yeah, I am."

"If I was there, baby…"

"Tell me what you'd do to me."

"Really? You want me to tell you?"

"Um…Yeah."

Her breathing is audible now and my cock is rock hard.

"Tonight I'd take my time. And first you're gonna strip for me. I'm sitting back on the bed, stroking my cock while you take off each piece of clothing, nice and slow. I love your tits, Veronica, and as you take off that bra all I can think about is sinking my dick between them, fucking those tits. They're mine. But you're naked now and I can't wait to get a taste of that sweet little pussy." She's panting now. "Come over up here on the bed and kneel, baby, sit right on my face. Hmm, my tongue's on you now and my hands are full, grabbing onto that ass. You're trying to move but I've got you pinned to me, licking and biting that sweet thing."

"Tell me, uh, more," she begs. I can picture her back arching off the bed right now. "How h-hard are you right now?"

"So hard I'm gonna break you in half when I fuck you." My hands shake opening the lube from my nightstand drawer, and as my hand makes contact, I nearly blow. "I'm turning you over now, fucking you on all fours, that beautiful ass sticking up right in my face, Veronica. I'm in so fucking deep."

She can barely utter the words coherently when she chants, "Fuck me, fuck me, fuck me." I can picture her, thrusting her fingers in and out. Then she lets out a soft moan and I know she's gone. I'm grunting now, my hand exerting so much pressure, imagining the tight grip she had on me the other night, but tonight I'm imagining us skin on skin. Just the thought of that has me blowing my load faster than a fourteen-year-old.

After a few moments with the two of us just breathing, my sweet girl giggles. Maybe she's never done this before?

"Guess the cat's out of the bag...Now you know I like phone sex."

There goes that theory.

"Just so you know, lady, I prefer live, in-person sex."

"Duly noted."

"But that was pretty hot. I just had to ignore the image of Chuck in the bed with you."

"Yeah, I think I'm going to have to rethink this whole sleeping arrangement thing before he gets too set in his ways."

"Yep, that's my side of the bed."

She doesn't say anything for a moment, but it's a moment too long for me. I don't make a habit of wasting my time and I don't waffle. I know what I want. Pretty simple from where I stand, she either wants the same or she doesn't. If she doesn't, it's going to hurt like hell but I'll move on. Try my best to move on, anyway.

Please, God, let me have this.

"Veronica, I want to do this. I want you in every way, every part of my life." I let out a frustrated breath. "Tell me right now...Do you want this too?"

"I want you." Her voice sounds serene and sated. "I do."

I breathe out a sigh of relief. "I'm crazy about you."

"You are?" she asks, sounding as light and playful as a child.

"You know I am." To myself, I add out loud, "I'm literally dreading this trip."

"You're going away?"

"That's one thing that sucks about my life...I'm always going away. At least this is a short one, just two days in L.A."

I like the disappointment in her voice when she asks, "What time is your flight?"

"Not until late afternoon."

"Can you get into the office a little late tomorrow morning?"

"You mean roll in at ten, like I'm a florist?"

"That's exactly what I mean."

"Why would I do that?"

"Because I'm lying here naked, I'm wet, and I want your cock so badly that I ache."

* * *

Pumping in and out of Veronica leisurely as the sun peeks through a slit in her bedroom curtains, I realize my dick hadn't been this happy in years. Correction: me *and* my dick. And feeling her reach between her legs and touch herself as I fuck her, it turns me on like nothing else. This girl is the real thing. Being with her is just so good.

Last night, laying side by side after we both came hard, literally looking into each other's eyes in that very moment, I had this pressing urge to remember every detail. Like when you're a kid and you wake up from a really great dream. It's so good that you struggle to hold onto it. It's a desperate feeling because you *know* the memory is going to slip away but you really, really don't want to forget. I felt similarly high in that moment last night and wanted to hold on to to every second of it. Last night I knew I was with the real Veronica, not the distant, shipwrecked version of the girl.

I'm in love with her.

"Don't go," she whispers, backing her ass up even closer as she leads my free hand down between her legs. "This feels too good."

Going harder, feeling that tingling down to my toes that tells me I'm close, I lean in and pinch her gently down there. "Never fucking you with a condom again, got that?"

She lets out a garbled cry that's a mixture of my name and what might be a Gregorian chant it goes on for so long, the both of us coming down from it a full few minutes later.

"Holy hell."

"Oxymoron."

"*You're* a moron," she says, laughing as she wallops me in the face with her pillow.

I wrestle the pillow from her and then wrestle her until I let her win. She sits on top of me, triumphant, my hands pinned on either side of my head.

"Nice view. Maybe I will stick around." We're no match in strength. Sitting myself up, her legs slip around my waist and I hold her close, the feeling of our bare chests pressed together like nothing else on this earth. "I really don't want to leave."

She tilts her head to the side and fixes me with a long, searing kiss. I can feel her slick center and her tight nipples pressed up against me. Will I ever stop wanting her like this?

She groans, breaking the kiss to look over at her phone on the nightstand. "Nine-thirty. I have a ton of arrangements to make this morning. Gotta hop in the shower." She rolls over and gets up, tossing her long brown hair over her shoulder. Veronica looks like a dream. I watch her ass sway as she makes her way across the room. She looks back at me, her eyes dark with desire. "Are you coming?"

* * *

"I'm taking a late flight on Friday night so I'll be back in New York early on Saturday morning. Spend the day with me?" She bites her lip, looking uncertain. I stop dressing with my jeans only half-way up my thighs. "What is it?"

"It's Henry's birthday on Saturday. Will you come with me?"

I need to sit on that for a minute, saying nothing as I finish getting dressed. "Do you think they're ready for this? I'm assuming this is going to be a big family get-together."

She comes closer, placing both hands on my chest as she raises herself up on her toes to plant a quick kiss on my lips. "I'm scared too," she says, "but I'm with you now." I want to roar and beat my chest like the king of the goddamn jungle at the sound of those words. "Family is everything to me, so if we're going to do this..."

"I'm in. Just maybe warn Jake first...And your uncle...And shit, Tomasz too."

"Good idea." She smiles wide, teasing me now. "Wow, this might be the first time I've ever seen you rattled, Dylan."

"I'll get you back," I say, pinching her perfect ass. "It's fall fundraising season in Manhattan, sweetness. Can't wait to see you in some fancy up-do and an evening gown."

She pushes against my chest, laughing. "As if!"

"Oh, you'll be on my arm, I guarantee you that. Consider November eighteenth your coming out party. That's Margot's big night…The Fresh Air Fund's annual fundraiser."

Her smile drops. "Really?"

I use her words as I cradle her face in my hands. "If we're going to do this…" Dropping a kiss on her forehead, I think about everything that could potentially go wrong. Visions of a drunk, knife-wielding Cecilia quicken my heartbeat for a nanosecond before I squelch those ridiculous concerns. "Don't worry, my mother is already a fan of yours."

"She knows about me…About us?"

"No, but she made a comment about how close you and Rachel seem to be, and how fortunate it is for Rachel to have such a devoted mother figure in her life now that Kasia's gone. Believe me, she'll adore you."

Veronica looks down at her feet, but she can't hide the smile that my mother's compliment triggered. "I like your mom."

"And don't worry," I say, tipping her chin up so we're eye to eye, "I'll make sure to keep the wolves at bay, all right?"

"Your ex will be there." I nod. Grimacing, she asks, "Mel?"

"Yes, but I promise you, she'll behave."

She shrugs. "I don't really give a flip about her anyway." She sits on the bed, pulling socks on before she dons her fuzzy shearling boots. Looking up at me, she asks, "Was Kasia friends with Melanie?"

"Ah." I mull that over for a moment. "They weren't friends, no. Kasia pretty much loathed her when they first met."

"My cousin was a good judge of character."

I sit on the bed next to Veronica, taking her hand. "She was, and she had no reason to like Mel back then. Mel could act like a stuck-up bitch at times, and she's also jealous by nature…Likes to be the only pretty girl in the room. And," I pause, shoring myself up, "I screwed Mel here and there back in the day." Veronica's eyes lock on mine. "Mostly before I met Kasia, but I, uh, cheated with Mel once."

"Wow, with *her*?"

"Yeah," I say, shaking my head. "Totally not worth it."

She looks at her phone again. "I wish we could erase the last five minutes of this morning."

"I know. I don't want to leave things on that note either. C'mon," I say, tugging her up off the bed with me. "It's five to ten... You'll be late." I follow her inside the store and wait for her to open up. "Veronica, I feel like I have to be one hundred percent honest with you, and sometimes, like just now, that's gonna suck balls. But I think it's the only way you'll ever really trust me."

"That did suck balls."

And so will this. "In the spirit of full disclosure, I have a breakfast meeting tomorrow morning with Winery Girl."

She braces her hands on the sides of the register. "Gia?"

"Her name is actually Georgianna. She introduced herself to me as Gia." I tilt Veronica's chin up. "That's what piqued my interest."

"I'm just gonna go vomit right now."

"She's been lobbying for me to take an interest in one of their subsidiaries. I looked into it and I'm not biting...Just giving Spectra the courtesy of a sit down so I can formally decline. She was pushing for a dinner meeting but I insisted on breakfast."

"And tonight?"

"Tonight I'm having dinner with my college roommate, his wife and their three children." I lean in to kiss her and I'm grateful that she lets me do it. "Tonight I'll be missing you."

Chapter Thirty-Two

VERONICA

I guess I could get used to this.

Dylan told me to expect someone at noon today, a personal shopper who works for his family. I protested at first, but really, I have nothing to wear to an event like this. Kasia generally designed more casual clothing, so the pieces I have from her older collections won't cut it. There isn't one thing in my closet that could pass for formal wear.

I don't take to the experience at first. I don't care for Diana, this bossy chick who is no more than thirty, eyeing me in my bra and panties, inspecting me from every angle as she determines which gowns to select from the garment racks that now crowd my living room. She pinches me in at the waist when things are too tight, plumps my tits up in some dresses, taps my tummy and simultaneously pushes my ass in to encourage me to stand up straight. She manhandles me.

But damn, standing here in this crimson red satin halter gown she decidedly tells me is "made for your body," I'm suddenly in awe of the woman. There's nothing to it, no beads, no dazzle. But the way the fabric outlines my curves, and the cut of the top, exposing more shoulder, skimming along the sides of my breasts and then dipping down to expose more than half of my back—the effect is tasteful and sinfully sexy at the same time.

"Classic and demure…It's your body that takes this dress from a Bentley to a Lambourghini." Stepping me into a pair of black strappy heels, she directs my gaze towards the mirror. "Evan and his girlfriend will be here at five…Hair and make-up. Tell Evan I said natural wave." Standing up, she gathers my hair into a soft, low ponytail that drapes over one shoulder. "Better, I'll send him a picture," she says as she snaps away. "You don't want to look like those stuck-up brats with their overdone up-dos. You're young and sexy, so let's go with it."

By the time hair and makeup are done, it's nearly seven and Dylan is due any minute. I wished I was one of those city girls you imagine, the ones with chilled champagne always on standby in the fridge. I was battling a case of giant-sized butterflies, their wings fluttering wildly in my belly, and I could use a sip of something right about now—anything.

Tonight I fear all eyes will be on me, with not so much as one friend in the room besides Dylan. Well, I reason, the Farrells will be there, and I do know Darcy, but that's about it. Some of Kasia's others friends will be there, Rene and Caitlin for sure, but I don't really know them all that well. And I sure as hell can't predict what any of them will think about Dylan going after Kasia's much younger cousin. Guess I'll find out soon enough.

Deep breath, I tell myself and then take one when I hear a knock on my door.

Dylan literally takes a step back when I greet him. He looks me over from head to toe, his eyes softening as he steps forward again, tracing one finger lightly along the side of my face, continuing down to where my hair drapes over my shoulder. "You're breathtaking."

"You like it?"

"I," he shakes his head, pausing, "I feel incredibly grateful right now and incredibly lucky. You always look gorgeous, baby, but right now? No one could even come close to you. I almost feel bad for the other women...Every eye is going to be on you tonight."

"Keep talking like that and I'll probably trip and fall on my face as we enter the room. I'm a nervous wreck as it is."

"Hmm...I should let you sweat it out. You did leave me alone in a room with Tomasz and Michal at Henry's birthday party. That was pretty mean."

"I *left* you? *I* was watching over Hyacinth if you remember correctly, and she was trying to feed Chuck a piece of sushi."

"Whatever, I felt like a piece of sushi in a shark tank that entire day."

I can't help but laugh, because Dylan did look like he was breaking out into a cold sweat once or twice that afternoon. But it all worked out. He was already a rock star in Rachel's book, but my cousin Michal's boys were also in awe, the oldest one a star lacrosse player like Dylan had been. I think he was escaping from the adults when he organized those impromptu lacrosse and soccer games, but whatever the reason, he made friends with all the little ones as a result. And he didn't really need to worry; all of the adults were more than cordial. Even Tomasz kind of, sort of came around. After pulling me aside early on in the day for a heart to heart that could be summed up on his part as: *What the hell are you thinking?*, Tomasz, at my insistence, gave him the benefit of the doubt. I don't know if Dylan would ever earn the level of acceptance Jake seemed to have been granted right off the bat, but I could say that after last weekend I wouldn't hesitate or stress over bringing him around my family.

We were a couple.

The thought alone made me sigh, made me feel lighthearted and content.

"Come on, gorgeous, we cannot be fashionably late tonight, and the longer we stay in this apartment, the more I'll be tempted to hike the bottom of that dress up and eat you."

"You better keep comments like that to yourself tonight, mister."

Wrapping my shawl over my shoulders, he says, "I always keep everything about us, every hot and sexy little thing about us, to myself."

I was glad I took the champagne Dylan offered me on the ride over to The Plaza, loosening me up some, because nothing could have prepared me for the barrage of camera flashes and paparazzi that descended on us as we exited the car.

Unlike other times, when I noticed Dylan would just walk by a lone cameramen without even so much as a nod of recognition, tonight he stops and grants them full access. He has his arm wrapped around me, his hand resting intimately on my hip as he turns us from the direction of one photographer to another, giving them all a chance to snap us.

"Who's the knockout, Cole?" one calls above the rest.

He answers, "My girlfriend, Veronica Petrov." They all start yelling questions then and the flash of the cameras becomes constant. He ushers us inside once he drops that line, and in response to my wide-eyed stare, he shrugs, brushing me off. "What? That *is* you name and that's who you are."

"Veronica, that dress is stunning," Mrs. Cole says, air-kissing me on both cheeks. Dylan arranged for the four of us to go out for a casual dinner last week, which I'm now so grateful for in this moment. It makes me feel more relaxed knowing I have two more people in my corner tonight. And while Dylan is being pulled in ten different directions the second we walk through the door, I barely know a soul in the room.

Picking up on my discomfort, Mr. Cole nudges me gently and hands me a champagne flute. "I'd like to tell you that one day you'll look forward to attending these events, but I won't lie to you."

"Don't listen to Vince," Mrs. Cole says. "This is a wonderful cause. It's the only big event I still care to be associated with."

"Vince, Margot...Who *is* this beautiful creature? Have you adopted another child?"

Margot's face stiffens. "Bunny."

Bunny leans in for a kiss from Vince, which he gives her, but his manner is stiff and uncomfortable too. The woman goes right on making small talk, acting as if she doesn't notice the sudden chill in the air. "You two are looking fantastic, as always." Vince moves in closer to Margot. Both of them smile but neither one feels the need to return the compliment. Undeterred, she keeps at it. "We missed you over Labor Day. I can't believe you came back to New York so early."

Now Margot's smile seems genuine. "I used to love the Vineyard but it just doesn't feel the same to me anymore. Actually," she looks to Vince, "we're thinking about putting our place up for sale. Dylan isn't interested in keeping it either."

At the mention of Dylan's name, the woman's smile thins and she turns back to me. "I'm sorry...I'm Bunny Tate, and *you* are?"

Vince takes a slight step forward, as if he's trying to shield me. "This is Veronica Petrov. She's a friend of Dylan's." Looking to me, Vince adds, "Bunny is a very old friend of the family's."

"*And* I'm Dylan's mother-in-law."

Margot's tone of voice is concerned when she asks, "How is Cecilia?" but the look on her face tells me she's anything but.

"She's doing well. You know this year's been difficult, but she's soldiering on. She's traveling, doing charity work."

"And the gallery?"

Bunny literally beams, tilting her head. "She's in the process of selling it."

Margot sips at her champagne, her tone clipped when she comments, "I'm sure the business isn't worth much, but that property alone will net her another nice windfall."

Bunny's look tells me she's gearing up for a comeback, so I take that as my cue to escape. Looking to Margot and reading understanding in her eyes, I say, "I see a friend, excuse me."

"Darcy?" I tap the woman's shoulder, praying it's actually her.

"Oh my God! Veronica!" She takes my hands in hers, backing up a step to take me in from top to bottom. "You look so," bringing her gaze back up to me, she smiles, "grown up." Turning to the group she's with, she makes introductions. "Tom, you remember Kasia's cousin, Veronica, don't you?" Then she introduces me to her brother, Luke Donovan, and another drop-dead gorgeous guy named Mick. With their six-foot-plus frames in tuxedos, chiseled jawlines and bright white smiles, they're like a Brooks Brothers advertisement come to life.

"I'm so sorry I wasn't able to catch you at that silent auction last month. The twins came earlier than Rene and Caleb expected, so I was on duty."

"How are they, and how's Rene feeling?"

"She's great. Nothing slows that girl down. And the babies are beautiful. Two boys and now two girls."

"Two sets of twins...That sounds like a *lot* of work."

"Caleb works from home one or two days a week and the boys are in school full-time now, so that helps. And tonight my parents are babysitting. Rene and Caleb bailed at the last minute. I think they just wanted to have a quiet dinner alone instead of all this," she says, gesturing around the room.

Darcy's husband Tom looks out over the crowd. "Veronica, I have someone you have to meet. My younger brother is around here somewhere. Terrence just finished law school and he's moving to the city next month."

"Um," I hedge, looking around for Dylan, feeling awkward.

Darcy nudges my side. "Terrence is twenty-seven, gorgeous, and like seriously, he's the nicest guy you'll ever meet."

I want to whisper to Darcy that I'm here with someone, but I don't get the chance. Tom, trying and failing to curb his laughter, taps my shoulder and gestures to a man making his way towards us with a pissed off look. With jet black hair and blue eyes, the boy is striking, but he still doesn't hold a candle to Dylan.

Towering over his brother, the man I assume to be Terrence says, "Would have been nice if you told me this thing was black tie, jackass. Your pants are wedged in my ass crack right now and this jacket..." He shakes his head, looking down at the cuffs that are definitely more than an inch too short.

"Terrence!" Darcy tugs on his hand and shoots him a look that says: *Mind your manners!* "I want you to meet someone." She shakes her head, placing a hand on my shoulder. "Ohmigod, I actually just realized you two have already met!" She's still smiling, but her eyes tell me that she's missing her dearest friend. "Kasia came down to the beach with you and Olivia once when you were...I don't know, maybe nine or ten years old. Do you remember, Veronica?"

I laugh. "You know what? I actually do! There was sandbar or something that day and I remember Olivia running out of the water with—"

"Those tiny little crabs on her fingers." Terrence is looking at me with a wistful smile, his gaze raking over me before he meets my eyes again. "I remember that too."

"Poor thing!" Darcy has her hands up, wiggling all ten fingers. "I remember she was screaming her little head off. How is Olivia?"

I guess Kasia never filled Darcy in on our family drama. "She's doing well. Olivia's a sophomore at Columbia." I'm tempted to add: *She's the good daughter.*

"That's great. And I know you're running Alex and Henry's entire operation now...That's impressive." Maybe Darcy *is* aware of my situation because that seemed like an obvious effort on her part to steer the conversation away from college talk. I begin to perspire when she keeps right on with the matchmaking. "Terrence, where is your new apartment?"

"I'll be on Eighty-first and York." He looks to me. "What about you?"

"I have a tiny one bedroom above the store I manage on Seventy-first and Madison."

"You're living large. I'm cramming into a crappy fourth floor walk-up with three other guys. I thought my living situation would get better after school but the rents are insane in this city."

Darcy is full-on beaming. "You're practically neighbors!"

I have to put a stop to this. I mean, Terrence is a nice guy and all, but Darcy's looking between the two of us like we're a forgone conclusion.

Sensing my unease, Terrence shakes his head and smiles at Darcy. Looking back to me, he says, "She means well."

I relax a little then, and Terrence is easy to talk to. He tells me about living in the south for the past three years during law school, and he doesn't miss a beat when I tell him I'm *on a break that may or may not be permanent* from NYU.

"You'll figure it out, Veronica. And I get it...Right now I'm just praying that I love being a lawyer, 'cause if not, I'll have to face the fact that I just wasted a whole lot of time and money."

"If you absolutely hate it, I'll hook you up with a job driving our delivery van."

His easy smile matches mine. "I'm gonna hold you to that." Leaning in slightly and gesturing his head towards the other side of the room, he lowers his voice when he says, "I was just about to get a drink...Come with me?"

"Nope, I've got Veronica covered." Dylan slides one hand around my waist and leans down to kiss my cheek. "I've been looking all over for you."

Darcy, Tom and Terrence are staring at Dylan's hand, which is now resting low on my hip.

As if on cue, a waiter appears at Dylan's side. "Club soda for the lady and a Macallan rocks for me." Looking back to the others, he asks, "Anyone else?"

Terrence isn't smiling anymore. He keeps his eyes on Dylan when he says, "Bourbon neat."

"My, my…I'd say you're all grown up with a drink order like that, T, but it's hard to keep a straight face when you look like you're wearing a suit from your friend Moshe's Bar Mitzvah."

Terrence looks down at his ill-fitting tux and then trains his eyes on Dylan. "Nice to see some people never change, Cole." Turning back to face me, he reaches over and takes my free hand. "Hey, I was really sorry to hear about Kasia. I always liked her. She made everyone around her feel special."

"Thank you."

He doesn't let go of my hand when he asks, "How are Jake and the kids doing?"

Dylan's fingers sink into my hip, pulling me in a little closer. Are these two in some kind of pissing match over me right now?

I slip my hand out of Terrence's grasp. I don't want to hurt his feelings because he does seem like a genuinely nice person, but I don't want to give him the wrong idea either. "It's day by day still, but things are getting better."

Darcy jumps into the conversation, obviously sensing the tension in the air. "I agree. The kids were all down at the beach house last Sunday. I think getting the dog was a great idea. Milo loves him, right?"

"He does, but lordy, my dog looks like a peanut compared to that hairy beast."

"I know, right? I can picture the five of them at the shelter, picking out the craziest looking stray, the one that no one else wanted. He's ugly but he's good natured."

The waiter comes back with our drinks. Terrence takes a sip from his, studying Dylan quietly. He seems to have come to a decision when he announces, "All right, I'm heading out to meet a few of my friends downtown." Looking down at his outfit and then at Tom, he adds, "I'm going back to your place to change first."

Dylan smirks and says, "Good idea," after taking a long pull off his drink.

Standing to his full height, which gives him a good two or three inches on everyone else, Terrence fixes his eyes on Dylan. "What can I say? Being the biggest cock in the henhouse occasionally has its disadvantages."

"Biggest dick...Got that right," Dylan mutters.

Mick asks Dylan a question, pulling his attention away for a moment. Terrence leans down to kiss Darcy's cheek. "See you later, Sis. That key still in the same place?"

"Yes. I'll let the babysitter know you're swinging by."

Terrence looks to Dylan's hand, still resting on my hip, before leaning in on my other side. "It was so good to see you again, Veronica." Kissing me on the cheek, he whispers, "Be careful."

Dylan gently pulls me in even closer. "Thought you were leaving, T?"

He nods, conceding the loss I think. "Adios, Cole."

Mick says something else to Dylan but he ignores him. "Dance with me?" he asks, looking a little shattered, if that's even possible for Dylan Cole.

No one else is dancing, but when Dylan leads me out onto the center of the floor, a few couples begin to make their way out. We slow-dance in silence for a few minutes, each second ticking by in what feels like slow motion, my anxiety ratcheting up steadily.

When he looks at me for the second time with a pained expression, I keep my voice low even though I'm beginning to feel panicked. "Tell me...What's the matter?"

"Nothing," he murmurs, leaning down to breathe me in. "I just think..." he trails off, shaking his head. "This is all happening so fast, Veronica, and I—"

My feet stop and I'm no longer following his lead. He's still holding me close, but his actions are telling me the opposite of his words. My heart is a heavy weight, anticipating the axe that's about to drop. It's all too familiar.

This is all happening too fast. I feel like I'm being torn in two. You have to understand how much I care about you, Veronica, but I can't do this.

Shaking off the feeling of being back in Larson's arms, half listening to Dylan plead with me as my heart slowly turns to stone, I tell myself that I'm conditioned for this, that I'll survive. But will I? For all my tough talk, Dylan's words are literally knocking the wind from my lungs. Confused, I back out of his embrace. "Excuse me," I whisper, unable to meet his eyes.

"No Veronica, wait."

He goes to draw me back in as we stand off to the side of the dance floor, but he's interrupted by an older woman. "There you are, Dylan. Do you need a formal invitation to stop in and see your favorite aunt? It's beyond rude...I haven't seen you in months!"

Dylan has a firm grasp on one of my hands, preventing me from making my escape. "Veronica," he looks at me pointedly, "I'd like you to meet my Aunt Colette."

"So nice to meet you," I say, trying my best to smile but knowing I can't muster up anything even remotely close to cheery. I feel dizzy and overwhelmed. I have to get away. I gesture my head towards the corridor. "Please excuse me."

He drops my hand, and as I make my way towards the ladies' room, I can still hear his aunt, her voice laced with disapproval. "Now this one is a little young, Dylan, isn't she?"

This one.

Yes, *this* one is young, naïve, foolish...All of the above.

DYLAN

"That wasn't wise," Anna cracks, fixing me with a look of abject disapproval.

"I can handle myself," Veronica snaps with her eyes trained on me. Turning to Anna, she adds in a softer voice, "But thank you for the save, Anna."

Anna squeezes Veronica's hand. "No one can handle those bitches when it's three on one. I've been on the receiving end before, so I should know. I'm just glad Dylan pointed you out to me earlier so I knew who you were."

"What is going on?"

"Nothing," Veronica says, shooting Anna a look, something unspoken passing between them. "It was nothing."

Well *nothing* comes traipsing out of the ladies' room snickering a moment later, Samantha Paulson and Delia Parker, tipsy and laughing alongside her.

I snap at Veronica, unable to keep my anger in check. "Don't run off again, do you understand? We're not finished."

I shouldn't have turned my back on Veronica but I was furious. Even without the full play by play, I know exactly what's gone down between my ex and my girl, and Cecilia isn't getting away with this shit anymore. I step forward. "Having a good time, ladies?"

Delia, always the doormat of the group, looks alarmed, while Samantha Paulson, greedy cow that she is, grabs a crostini from a passing server's tray as she flashes me her signature fake smile. "So good to see you, Dylan! Your mother has done it again...*Such* a fabulous night."

I ignore her lame attempt to ingratiate herself with me. "A word, Cecilia, right now."

And just like that, her two steadfast friends drop her like a bad case of the clap. Cecilia raises her chin in defiance, but then I notice her looking over my shoulder smiling. I turn to see Veronica's back.

"Your date's in a hurry to leave."

I spin back to my bitch of an ex-wife. "What did you say to her?" No answer. "What's happened to you, Cecilia? You used to be better than them! All this time, were you really just as shallow and empty hearted as they are? Are you *that* good of an actress?"

She staggers just slightly, either from drink or from shock, holding on to the wall for support. "You're calling *me* empty hearted? You parade that *child* around here, in *our* circle, calling her your *girlfriend*? You're the one who's cruel, Dylan. And if she has any sense, she'll run away from you as fast as she can." She angrily swipes at a tear that's stained with mascara. "It looks like she just did."

My phone chirps, signaling an incoming text. It's James: *Bringing her home.* I shoot off a text telling him to come back around for me. A full minute later I get a reply: *The lady says no.*

What in the actual fuck just happened? Why did Veronica flip out on me, zoning out when I was trying to talk to her and then backing away from me on the dance floor?

I want to scream at the cabbie, who is purposely taking the scenic route uptown. When I see James's name flash on my screen, I have to breathe for a moment, knowing I'm about to unleash on him.

"Where are you?"

"Sorry I couldn't come back 'round for you, Cole. She was pretty upset."

"I'm almost there."

"I'm gonna stay put. I have a feeling she won't be opening the door for you tonight."

We pull up just then. As I'm paying the cabbie, Veronica comes storming out her front door dressed in sweats with a small duffle bag slung over her shoulder.

"Can I take you somewhere, Miss Veronica?"

"I have my own car, James, but thank you." When she catches sight of me stalking towards her, her polite smile drops and her features harden.

"Where in the fuck do you think you're going?" I twist the keys out of her hand, lift her up and throw her over my shoulder.

"Put me down!"

"Simmer down!" I bark, seething, giving her ass one hard swat. It's hard to open the vestibule door with her pounding on my back.

"James!"

"He's not coming for you, sweetness. Got that?"

In my periphery, I do see him getting out of the car, but I kick the door closed behind me, listening as the lock catches. He'll find himself heading back to that shithole town outside of London with his visa revoked if he takes one step closer. I think he knows that. And more importantly, he knows I'd never hurt her.

There are thirteen steps to that first landing. Her body is tense as she curses me and rains hits down on my back for the first half, her pace slowing the higher we climb. By the time we reach the landing, it's as if all the fight has left her. Opening the door and taking her inside, I hear her whimper, her body limp as I lower her to the couch.

"What happened, Veronica? What did she say to you?" She looks at me for a long moment, says nothing. "Please talk to me."

"Do you think that's what this is about?" Veronica wipes at her eyes. "You think I'm upset over something your wife said?"

"I—"

"Why don't you tell me what's been going through *your* head all night...And tell me the truth."

I *was* acting strange, but how could I explain my behavior? Should I tell her I couldn't stand to watch as nearly all the men in the room stared at her? How when I pointed her out as my girlfriend, everyone invariably commented on her age—the younger ones also feeling free to comment on how hot she was? How I had to put one of my board members in check when he asked if Veronica had any friends for him, like she was a fucking call girl or something? Standing by as Terrence Farrell practically fell at her feet tonight— should I tell her how that gutted me? With no baggage and a full decade younger than me, Terrence was a better choice. I wanted to choke the life out of him because I knew without a doubt that he was the better man.

I sit on the couch beside her, looking off at the far wall. An odd feeling comes over me, as if I've been in this very place before, knowing it's all about to crumble. "I don't deserve someone like you and I know that."

She cradles her face in her hands. "If this is the start of some lame *you'll be better off without me* speech, just save it. I've heard it before."

"You don't understand."

"You're right, I don't."

"Tonight..."

When I trail off, she murmurs from behind her hands, "Tonight you realized that we don't fit, that we don't make sense?" I don't answer because I'm desperately trying to put what I'm feeling into words. "That's what everyone else thinks," she raises her voice just slightly, "but I don't. I *know* I belong with you."

Does she? I want it to be true. Since that night at my apartment when we both laid everything out there, we've been inseparable. It's been less than six weeks but I'm already completely gone over her. I come home to her every night that I'm not away on business. We're hardly ever apart. And waking up with Veronica Petrov in my arms? It's so good that I'm nearly selfish enough to go on pretending, to keep my mouth shut just so that I can have her.

My face reddens with shame when I think back to a day last week, the day I stood in her tiny bathroom shaving before I left for work. I paused to pick up the little plastic packet that sat on the lip of the sink to examine it. Half of the days were empty, the remaining small blister packs holding the pink pills. I was tempted to take the pack, to misplace it so maybe she'd forget for a day or two. Yes, I want her *that* badly.

"Veronica, I'm so selfish when it comes to you. And tonight...I just wonder if I'm doing right by you." I'm too ashamed to meet her eyes. "The first person I ran into tonight was Anna's husband. Declan's a pro hockey player and he always brings some of his team-mates along to these events as a favor to my mother because they've got deep pockets. A few of the rookies noticed you walking across the room towards Darcy. Before I could tell them who you were, they *all* started talking about you. Every one of those guys wanted you. And not like, piece of ass wanting you. Those men *saw* you, they thought you were spectacular. I finally get away from those toothless morons and then some dipshit I work with asks me, dead serious, if maybe you have a friend to set him up with. He's married mind you, and I couldn't even call him out on that because I've lived so many years of my life just like him—like a fucking cheat. And then I'm finally making my way towards you when I see Terrence lock eyes on you. I love that kid but I wanted to strangle him with my bare hands tonight."

She cuts in. "Are you telling me you're jealous or something?"

"No. I'm telling you that this is moving fast...Maybe too fast for *you.*" Veronica starts to cry again but I keep going because I have to get this out. "Are you going to regret this?"

"What do you mean, Dylan?"

I pull her up and over my lap, cradling her face in my hands. "I can offer you a good life, a *very* good life, but will it be enough? I want everything and I want it now."

My instinct is to look away but I fight against it. I'm pretty sure that what I'm about to say will sicken her, make her reject me outright, but I have to take what's coming. "Do you remember when I told you I didn't want to use condoms anymore?" When she nods, the words nearly catch in my throat. "I know you're on the pill, but I wanted...I want...I-I dream about you being pregnant. I basically want to trap you, Veronica, and that's beyond fucked up on my part."

"What?"

"You heard me. I want to be everything to you, the only man you'll ever want to be with."

Running my hands slowly down her sides from breast to hip, feeling her curves for what might be the last time, I lay it all out there. "Every time we fuck I want to plant myself inside of you, give you no choice but to marry me and spend your life with me. And tonight I realized just how desirable you are...That *every* man sees you the same way I do. If I wasn't so certain you're going to wake up one day and realize that I'm not good enough for you, then I wouldn't be so hell bent on possessing you."

"You *are* good."

"I'm not and you know it."

"I thought you were breaking up with me tonight."

"Maybe I should be, baby."

"No," she whispers.

She goes to raise her shirt over her head but I catch the hem in my hands. "Don't do that."

Those whiskey brown eyes narrow on me. "You think I'm

playing the damsel in distress right now? I'm not. You don't get to decide for me. I'm not a child. No one gets to judge me anymore, to tell me I'm good or bad. No one gets to decide if they'll keep me or if it's time for me to go. I make my own decisions now." She jabs a finger into my chest. "And I don't *need* you, Dylan...I know that." I rub at the spot on my chest, not because the jab hurts, but because those last words feel like a crushing blow. But her eyes soften when she takes my hand and places it over her own heart. "I decide who I love...And I love you. So maybe instead of talking about breaking up with me, maybe you should be touching me, fucking me...loving me."

"I do love you, Veronica."

She holds my face firmly in her two hands. "If you love me then don't leave me."

Her plea guts me. For all the talk of being in control, of making decisions for herself, there's still a part of Veronica that fears being abandoned again above all else. And fuck it, why am I even floating the idea of something that will crush her when it's also the last thing I want? Here she is telling me she wants me—why am I fighting this?

"I've never felt as happy as I do when I'm with you, Dylan. I feel safe and I feel so...precious. You make me feel like I'm precious to you. Am I?"

"Don't you know by now that you're everything? I don't even know who I am without you anymore." I repeat it again because it feels so good to finally say what I've been feeling for so long. "I love you."

Standing up, Veronica lifts the cotton shirt over her head and unclasps her bra, letting them both drop to the floor. She slides her sweats down, revealing all of her bare skin to me. She lets me get a long look before she sits back down astride me, pushing her hips in close to mine.

"So now I know that you love me, Dylan, but I really need you to show me."

Chapter Thirty-Four

DYLAN

Tom claps me on the back, so hard I nearly choke on an ice cube. "You look happy."

"Does that bother you for some reason?" I ask as I wipe the droplets off my lapel.

"Jeez, I thought love would make you a little less cantankerous. And of course I'm happy for your cranky ass."

I look across the room at Veronica, standing next to Terrence and his new babe, a girl from high school he reconnected with over Thanksgiving weekend. I *am* happy, but the sight of her with people closer to her own age still eats at me sometimes.

"She's it for me," I say with resignation. Meaning that if she does wake up and decide to dump my ass someday, I no longer believe I'll be capable of recovering from it.

Mr. and Mrs. Donovan each hold one of Caleb and Rene's new twins, making their way around the party, saying their goodbyes and wishing everyone Happy New Year a few hours before the ball actually drops. Mr. Donovan stops to talk to Veronica. A lump forms in my throat when she takes the baby girl from him for a moment and nuzzles into her neck, breathing in that baby scent before cradling the baby close to her own breast. Looking back to Tom, I say, "I've got it bad."

"That's a good thing. And don't question it so much, all right?" It's like he's reading my damn mind.

"Question what?" Darcy asks, fixing her man with a sexy smile and a little hip check.

"Just telling Dylan not to let his pubes turn gray while he's deciding whether or not to make an honest woman out of Veronica."

"You're so gross!" Turning to me, Darcy raises her eyebrow and smiles. "She told me you two spent Christmas with Margot and Vince?"

Yeah, it was surreal. Many things have changed about life in the Cole household, but Christmas is still a fabulous affair with lots of extended family and business strangers. That's what Veronica calls them instead of business associates—it's fitting.

I caught her looking at me that night the same way I'm looking at her now. She was standing with Aunt Colette but I could tell she was only half listening as my aunt prattled on. Her attention was fixed on Mason, who'd fallen asleep in my lap. He'd been a cranky little monster all throughout dinner, probably hopped up on opening all those presents and eating too many cookies. Declan shot me a look when his son wailed and called out for me. I snickered, knowing the kid only wanted me above his father in that moment because I had a warm sip cup of chocolate milk in my hands, whereas Declan had the almond milk smoothie that Anna had most likely infused with kale, hemp seeds and who knows what else. Mason wriggled out of his father's arms and came over to me, climbing into my lap as I sat in a big, comfy chair next to the twinkling lights of the Christmas tree. The kid was conked out and drooling within five minutes. When our eyes met I wondered if she felt like I did. Was she as ready for this as I was?

Watching her tonight, I wonder the same thing. Veronica will be twenty-three in February and I'm turning thirty-eight this month. Her biological clock isn't ticking but my emotional clock suddenly is.

Maybe she thinks I'm struggling with the crazy side effects of old age when I roar, "Move in with me," later on that night as I rock into her, spilling myself into her body as her hands hold tight to the rails of the bed frame above her.

She doesn't say anything at first, our bodies stilling as we both come down from the high. I'm not tense, uneasy or feeling anything other than euphoria in that moment. First and foremost, I've just had a spectacular orgasm, and second, I meant what I said and the request came straight from my heart.

I lean over her, undoing the necktie that binds her hands to the bed frame with one hand while cupping a breast with the other. I rub her wrists while I lick and kiss a trail up and across her shoulder to her neck, tasting the salt on her skin.

She lowers her hips down to the bed and I follow, then she rolls her body so that she's nestled into me. "You want that? Is it because you hate this little apartment or something?"

"Definitely the *or something* part of that statement." I nudge her with my cock, which is already getting hard again. "I want your clothes hanging in the closet next to mine. I want to cook dinner together when we get home, wake up next to you every morning." I reach down and traced the semen on her inner thighs, circling it back up and pressing it into her opening. She's still on the pill so it's a meaningless act, even though it means something very real to me. "I need you." She doesn't answer other than to breathe a contented sigh as she gently rocks her hips against the finger I now have lodged inside her. And my girl is definitely in for at least three glasses of champagne at this point, so I'm not really pressing for an answer. Pulling her in close, I kiss her temple. "Go to sleep, baby."

* * *

Veronica watches as I pull on the same clothes I wore the night before. "Don't you see?" she grumbles, "If I moved in with you I'd still be all alone tonight."

"If you came on this trip with me, like I *asked* you to, we could be wining and dining at all the best spots *and* living it up in my fancy hotel room." When she goes to protest with that cute frowny face, I raise my hand. "I know you have to work, I get it." In truth, I like that she doesn't drop everything for me, but damn, I miss her so much more now every time that I'm away. "I'm just saying that if we lived together, I wouldn't have to run back to my place right now to pack and get ready. We could lie around in my big giant bed for the next few hours."

I'm leaving for Zurich this afternoon. One of my senior executives is coming along, my sole objective for this trip to ensure that I'm no longer needed to oversee operations there. It's a transfer of responsibilities. I have no need or desire to go there anymore.

Checking the time on her phone, she sighs before flopping back onto the bed. "The flowers aren't going to arrange themselves."

"It's probably going to be dead today, no?"

"It's New Year's Day, so the store is technically closed, but it's Monday, silly. I've got a van load of white lily arrangements that have to go out first thing tomorrow morning to Cole Industries," she teases, tossing a pillow my way.

Crawling back on top of her, I pin her hands above her head. "Maybe I'll cancel the order."

She's play acting now, putting on that pout. "Please Mr. Cole, don't cancel your order." Letting her knees fall open to the sides and looking down at her own tight nipples, she asks, "What can I do to convince you to change your mind?"

I shift so that both of her hands are trapped by one of mine as I push my pants down just over my hips and draw my cock out. "You want to play it that way?" I tear right into her, her moans and the way she presses her hips up to meet mine telling me she likes it hard like this. "Come live with me and I'll fuck you like this every morning, baby...Morning, noon and night."

With hooded lids and one side of her mouth ticking up in a smile, she gasps her words out in between thrusts. "Oh—Oh, yeah—I'll—Give—It—Some—Yeah—Serious—Yes, yes—Thought."

Chapter Thirty-Five

VERONICA

My toe is tapping of its own accord. Dylan reaches over to still my knee when the utensils on the table strike one another with a loud clatter for the second time.

"She's not coming...Let's just go."

"Whoa girl, it's only five after...Let's give her a few minutes."

We sit quietly for the next five minutes, Dylan checking his phone and answering emails while I stare at the door. When I see her I jump to my feet nervously, but then sit down quickly when I see that my mother is trailing behind.

Olivia approaches, looking nervous, while my mother is looking at the ceiling, at the other tables, at her fingernails...basically anywhere other than me.

"Olivia," I breathe out, pulling her in for a hug. She hugs me back, giving me hope. Dylan stands up and pulls out a chair for Olivia and then for my mother before taking his seat next to me. I feel him give my knee another reassuring squeeze.

"Mom," I greet her, trying not to sound as irritated as I feel. I want to say, *Who asked you to come?*

"I don't know if you remember me, Mrs. Petrov." Dylan offers his outstretched hand. "I'm Dylan Cole."

She shakes his hand once, the gesture stiff. "I know who you are."

"I have to admit," Olivia speaks up, trying to ease the tension, "I don't remember you very well."

"It was a long time ago," he offers with a soft smile.

My mother has the nerve to look indignant when she says, "I read in the paper that you're getting married."

Olivia looks at Mother as if she's telepathically willing her to shut up, then looks back to me apologetically. "It was a gorgeous picture."

"Thank you, Olivia. The wedding is at the end of June."

Mother glares at Dylan. "When is the baby due?"

No one knows about the pregnancy. I'm only ten weeks along and not showing one bit. But he smiles wide. And I know this smile —it's his *fuck you* smile. "The baby is due in November. We can't wait."

"A Church wedding?"

"No," I snap. "If you've been following our lives in the papers, like you said, then you know Dylan is divorced." Deciding to dig in, I add, "Henry, Alex's *partner*, is an ordained minister. He'll be performing the ceremony and the wedding is being held at their home."

My mother reaches across the table to take my hand but I pull mine back out of reach. "Veronica, you know this is a bad way to start married life." I stare at her, stunned. *What in the fuckity-fuck do you know about starting off married life on the right foot?* She looks down at her own hands. "I know we are not close, but you do know that I love you. When I found out Olivia was meeting you today, I insisted on coming."

"Too little, too late, Mother. I don't need your approval or your counsel anymore. I *needed* you when I was seventeen."

"Your father—"

I can't let her finish. "My father is a pathetic excuse for a man."

"No! He's always tried to protect you girls!"

"From what? I needed protection from *him*!"

Olivia, as per usual, looks like a deer in the headlights. She's staring out the window, and only when my gaze follows hers do I see what holds her attention. Shaking my head and laughing, I say, "Look, your ride is here." My father is glaring at me from across the street. Total déjà vu, but I'm not seventeen anymore. I'm no longer afraid of him. To my mother, I say, "You'd better run along...Don't want to keep Daddy waiting."

My mother stands and gestures to Olivia. Her anxious expression tells me this was a covert operation, and I feel bad for my mother for a moment, knowing there will be hell to pay for her disobedience.

I grab Olivia's wrist when she turns to go. "I asked you here to invite you to the wedding." I hand her an invitation, which she folds up into a small square before stuffing it into her front pants pocket. She smiles at me with the word *sorry* written into her expression.

I sit back down, exhausted. The real reason I asked Olivia here today was to see if she would be my Maid of Honor. Obviously that's not happening.

"Guess I'm going with my original plan for junior bridesmaids only?"

Dylan leans over to kiss me and then rests his forehead against mine. "I'm your family now, baby, understand?"

He's serene and calm, then darting up out of his chair and knocking it over in the process a moment later. He's out the door and in the street, towering over him and pushing at his chest. I heard my father out there ranting like a lunatic too, but while his words still hurt, ignoring him was second nature to me by now.

"Go ahead...Call her a whore again, old man, and see what happens to you!" My father tries to push back, but he's no match for Dylan. One, two, three pushes until he has him pinned against his car. "Get in your car, start fucking driving, and don't look back. Come near Veronica again and I'll bury you."

James is standing across the street a good thirty feet away, but I see my father glance at him, awareness overtaking his features. He spits on the ground at Dylan's feet before looking back up. "You deserve her."

I leave a twenty on the table, shaking as I make my way outside. James ushers me into the car and Dylan is beside me in the back seat a moment later. His face is red and his fists are still clenched. "Never again, Veronica...I never want them anywhere near you again. They don't deserve to call you their daughter."

"You're all I've got, Dylan." I rest my head against his chest as he slides his arm around my waist. "And I'm all right with that."

Chapter Thirty-Six

VERONICA

I laugh out loud examining the contents of the package. A sheer lace bodysuit from Sarreri, Lollia bubble bath, body oil probably sourced from Cleopatra's very own private collection, and a vibrator with a bedazzled handle. The card tucked inside reads: *Thinking of You*.

Every month I received a package. It might be chocolate-covered fruit, exotic teas, luxurious soaps, or a selection of salsas to top my famous huevos rancheros. More often than not, it's lingerie. The packages arrive while Dylan is away on business and the cards always read the same. He never *ever* sends flowers.

I shoot out a text: *You think I'm going to look hot in that bodysuit right now?* He replies immediately: *You're barely showing. And yes, the bump looks totally hot.* A few minutes later, he follows up with: *No comment about the electronics?* I answer: *I don't even know what to say about that!* His parting text before he boards the plane makes me ache for my man to get home. *What did I tell you when I proposed, V? For the rest of my life, I'm going to give my woman* everything *she needs.*

Taking myself in as I look in the mirror, I'll admit, I do look pretty good. I laughed when I saw that Dylan purchased my pre-preggo size. I think he appreciates the way my slightly fuller butt and hips stretch the fabric, not to mention the way my breasts now push up and over the cups. Turning profile, I see that at five months along I do have a bump, but I'm still not very obviously pregnant yet.

Last month at our wedding I wasn't showing at all. Not that it mattered; every guest knew we were expecting and was excited for us. And everyone who mattered was there. Alex was my Man of Honor while Melanie stood beside Dylan. He didn't like the idea of having Tom as his best man the second time around—thought it was bad karma—and I no longer despised the bitch.

In our own odd way, Melanie and I have bonded. She's bad mannered and vulgar despite her blue blood, which I find funny, and we have one very important thing in common: a fervent stake in Dylan's happiness.

Nell managed to fly in from the West Coast, just having snagged an internship at The Getty. I hope time and distance don't eventually come between us, because that girl will always have a place in my heart. It takes a special kind of person to notice when someone else is in distress and to reach out a helping hand, no questions asked. And I was especially grateful for her presence on my wedding day. Dylan had plenty of friends to fill the chairs behind him, but mine were filled almost entirely by family. And while Darcy, Rene, Caitlin and the rest of those women had taken me into their circle, expressing nothing but acceptance and friendship once Dylan and I were firmly a "thing," I couldn't help but feel sort of like a mascot when I was around them. I would always be fifteen years younger and at a different stage of life, and in a way, I would always think of them as Kasia's friends.

As my aunt and Darcy helped to fix my veil in those last minutes before I walked down the aisle, I missed my own mother and my sister terribly. I wouldn't let the disappointment settle in and ruin this perfect day, though. I reminded myself that I have plenty of family, and family can be defined in many ways.

Henry was the first person I saw as I started down the makeshift aisle that was set across their gorgeous expanse of land looking over Long Island Sound. He trained his eyes on Hyacinth and Rachel, outfitted in matching cornflower blue dresses, looking adorable. Just about every guest looked on smiling as Rachel tried to corral Hyacinth when she went to hand every person sitting in an aisle seat their very own personal rose petal instead of dusting them along the ground. Henry looked beyond them then, smiling at me with the kind of love I imagine most girls receive from their fathers. And when Dylan took a step forward, flashing his loving eyes my way, I couldn't possibly feel as if anything was missing in my life.

But just before Alex joined my hand with Dylan's, I saw a figure moving in the distance, quickly making her way towards us and taking an empty seat in the back row. A fair-haired beauty dressed in a floral dress smiled shyly and blew me a kiss when we locked eyes. No, Olivia wasn't standing beside me that day as I'd hoped, and no, we weren't even really friends at this point, but we are and will *always* be sisters, and she was here—for me.

After we recited our vows to one another, vows Dylan and I wrote ourselves, I was fixed with a searing kiss. My husband—did I mention how much I love, love, *love* using that word? My *husband* pulled me close to his body, his touch, the breath in his lungs, and the soft contours of his mouth telling me exactly what his vows had told me just moments before:

I finally found you
and I'm *never* letting go.

Epilogue

MARGOT CLARKE COLE

Sometimes love fills you, seeps into every fiber of your being as if you're breathing it in, or it's the very blood pumping through your veins.

Every woman will tell you that holding her child for the first time is the most profound and magical kind of love you will ever experience. I do not dispute that. But I cannot remember feeling so much love, such unbridled, overwhelming joy, as the first time I held my grandson in my arms.

Matthew. It means gift from God, and that's exactly what he is to me and to Vince, and of course to his parents as well. A boy. Maybe it's wrong that I prayed for a healthy boy, and I certainly would have been overjoyed with a granddaughter, but I suppose a part of me wanted to relive those years, the years when I held my own boy and then stood beside him, watching as he grew into a confident and capable man.

Today I watch my son Dylan lift Matthew into his arms, and watch with gratitude as his beautiful wife Veronica comes to stand beside him, gently nuzzling her nose into her baby's belly before rising up onto her tiptoes to kiss Dylan just underneath his ear. The kiss makes him at once smile and look on at her with hunger.

Is it good parenting or is it luck? When you get to this point, when you finally let out a sigh of relief, realizing that your child isn't just through school, gainfully employed, married and settled—when you realize they are thriving, flourishing. Is this when you pat yourself on the back or is this when you take a moment to thank a higher power?

Recognizing the myriad of things that *could* have gone wrong, acknowledging the times that your input was not a positive factor, but something that maybe set them off track for a spell, and being aware that wealth and privilege can sometime be a catalyst for failure rather than success, I take this moment and raise a silent prayer of gratitude to my God.

I also did this on the occasion of Dylan's wedding the June before last, a day so different from his first wedding day. When he married Cecilia I hid my misery with a smile. So conflicted over what I knew in my heart was not a good match, despite everything looking so perfect on the surface.

Like his first wedding, on the day he married Veronica there was not one cloud in the sky, the bride was breathtakingly beautiful, the flowers were perfect, the music and the ceremony were moving. The similarities, however, ended there.

Dylan and Veronica didn't stand on tradition. In fact, she wore no shoes, her silver toe ring gleaming in the sunshine as she made her way down the grass "aisle" in a strapless white dress that I believe she purchased at a vintage clothing store in the East Village. We were not in a church as they exchanged vows and there was no priest. A "minister" ordained via the internet presided over the ceremony—I'll admit it wasn't easy, but I was able to come to terms with it. But the most notable difference to me was the look on Dylan's face. It was one of pure joy, and of relief. He looked like a man who was finally granted the one thing he'd wished and hoped for, when for so long it had been nothing but a vision or a dream.

I said a prayer for Cecilia last month on the day of her wedding, even though I was not there to wish her well in person. I know Dylan is also grateful that his ex-wife has found happiness with a good-hearted man, and like me, I'm sure he hopes they'll be blessed with a child soon, just as he has been.

Today, on the occasion of my grandson's first birthday, I say the same prayer of thanks as Dylan lowers Matthew to the grass and he toddles over to me on unsteady feet. Matthew raises his arms and I pick up my precious angel and lift him towards the sun.

Once I've lowered Matthew and hold him close to my heart, Vince comes up behind me and wraps the both of us in his embrace. In that moment I see Veronica, who is watching us and smiling. *Stay strong, young lady*, I want to tell her.

She is my daughter now and I will strive to show her by example how to love with your whole heart. I will be her rock when she needs me to be, because Lord knows being married to a Cole man comes with its challenges. But I don't really worry about Veronica.

Although I don't say it to her, for fear she'll think I'm comparing the two of them, I do see the same enviable qualities in Veronica that I once saw in Kasia. I'm convinced Veronica will never lose herself in Dylan's shadow, even when his larger than life existence threatens obscurity. I am confident she'll demand what she needs from my son, and will not stand by silently if he makes choices that are not in their best interest as a couple or as a family. And as I watch her make her way across the backyard and sit herself on Dylan's lap, wrapping her arms around his neck and whispering in his ear, I'm certain she will love my son for every spectacular day this life grants them.

No mother could ever hope for more.

* * *

A Note From Lily

A heartfelt thank you for taking this journey and reading the Let Me series. There are so many characters I love from these books, but Dylan Cole his one of my absolute favorites, and has been since he made his first appearance in my debut novel, *Let Me Be the One*. I sincerely hope you've enjoyed your time in their world, and if I was a new-to-you author before, I hope you'll keep coming back for more.

With Gratitude,
Lily

* * *

The Blackbird series is available now. Enemies to lovers, a sexy single dad who falls for the nanny, a heartbreaking military romance and more...If you're into love stories that leave you holding your breath and begging for more, you'll be hooked. The Blackbird Series kicks off with *When the Night is Over*.

Are the bonds of our first true love as strong as they feel when we're young, innocent and consumed with the promise of forever?

The last time Charlotte Mason saw Simon Wade, he was shoving a paper bag from the pharmacy into her hands with a morning-after pill inside.

Even though he literally left her holding the bag, when love is true it's limitless. She wants more for Simon than the ties that bind him to their dead-end town. He has one shot at a better life, and she'll stand aside so he can take it.

Nearly four years later Charlotte is still nowhere to be found, and it's not as if Simon hasn't been looking. How can he forget the girl who still haunts his dreams?

Also by Lily Foster

LET ME SERIES

Let Me Be the One

Let Me Love You

Let Me Go

Let Me Heal Your Heart

Let Me Fall

When I Let You Go

BLACKBIRD SERIES

When the Night is Over

Your Hand in Mine

Ghost on the Shore

All Your Life